EMBRACING THE TIDE

The Inner Circle - Book 3

Rogue London & N.M. McGregor

ROTTIE BOOKS LLC

Published by Rottie Books LLC
A Tennessee Organization

Copyright ©2025 Rogue London & N.M. McGregor.
All rights are reserved.

No part of this publication may be reproduced, stored in a retrieval system and/or made public in any form or by any means, electronic, mechanical, photocopying, recording or otherwise, without the prior written permission of the publisher. deborah@rottiebooks.com.

This book is fiction. Names, places, locations and events are either created in the author's imagination or are used fictitiously. Any resemblance to actual persons, places and events is purely coincidental.

Blurb by Alluring Blurbs
Cover art by Rogue London and Western Sky

First printing edition 2018
West End Lass by N.M. McGregor
Published by Nadine Jolly
ASIN: B07QX98K7R
ISBN: 978-0-9958974-9-6 ebook
ISBN: 978-0-9958974-8-9 paperback

ISBN 979-8-9925234-3-0 (eBook)
ISBN 979-8-9925234-4-7 (Paperback)

Contents

Series Blurb	1
Blurb	3
Warning	5
Chapter 1	7
Chapter 2	13
Chapter 3	23
Chapter 4	35
Chapter 5	51
Chapter 6	59
Chapter 7	69
Chapter 8	81
Chapter 9	93
Chapter 10	103
Chapter 11	111
Chapter 12	131

Chapter 13	149
Chapter 14	161
Chapter 15	173
Chapter 16	183
Chapter 17	193
Chapter 18	201
Chapter 19	215
Chapter 20	235
Chapter 21	247
Chapter 22	261
Chapter 23	269
Chapter 24	279
Chapter 25	287
Chapter 26	295
Chapter 27	311
Acknowledgements	323
Join the Inner Circle	325
About Rogue London	327
About N.M. McGregor	329
About the Publisher	331

Series Blurb

Sure, the '80s seem fun, but there's more to it. A sinister side no one talks about. Dark alleyways and shadows dogging our every step.

This is our tale of overcoming, having each other's backs, and accepting the dare to live and love through it all.

Blurb

"...you were thrown into situations you weren't ready for. That trend seems to have continued for you, Montana... I understand you feeling lost. But what you have control of is how you approach life and live it. Your choices are what make you, so choose well."

If I thought my life was interesting before, it's nothing compared to now. At heart I'm still just Montana Stanford, West End Brat. But now, I'm also garnering fame, wealth, and power I could never have dreamed of. With those things come new perks, but also new responsibilities and, *of course*, new dangers.

It seems no matter how hard I try to stay out of trouble, it still finds me. From assassination attempts, to stalkers, and what is shaping up to be an all out war, it's consuming my life like a tidal wave.

I'm trying to choose my actions wisely but it's becoming more difficult by the day, as the threats that once affected *only* me are now trying to drown those I love most. I *refuse* to be their downfall and I *refuse* to lose a single one of them.

It's time to make a stand. It's time to take back control. Win or lose, it's time to embrace the tide.

Warning

Hello again!

If you're reading this, you've read the first and second installments of my story already. I'll even take the chance of assuming you read my welcome letters in those stories too.

If that's the case, we don't need to go over how *different* the '80s were. We've already discussed that, and how that decade wasn't all sunshine and roses, fun and games, or alcohol and parties with *iconic* music. A secret I've learned on my journey is, it wasn't *just* the '80s that had sinister shadows.

I know you're wondering what my point in all this is, and I'll tell you. My story has been gritty from day one. That's because life is gritty and I don't sugar-coat shit. That's never been who I am. The older a person gets, the grittier life gets. Think of it this way, life is like a video game. Every year you level up, and each new level leads to newer, more difficult challenges and more badass boss fights.

As this story progresses, the hurdles and enemies get steadily more dangerous. So do the love, passion and success. The outcomes are not always as pretty as we might like. So, the dare still stands...

I'm Montana Stanford and this is my story. It's grittier, more raw, and definitely not for the faint of heart. Come with me on the last leg of my journey... or are you chicken?

Chapter 1

I was contemplating doing something stupid. As much as I loved touring, it was exhausting. Seven weeks on the road with a concert per day had taken its toll on me. Alex never appeared to tire, and Otter seemed to know how much of himself to keep in reserve and maintain an enviable neutral state.

Not me. I went into every situation with the best intentions, repeating to myself, *this time will be different,* and I always ended up in the same place. That *'same place'* when all those best intentions flew out the window wasn't happening as frequently, so I had to be thankful for that.

I knew Adam was coming. Not that anyone had told me, but solely based on my actions these past few days. Alex or my bodyguard would have no choice but to call in my cavalry, which was Adam. He was my regulator, and without him I don't think I could have done half of what I did.

I pictured my beautiful Greek god—my rich philanthropist artist whom I missed terribly. He was coming and I didn't want him to find me losing my shit, so I made a pact with myself to avoid any potential trouble tonight by avoiding people.

If need be, I'd hide in my dressing room and allow Alex and Allyson to handle PR and the fans. Alex had brought his support on tour and through the entire tour she'd held his hand while learning the ins and outs of the music business.

Allyson was being groomed to be our official publicist for our new record label. She would also be our liaison, as well as lead contact for touring dates, and would team up with the head of security to work out schedules for all the bands that signed with our label. We were still under contract with Atlantic Records for our music, but starting our own company and signing artists to our label wasn't breaking any rules.

That was what we were working on while on tour. You'd think that my brother would have known me better by now and would have waited before going ahead with such an ambitious plan. But as he said, it takes a long time to put a project of this magnitude together, so we had begun early, which added stress to our already demanding schedule.

We were playing to a thunderous crowd. I was a little surprised as I always pictured the Japanese as a race of quiet, polite people. My stereotype was way off. They made just as large a racket as any other country we'd played.

Allyson was born in Japan and this was her first time home in a year. She'd planned a luncheon, so Alex could meet her parents, but they didn't show up. Alex was very disappointed to not be given the chance to woo her parents into liking him.

Allyson wasn't surprised at her parents' no-show. They wanted her to either marry from their culture or marry a rich American business tycoon. Despite my brother becoming that very thing, her parents viewed him as a musician and didn't care about his money or his investments. She said that, by coming to lunch, it would show approval of her choice in Alex. In their antiquated thinking, a rich business tycoon is all that would do for their only child.

Unlike my situation with Adam's wealthy, part of the Vancocuver elite, parents who had accepted my feral monster self without question. If they could only see Alex and Allyson together, I was sure their dynamic would impress them. The love they shared was deep and beautiful and watching them the past weeks without Adam here to complete me was triggering my backslide. I would never tell my brother that.

Adam was coming, he would always be my knight in black shiny chrome. He was the most unselfish person I'd ever known and he always found a way to be by my side when I needed him the most.

When the concert was done, I kept my word and avoided all unnecessary contact with fans and stagehands. I closed my dressing room door and leaned back against it for momentary support. The performance felt off, but only Alex seemed to notice. Which made me wonder, was it my performance or just my feelings that were off?

Before disappearing to my room, I made Alex confess that Adam was coming and when he would arrive. I wanted him to find me in fine form. So, off I went to shower and change into a special outfit I'd brought along.

I was grateful to have a dressing room with a private bathroom. I found that I sweat so much on stage, it would dry on my skin as soon as I was done. Then I would be freezing by the time we got to the hotel. Not having one had led to some health challenges while touring. A standing request was put in for my own bathroom, but it wasn't alway feasible.

I'd just finished applying some lipstick, when there was a knock on my door.

"Montana, Montana, are you in there?" I smiled as that voice confirmed my feelings from moments ago, Adam had arrived. He must have panicked when I didn't respond right away. I opened the door to see Adam backed up, foot in the air, ready to kick down my door.

I stood in shock at the sight of Adam about to break in my door, which quickly changed to heat as his eyes roamed my body with a hungry look. I stood before him in my tight form-fitting white cocktail dress with matching heels. I imagined I made quite a sight. Adam loved me in white, always his first choice when he picked out my clothing. He said I was his sexy angel.

I'd changed the harsh stage make-up for a dusting of foundation, mascara, and light pink gloss. Quite a change from the heavy rocker makeup I'd had on an hour ago. I leaned on the door handle and smirked at Adam.

"Hello, darling," I purred.

"Why, you little minx, you knew I was coming."

"I'm sure I don't know what you are talking about," I batted my eyelashes, doing my best to look innocent.

He was catching up to my surprise, his eyes sparkled with a *challenge accepted*, and it drove a stake of desire right to my lower belly. He tugged me to his chest and kissed my neck, my cheeks, and my lips, taking his time and devouring me like a starving man. I shuddered with the intensity of the sensations, emitting soft mewls.

"Montana, I wonder if subconsciously I wanted you to have a meltdown, so I could come and hold you in my arms."

I didn't answer, instead, I released the door and pressed into him, becoming limp with the sheer pleasure I was receiving just from being held in his strong arms.

He whispered in my ear, "Are you hungry? Let's go and have some late-night sushi and sake and you can tell me about the tour. We can get back to this later, hmmm?"

"I know the perfect place," I muttered, stepping away. I was hoping my sexy outfit would do the trick and we'd have an indulgent rest of the night together. I booked a private booth in a Japanese restaurant that had been recommended by the concierge at the hotel where the band was staying.

Chapter 2

When the elevator opened to the restaurant, I was arrested by the spectacular views. I could tell Adam was impressed by my choice, since he usually handled reservations.

I sauntered to our private room swinging my hips suggestively. Adam glanced at our host, who seemed completely unaffected by my strutting. Adam assisted me into the room. He held back from closing the door, speaking in Japanese with our host for a moment. I shook my head and giggled, he was probably telling the guy to not bother us, but I'd taken care of that when I called.

I was positively vibrating, oozing with anticipation. Adam finally closed the door once the sake was delivered. He poured us each a steaming cup and we toasted to *meltdowns*.

He held my gaze. "I love you, Montana."

"I love you back."

"Maybe it's time you drop the act and fess up. I was under the impression that you were struggling and I was called to bring you back to yourself. I see that is not entirely the case."

I gave him my quirky side smile, eyes glittering in amusement. "But, Adam, I do need you. I need you in every way, can't you feel my need right now?"

I was pushing to not talk about how I'd been struggling these past few days. I didn't want that shadow hovering over us, I just wanted to enjoy being with him.

His eyes glittered darkly. He chuckled and shook his head, and excused himself, saying he needed to pee after the long flight. Adam slid open the door to our private table and disappeared down the corridor. I leaned back against the screened wall behind me, wearing a small satisfied smirk.

Adam looked quite satisfied with himself upon his return and I briefly wondered if he had gotten up to something when he went to the bathroom. Something more than a satisfying pee, I mean. He had a far better game face than me, so it was hard to know if he was up to something or just messing with me and wanted me to think that way.

He poured us more sake. All the tension drained from my body and I sat back completely relaxed. "How was your flight?"

His eyes still glittered and I wondered what was going on in that head of his.

"You know the rules, Brat, first you tell me what's going on, then I'll share."

Fifteen minutes later, after complaining about my brother and Allyson, yes I was totally throwing them under the bus for my actions, a knock startled us. Our waiter slid our door open and set down a large tray on the table. He placed each item before us with speed and precision and then left us in peace.

"I met an amazing woman on the plane over."

Say what now, where was he going with this? A flare of jealousy stabbed me in the belly. My brother Alex may attract all the fangirls, but Adam had always attracted all types of women in general. Despite knowing I had absolutely nothing to worry about, I could still fall prey to the jealousy monster from time to time.

"She told me that one should choose a life partner that encourages them to be better, not someone who wishes to change them. I found that in you, Montana. You make me a better man, a better artist, a better human being."

"She sounds like a wise woman."

Adam smiled. "Indeed, she was."

I observed him through my peripheral vision... the man was definitely up to something. When we were done eating, Adam opened the screen door and our waiter appeared a moment later and removed all the dishes in that same efficient way.

He came back with champagne and a small wrapped gift. Aha! I knew he'd been up to something.

Our waiter left and Adam once again slid the door close. He handed me my champagne. "To us," he cheered, clinking my glass

"To us," I repeated and took a sip of the crisp bubbly liquid. "Mmm, yummy."

Adam put his glass down, picked up the box, and held my gaze.

"Montana Stanford, will you marry me?"

Adam opened the box toward me. I guess he wanted me to see the ring, snug in its little home, before removing it and I could understand why. The box was a tastefully done diorama of a sparkling undersea world, complete with a clam in its center cradling the promise ring Adam had given me for Christmas a few years back. It was only then I realized it was missing from my hand. He laughed at my shocked expression.

"Are we adding magician to your list of skills now? How did you accomplish this?"

"I snuck it out of the bathroom in your dressing room while you grabbed your purse. I guess you were too rushed to remember it."

My shocked expression quickly changed to a sheepish one, since it was not the first time my ring had gone unnoticed.

"Montana, when I gave you that ring, it was symbolic of what I felt for you. I wanted you to have something that spoke of my commitment to you. But your tastes have changed as you have grown, as have mine. I wanted you to have something to show my undying devotion to you, my unwavering commitment to us, and acknowledge that we all change and grow, and that is welcomed, and encouraged."

He withdrew a second box from the inside pocket of his sports coat, and opened it toward me. Inside was another delicate clam that held a gorgeous ring of woven diamonds in an intricate infinity loop. Where it met in the center were two blue diamonds. I gasped, mesmerized by the beauty.

Adam slid closer, barely dropping to a knee squat below the recessed table. "Montana, are you going to make me repeat the question?" Adam asked with gentle amusement colouring his tone. My gaze travelled up from the box into the green depths of his eyes.

"Adam Northrop, I would like nothing more than to be your wife. I have loved you since the first moment I saw you and love you even more now. I never want to be without you. I Do."

I squealed in pleasure as Adam removed the ring from its watery looking home and placed it onto my left ring finger. Then placed my promise ring on my right ring finger.

"To Mr. and Mrs. Northrop," Adam said and held his glass aloft in another toast." His eyes glazed in happiness. We drank deeply and then kissed to seal our vow.

I fell asleep in Adam's arms on the ride to the hotel. When we arrived, he had hotel security go ahead of us to ensure our room was safe. I'd been receiving notes from a stalker. The message was always the same. "Your ass is mine. I'll finish what I started."

In addition, there had been a few overzealous fans, and one failed attack-attempt on me already on this tour.

The studio was taking threats seriously since the bomb explosion in my hotel room in London on our last tour. Thankfully, Adam had taken my safety into his own hands and had hired Charlie, a private security guard, affectionately nicknamed, The Babysitter. Charlie had thrown the bomb out the window and covered me with his body, saving my life.

Eddy, my best buddy and a detective back home, was spearheading the investigation. He felt the bomb was part of a larger plot, and possibly being controlled by a nemesis who was doing time for attempting to kill me, twice.

There were no other leads and all roads seemed to travel back to her although they couldn't prove it yet. Personally, I didn't feel this was her M.O. That didn't mean that she wasn't a part of it, she could be orchestrating it, but this felt different.

With the all clear given, Adam carried me to the king-sized bed and undressed me.

He pulled the covers down and tucked me in. "Where are you going?" I asked in a sleepy voice.

"I'm taking a shower, Brat, go to sleep." That's all I needed to hear. The sounds of running water lulled me to sleep within seconds.

The morning light brought with it a feeling of elation and pure happiness, a residue of last night's hot date, proposal, and dreamless slumber. Adam had left a note to order room service and wait for him. He'd had a meeting with Alex and the head of the security team early this morning. I was just finishing when he arrived. I gave him a radiant smile and drew him into an embrace.

"Good morning, Mr. Northrop." I stood up, my words lost when I pressed my lips to his neck and snuggled in close. His scent was like heaven. I could inhale him for fifty years and never tire of it. He was a blend of Italian aftershave, and his unique man-smell, with a faint hint of the paints he used in his work.

"Hello, soon-to-be Mrs. Northrop, I see you were a good girl and ate all your breakfast." I leaned back and crossed my arms. I hated it when he did *that,* and he knew it. He pushed me back toward the bed until it hit the back of my knees and I sprawled on my back.

He straddled me, leaned down, pulled my arms gently above my head, and ran his hands up and down my arms.

"Gee, Mo, with all this added muscle from drumming I guess I should be afraid of you now." He grinned wickedly. Why, the cheeky man was doing a fine job of awakening my feisty side.

"Meh. I guess it helps. Some guys do need to be controlled."

He chuckled and rolled us on our side, tucking me to his front.

"I feel bad that you traveled all that way, put me to bed, and then got up early for a meeting regarding me, while I got to lounge in bed and stuff my face with really good food."

"Don't worry, I stuffed my face too, during the breakfast meeting."

"What was the meeting about?"

"You, what else?" His eyes glittered with amusement.

I huffed, "Seriously, Adam, what about, specifically?"

His green orbs shifted, gone was the humor. I knew this look and braced myself for a lecture.

"I've put a time stipulation on your post concert obligations. Honestly, Otter was there and relieved, as he's just as tired as you are."

That really surprised me. He never looked tired, and I'd never asked, just assumed he was doing fine.

"I guess I'm a bit of a shit bandmate. I just assumed he was doing fine."

Adam agreed. "Otter doesn't give much away so it's easy to overlook. He's the proverbial strong silent type."

I laughed. "Yeah, pretty much. What else?"

"Charlie gets more say on your behalf with the tour manager. I let that guy know in no uncertain terms that I will sue the studio if they don't take the band's personal needs into consideration."

I opened my mouth to complain but he cut me off before I could utter a word. "Let me finish before you tear a strip off me. They are making a killing from Behind Blue Eyes, more with you than with any other new band in their history. And, they tend to give nothing unless asked. So I took it upon myself to do the asking."

I digested that. Alex did say that the label was very happy with their profits, surely they could be lenient on us when we'd brought so much to the table. Okay, I got it, Adam was drawing the line for us.

"So, they've been given boundaries as to how far they can push us?"

"Exactly so," he smiled. "Charlie will be there to make sure everything goes according to plan." There was a pause. "Now, Little Miss, we need to talk about your unhealthy way of getting my attention. If you need me, tell me, don't backslide and wait for someone to notice and call me."

I blushed at being called out. His expression softened. "I know it's hard for you, Mo, I really do, but I don't like worrying on a twelve hour flight if I don't have to."

My blush deepened. He was right, that was shitty of me. "I'm sorry. You know I don't usually think through what I do. You'd think I'd be better at this by now."

"Hey, it's okay. Just talk to me, okay?"

I buried my face in his chest. "Okay." My words were muffled. I pulled back and repeated it.

"That's my girl. Now how about you, me, and The Babysitter go on a hot date."

I burst out laughing, then groaned. "Really? Do we have to take Charlie? I mean he's great but I want to be alone with you."

Adam's eyes were sparkling with merriment. "Don't worry, Brat, where we're going won't require him being in our direct proximity. He's going to follow in a car while I tour you around."

I buried myself tight against his chest, and wished, not for the first time, that I could just crawl inside him where I would be safe.

Chapter 3

Adam preceded my arrival home by a few days and I couldn't wait to see him. Yes, the rest of the touring had gone off without a hitch, but it didn't, in any way, make me miss him less.

Adam was walking from the kitchen when the elevator pinged and the door slid open. I charged at him and threw myself into his arms.

"Hey, beautiful."

I wrapped my legs around his strong hips and buried my face in his neck. "You taste like mint and wine," I accused light-heartedly, "I want whatever you're having and what is that heavenly smell?" My tummy grumbled right on cue.

Adam smirked. "That could be the roses or the dinner I'm making to restore you to perfect health. You never eat well while on tour."

Truth. I slid down his body and took a look around. "You really outdid yourself, Northrop." Flowers covered every surface and he had lit candles throughout the kitchen and dining room. Pots on the stove emitted intoxicating scents.

My stomach rumbled again. "And you're wearing my favourite jeans, my kryptonite. If I didn't know better, I'd say you were trying to seduce me."

"It looks like I wasn't the only one planning a seduction. You know what you do to me when you wear white."

A smile curled my lips seductively. "You don't say?" I said innocently.

Adam shook his head in amusement. "Let me pour you some wine." I leaned on the counter and took in all the details of what he'd done. "Nice welcome home, Adam, thank you."

"You are welcome, my queen." He handed me my glass and held up his. He clinked my glass with his.

I took a long sip, savoring all the crisp fruity notes. "Adam, when we landed, I wanted to run outside and kiss the ground. So, I did. Alex laughed at me and asked, 'Happy to be home, sis?' I mimicked Alex. I stuck out my tongue at him, of course. 'Is it wrong to want to run down to the beach and stick my feet in the ocean, like right now?'

Alex said, 'not from my perspective, but I have it on good authority that someone missed you and is waiting for you right now wearing nothing but a pair of work jeans? Is that a thing? Wait, don't answer that.' So, I jumped into the waiting car and beckoned him and Allyson to hurry the hell up! They both teased me all the way here."

I set down my wine glass and hugged Adam. He was my home and he filled my senses completely.

"Well, I'm not surprised that was your first reaction when you got out of the plane. Because you, my Brat, are a whirlwind, even after a grueling tour schedule."

I chuckled and took another deep drink of my wine and felt my shoulders relax. "Maybe dinner could wait?" I moaned as he nibbled on my ear, sending goosebumps down my neck. I squeezed his ass.

"I think you're the brat, Adam, because teasing me while wearing those jeans is just plain rude,"

"Shhh, less talking and more kissing — and you're still the resident brat," he muttered into my mouth as he kissed me, making his words sound more like— *es tkng ore issing*.

We stayed like that for long enough to set my senses on fire. I missed him in more ways than one. He held me tighter and then suddenly let go, much to my annoyance.

"Sit down, penthouse goddess, and let me feed you food. The rest I will feed later."

"Oh fine." I pretended to sulk, but I really was hungry for food after not having eaten in at least ten hours.

"How are you feeling?" Adam was stirring something that smelled divine.

I sunk onto a dining room chair and let out a long sigh. "Second tour, how should I feel? Disconnected comes to mind," Adam gave me a quizzical look. "I mean, I've been gone so long that I'm disconnected from me. From my life here. For ten weeks, I've lived as an extension of my drum kit. I want to sleep in and lay in the sun and hit the beach. You know, do my thing."

He smiled in understanding. "I bet you do, but, honey, you left in September and you were gone for an entire season." Adam looked at me expectantly with a raised eyebrow.

"Did you have a point?" Whatever I was supposed to get was like air flipping all around me. My brain wasn't working.

"Winter, Montana, it's winter. You did notice on the car ride home, didn't you?"

"I noticed, but did you notice it's a balmy nine celsius on the beautiful west coast. I'll just wear a sweater, like duh!"

Adam made a face but didn't say anything, just checked something in the oven. I was amazed he could do all this, being a rich kid who'd never had to cook. Then again, Adam prided himself on being a renaissance man, whatever that was.

His expression was serious when he turned back to me, "Montana, we need to talk."

Oh-oh, when Adam said my first name, he wasn't beating around the bush. He had this game face when he was serious, and before I knew him well, I didn't know how to interpret his *serious* expression. I hated *talks* and likened them to lectures.

"Ah, I see, the aromatic garden and subdued lighting was to put me in a relaxed mood, so you could, what? Drop a big heavy on me? Thanks, Adam, very clever."

He sighed and put down his wine glass. "This was meant to be a special welcome home, my love. About a half an hour before you arrived, I received a phone call from Eddy that threw a wrench into my plan."

Adam placed a bowl of aromatic soup in front of me, "First course. I hope you like it."

I dipped my spoon in and tried a small amount on my spoon, "Mmm, this is exquisite, Adam."

"I'm glad," He tried it as well and seemed satisfied. "I know you need time to think about things once you're made aware of them, but we are limited for time and I want to give you as much wriggle room as you need."

He was going to spoon feed me, pun intended, the news instead of doing an information dump. I would play along because the way he was looking at me, whatever it was, would be serious and I didn't want to melt on my first night home.

I took a breath as if to steady myself, "I know what this is all about."

"You do?" Adam looked surprised.

"Sure, you're pregnant?"

Adam's laughter quickly turned into choking on a spoonful of soup. Ha! Got him.

"Why, yes, I am, and I wanted to talk to you about supporting us, so I could be a stay at home dad."

It was my turn to laugh. Humour was always good for me and I continued with my soup while Adam checked on the next course.

My bowl empty, I sat back with my glass taking sips and feeling less hungry and more relaxed. *I got this.*

"A penny for your thoughts, Montana." I flinched at the use of my name.

"Just admiring your fine ass, Mr. Northrop." I added a heavy emphasis popping the p. Ace called it disrespectful and snarky when I did that, but Adam always enjoyed my humor. Besides, it was my go-to when life felt too heavy, that or rum and coke.

He removed our soup bowls and set down a plate loaded with baked chicken, mashed potatoes with gravy, and a whole whack of grilled veggies. I dug in.

"Good?"

"Delish."

We ate our meal in silence for a while and it was a nice break. Even the hotels had felt loud while on tour. Being here in my familiar environment offered the silence I needed.

"Dan and I have to head out of town for a few weeks."

I stopped chewing and reached for my wine. Adam was watching me intently. He could read me like a book, and probably knew my mouth had gone dry. I kept my face neutral but that wasn't my only tell. My back rounded on instinct, an outward sign that my dinner was turning into a lump in my stomach.

"If this is all you had to say, couldn't it have waited?"

"We leave in a week or so for three weeks. Ace will be out of town for a part of that time on a project for my dad. I know the timing stinks, and I'm sorry. Thankfully, Alex is across the street if you need him. I tried to change the schedule around, but I am worried about putting too much pressure on Dan, as he's still recovering from his drug addiction."

He stopped talking and gauged my reaction. What he was saying was I would be free flying without a safety net. I'd just come from a tour where it had been on me and Alex, minus Adam's brief visit. I could do this.

"You're not considering putting me on lockdown like you did when you came home from New York, are you?"

He laughed. "If only I could. I'll never forget you showing up in the middle of one of the hottest days of the year in a long-sleeved shirt and a baseball cap, driving my Porsche. Really? You think I wouldn't have figured out that something had happened, again."

I laughed, "Yeah I was an amateur back then, I'm much better at pulling the wool over your eyes now, buddy." I was joking, but I could see Adam wondering if he'd been getting too soft when it came to my safety.

"You're right, grounded it is."

"Wait, Adam, I was totally kidding. Our lives are so busy there's no time to get into trouble." I wondered if I looked as nostalgic as I felt. No one knew better than me that I lived in a perpetual state of collateral damage. What I wouldn't do for a little peace. "You're right, showing up with long sleeves to hide the stitches was stupid. I'm not talking about that, specifically, but why it happened, not what came after, but what drove me to the park in the first place."

Of course, he knew, but I wanted him to know where my head was at now and used the story to get my point across.

"That night I was longing for simplicity, to have a little of the old me. The band is great, playing drums and getting paid for it is awesome. Being on top, at least for now, is amazing. Being with you is the absolute best. But sometimes, I just need to be me. The girl from the West End, the girl that hangs at the beach and forgets all the shit that she can't do anything about."

I paused and took a sip of wine for some liquid courage. "I miss laughing and joking around with my tribe and dreaming about the future. I no longer dream 'cause everything I wanted has happened. The only thing I don't have, which being at the beach gives me, is peace."

I pushed my plate away. Adam was wearing his artist face, that is what I'd come to call that far off all seeing look he'd been giving me since we first met.

He was probably seeing something and committing it to memory for a future painting. I didn't hide. I never did and let him explore the contours of my face. I was his muse, after all. He'd said once that with the amount of ever-changing expressions I should have been a movie star. Still, I always squirmed under his intense scrutiny.

"You've lost weight, and you have dark circles under your eyes. Are you having nightmares again? There is a fragility about you, Mo, that makes me worry that all of this life is too much for you."

I choked out a laugh. "You think? That is precisely my point. I don't want to talk anymore about it. You said Eddy called, so spill already."

He sighed in resignation before taking a sip of wine. "Okay, I will just come out and say it. The court case, Stanford vs. Stanley…"

"You mean the bad decision I made that fateful night to stop at Ceperly Park for a swing until midnight that got me followed and attacked." His eyes narrowed. I had woken up Adam's dark side.

"Yes. That night when the only thing that saved you from being raped and butchered was a fucking Coke bottle and a good Samaritan."

I flinched. Look what had happened when I wanted something simple, disaster. There were still two of the four attackers on the loose.

"The two you identified were just broken out of prison. They are on the loose, Montana. I would imagine that they will want to," he made air quotes with his fingers, *"'finish what they started.'"*

I felt the blood drain from my face. I downed the remaining contents of my glass. "Jesus H bloody Christ, are you kidding?"

Adam poured us each another glass of wine, probably realizing that I needed it to cope with the shock and I hated whiskey. I would be hammered by now if it wasn't for adrenal overload. I wished he'd take me to bed and make me forget everything.

"There is more. Mercy has developed some important contacts in prison. She is no longer just a girl with a hard-on to get rid of the girl who made her jealous in high school. We knew she made connections with an Asian gang from Chinatown, but she has remained busy with extracurriculars during her incarceration, and now has the ear of the Triad, the Chinese mafia."

I chewed on this new information and what was being implied. The noose was tightening, that's why Adam started with their schedule. This wasn't just being alone, but possibly being hunted and being alone. Crap!

Mercy hadn't come up since she stabbed me in the back, just missing my vital organs by a hair's breadth. I'd found out about her plot to remove me from the band and called her out. Had she not pulled a knife on me, it would have been a clean fight, but I'd underestimated her hate for me.

"What is the significance of Mercy's prison activities to me, Adam?"

He seemed to choose his words carefully. "Eddy said the word on the street is, she joined the Triad for one reason only."

"And what is the reason?"

"In exchange for having you taken out."

The Band-Aid had been ripped off. "Fuck! Fuck, fuck, fuck! Why?"

Adam watched me carefully, as his words pierced every part of me. My thoughts were roller coasting all over from it being my fault and wanting to end my life, to wanting to get sent to prison so I could shank that bitch in the bathroom.

I began to shake, the enormity of it all made the walls close in around me. The light was dimming and I slunk to the floor. I could hear Adam calling my name but I felt like I was in some type of limbo, unable to respond.

I heard Adam on the phone, "Alex, can you guys come? She just fainted."

I didn't hear what the response was but I immediately felt Alex's presence. A few minutes later, all three of my brothers stepped off the elevator.

I was aware of them and of Ace picking me up and carrying me to the couch. Alex took my hands in both of his. *"Montana. I know you're hiding."*

Alex's voice wasn't coming from outside my body, but right inside my head. "What the hell?"

"What's happening right now?" I heard Adam ask aloud.

"He's in her head. I saw him do this at the hospital once. It's kinda wacky but somehow he can get right inside," Danny answered.

"Alex? What are you doing here, get out. How did you get in my head? You're here, right, and not a figment in my alternate reality? How is it you are here without me inviting you in?"

"I followed you, and I'm not leaving until you're ready with me."

"You can do that?"

"Apparently, I can. Now take my hand. We're going back."

I physically jerked away from him. "Alex, I can't go back. Surely you understand, it's better to have me gone, out of the way. I can't control the future, but I can control this. I couldn't live with myself if anything happened to any of you, I couldn't live knowing I could have prevented it. Please, let me go."

"You are so damned selfish, Montana."

"Maybe I am, but you know this is for the best. I draw so much danger to me, to us. It's not right. Besides, that's kinda calling the kettle black, isn't it? You just took my last stronghold from me, my last hiding place."

"You have always been selfish, Mo. You think, because you choose to get out early, that any of this could be avoided. We don't have enough information yet. If you were gone who would be chosen to vanquish Mercy's thirst for revenge? The notes, we don't know who they are from. With you gone, maybe they would choose a new target? Kristine or Allyson or myself? You're not giving us the chance to make our own choices. Your actions are taking them from us. Totally a you move, by the way. As I said,

Mo, you are selfish. Now, take my damn hand or I am going to carry you back to consciousness."

I heard the sneer in Alex's tone and the conviction.

I opened one eye and saw all four men staring down at me with varying expressions of concern. These were the four horsemen of the Montana Apocalypse.

"You had us worried." Ace reached down and gently helped me to sit up.

"Drink," Dan said, handing me a glass of water. Alex grinned, holding my gaze. "Interesting hiding spot you have there, sis. It reminds me of a book written about Leonardo da Vinci. In it he creates a memory cathedral. It's a monstrous structure and he stores everything in it, every room full of things he wishes never to forget or ideas for inventions yet to come. Nice place to visit, Mo, but I wouldn't want to live there."

For some reason, his making light of something that had seemed so serious was hilarious. I began to laugh and the others joined in. We all laughed until tears rolled down our cheeks. When our humour died down, the panic had been replaced with something I had missed on the road, kinship.

"Thank you," I said to Alex and pulled him in for a hug. "Thank you for finding a way in and bringing me back. It is a haven, but it isn't safe, that's just the illusion that draws me there. You're right, Alex, it is selfish to check out. So, I guess we need a plan."

Chapter 4

Eddy's advice to us was to carry on as usual. Acting paranoid would only alert anyone who could be watching us. He wanted whoever *they* were to feel secure and hopefully make a mistake that would lead to their capture.

It was decided I would continue with my schedule while the guys were out of town but with amped up undercover security. Appearing normal and keeping things the same, at least to outsiders, was the new reality. Being safe had always been a priority, we would just take it up a notch.

Geoff, Adam's father, made his private team of investigators and security available to us as we were not updating the studio. It wouldn't have changed much anyway as, in their opinion, we were already costing more than any new band they had signed.

Geoff and Eddy discussed the pros and cons of blending undercover cops with private security. I felt more comfortable with Geoff's team for a few reasons... I knew them, and they never stood out. Since I was a family member they had a vested interest in keeping me safe, whereas

Eddy's team I didn't know. I'd always been able to spot undercover cops and I was pretty sure others could as well. In the end it was decided that the cops would do the reconnaissance work and leave Geoff's team to be on my detail.

A week later, Ace, Danny, and Adam were gone. Alex and I were the ones remaining behind for a change. He and Allyson had asked me to stay with them while Adam was gone, but I had declined. Alex knew why without me having to say it aloud. He would never admit it, but I knew deep down he agreed, why put Allyson at unnecessary risk?

We kept ourselves extremely busy juggling our commitments with Atlantic Records and our new record label, Twin Spin Records, located in a warehouse space on the same block as our current label to keep things convenient.

Alex was proving why it was important to listen and learn by showing off the skills he had newly acquired from watching closely and asking questions in our own recording sessions with Atlantic.

Our label, TSR, was headed up by Alex. As we were just getting going, our team was Alex, Allyson, and me. Otter helped but had no desire to be anything beyond being our bass player. More commitment would interfere with his fun, he had said.

I couldn't argue with that, and kinda agreed, but I was in this thing with Alex. I trusted that the benefit would far outweigh the short-term time restraints that had been placed on us to get such a monumental project up and running.

We decided we were ready to officially work with a local band, Turning Jane, and started with our friend, Cole. I'd introduced him and Stella, not long after she'd become our back up singer for Behind Blue Eyes.

She worked with them whenever she didn't have label commitments with us. Her contract with us was due to be renewed. Instead, she'd be going full time as Turning Jane's lead singer. I was sad to be losing her, but super happy that she was moving on in her career.

Alex spent a lot of time helping develop Turning Jane, and preparing Stella, for the role of lead singer. The group had grown a lot and having a professional like Stella had helped to streamline their sound and given a professional edge that they had been lacking.

I was a little envious, I wished I could sing. Well, that's not quite accurate. I could sing, I was just too chicken. Alex never pushed it, he said when I was ready, so was our label. Yeah right, like I would ever be ready enough to ever share my voice. I think not.

That first week with the guys gone, Alex kept us working late hours. His attempt at keeping me from being idle. An idle Mo was a dangerous Mo.

Alex brought in Cole's band to record their first single. He and Allyson would use the vast network of contacts they had cultivated to get the single playing on a variety of radio stations, both local and abroad. Europe was important. European tours always came before North American tours, so building a band's popularity was super important. Allyson was well connected, and that was working well in our favour.

By the end of each day, all I wanted to do was go home to Adam and fall into his arms. Instead, after a shower or bath, I'd crawl into one of his t-shirts.

I hated feeling like a sitting duck and to banish it I became the studio clown. Played silly games, hid things on people like I had done in our garage when Ralph was the drummer and not me.

Without Ace to frown me down, I fell back into my young teen shenanigans. I was having a great time until I was alone. That was the toughest, being in the penthouse, feeling swallowed up by the empty space with the sitting duck feeling at its worst.

When the guys had been gone for two weeks, and nothing had happened, I started to loosen up a bit and decided if going out was a problem, I'd bring my friends to hang out in my ivory tower with me. Down time had been non-existent since returning from the tour. I hadn't made it to the beach yet, despite my proclamation of needing to on my first night home.

The gap of disconnect was growing and I was in serious need of letting off some steam and connecting with my tribe. Those people reminded me of who I was before jobs and careers became a priority.

I called my girls over. We shared some drinks and plenty of laughs, then decided we needed more friends and drinks. Alex and Allyson showed up within minutes of the invite. A few trickled in later that night. I enjoyed the blend of my old crew and my new crew. We just clicked. We rarely talked about things that mattered, instead we told stories from our childhood. I had Much Music playing on the big screen, and we did goofy dancing, followed by falling on the carpet in peals of laughter. I hadn't had so much fun in ages. Even Alex let down his hair and joined in the fun. Allyson got to see my brother's goofy side and seemed to enjoy it very much.

I was feeling fantastically nostalgic as I soaked up the camaraderie in the room. This coming back to self was what I missed, being my goofy side, and I promised to make an effort to never lose this part of myself regardless of how serious life became.

There was a commotion at our elevator. Charlie, my personal bodyguard, entered the apartment along with a bunch of other men I didn't recognize. He grabbed me and headed for the back staircase. More guards pounded up the stairs and passed us on their way up.

"Alex!" I panicked. He and Allyson quickly followed with two more bodyguards, and when we got downstairs, they were escorted to a separate vehicle. As our vehicle pulled out, I saw all my friends with guards being escorted into a variety of vehicles that sped off in different directions. I was suddenly reminded of an old Russian movie where people are taken from their homes in the middle of the night, never to be seen or heard from again.

The shock of the fresh air, after the copious amounts of alcohol I consumed, had me reeling. Suddenly feeling sick, I opened the window and hurled, taking my time before sinking back into my seat. My inebriated thoughts strayed to where I was being taken and trusting in Charlie that I'd get there in one piece. But what about Alex, where had he and Allyson gone? My location question was soon answered when we parked in front of the Northrop mansion.

"What the hell is going on, Charlie?" Instead of answering, the silent giant scanned the enclosed parking area adjacent to the mansion. Then hustled me out of the car and inside the front entrance where Geoff was waiting.

"Thank goodness you're safe," he said ignoring the stench of booze on my breath. He thanked Charlie and gave him some further instructions. Then he headed to the kitchen and I stumbled after him.

Geoff handed me a glass of water. I drank it, while he brewed coffee. If I didn't know him well, I would assume this was just a test or a run-through of some kind to prepare for a future emergency, but he was tense. I could see it in his shoulders and the line of his mouth. Something was wrong.

"Geoff, what's going on? Where was Alex taken? Why did the guards just show up in the penthouse like that? It's a bloody good thing it was Charlie or I wouldn't have gone anywhere without a proper explanation."

"Good," he said without preamble. "I would expect no less from you, Montana. You're a smart girl, when you're sober." His tone was bland, but his eyes spoke a completely different message. His attempt at humour? Or a not so hidden barb?

"Why the secrecy and the urgency?" I was becoming agitated. "And where is my brother, damn it?"

"Follow me and I'll answer your questions." With water and coffee in hand, I followed Geoff into his office.

"Sorry for the cloak and dagger, but you were not answering the phone and we thought the penthouse had been breached already."

"Breached? Already?" My alcohol laden brain was having a hard time keeping up.

"Our agent that penetrated the local branch of the Yakuza, the one Mercy is affiliated with, sent word that an assassination crew was on its way. Somehow, they got wind that you were having a party and decided to strike while you were distracted."

"Are my friends okay? This doesn't make any sense, Geoff. I've been alone for two weeks. Why not then? Why wait for a distraction?" I shook my head in frustration and ran my hands through my hair. It brought to mind an old quote, *let your hair down and have some fun*. Oh yeah, I had let my hair down alright and look at what happened. My friends must be totally freaked out.

Geoff seemed to read my mind. "Not to worry, young lady, all your friends were given an escort to the location of their choosing. They know you, Montana, you have always been in trouble. I'm sure they understand."

"And Alex and Allyson?"

"In a heavily guarded hotel room for the night."

"Thank you," I said and truly meant it. I felt tremendous gratitude that everyone was safe. Maybe the booze and the nostalgia were making me morose, but the sense of gratitude was strong, and it not only filled my heart, but my eyes as well.

"Thank you for being on the ball, Geoff. It's been some time since I had friends over. I wanted to hang out with the people that help me feel like the real me, not Montana the drummer, or the Vancouver socialite's fiancée, not even one of the famous Stanford twins. Just plain old me. I was missing Adam and wanting some company other than work."

I hoped I didn't sound sulky or stupid, but with Adam gone, there was no one to share my feelings with. Alex didn't need the extra burden right now, and he knew my feelings anyway. He couldn't help it; he had a built in Montana radar. Right now, the nostalgia that inevitably comes with drinking too much was hitting me hard and I felt it important that Geoff know how I felt about the enormity of the situation.

"I was feeling lost. Do you understand what I am saying, Geoff, or do I sound like a drunken idiot?"

"I understand completely," he said rumpling my hair as he stood up. "Now, if I'm not mistaken, you're going to need some ibuprofen and more water before heading to bed. I'll send some up. Why not have a shower, Montana, to wash away your night. Adam brought over some clothing before the trip in case you needed to hide out here."

"Of course, he did. That's my Adam." I rose to my feet a little shakily. He grabbed my arm to steady me, and I moved in for a fatherly hug. I remembered the last hug from my dad. How old had I been? Sixteen? So much had happened since I last saw him. Ace's hugs were nice too, but they were brotherly, not fatherly, and always had a tinge of desperation in them like he was afraid it was our last.

There is something very unique and comforting about a hug from a parent. I had almost forgotten what it felt like. For the briefest of moments, I was just a girl, and it was wonderful. I sighed and reluctantly let go.

"I miss him. I feel empty when he is so far away. I think that's why I needed my crew tonight. The tour felt like an eternity and I wanted to get home to him and then he left." Geoff smiled in understanding and escorted me to the guest room.

"I took up the reins in my family early on, so my younger years were a lot like Ace's. I think that's why I like him so much. I can empathise with the circumstances he was thrust into. But you, I can't imagine growing up was easy. I imagine you were thrown into situations you weren't ready for.

"That trend seems to have continued for you, Montana. You strike me as someone who has circumstances outside of their control coming at you all the time. I understand you feeling lost. But what you have control of is how you approach life and live it. Your choices are what make you, so choose well. And there is nothing wrong with hanging with your friends, they are fine, you are fine. Relax and get some sleep, young lady," he said, closing the door.

I smiled, *young lady*, I hadn't heard that term too often in my life. I certainly had never felt young, and lady was pushing it. Although, I had grown in my social etiquette and would be considered a lady by society standards now.

Regardless of what the rest of the world saw, I was just me. Often I wondered how my life would have turned out without all the tragedy or Adam to bail me out. Many unanswered questions swirled around.

There was a knock at the door and Bridget, the Northrop's long-term housekeeper, entered placing water and pills on my nightstand. I thanked her, and we chatted for a few minutes. She asked me if I'd been in Adam's apartment over the garage yet. Apparently, changes had been made, and I might want to check it out.

After the pills, I headed into the shower. Dried and put on my white silk nightie. I should have been tired from the booze and the late night, but I wasn't.

The beast inside was restless. I decided to take a stroll down the connecting wing that joined the house, to Adam's apartment. The wing itself was a lovely space, wider than the other hallways and filled with art and comfortable furniture. I called it a wing instead of a hallway as it was wide enough to entertain, and it led to this beautifully painted door that screamed artist. Once I crossed the threshold, I was in Adam's domain.

His parents had built it for him when he started art school, and this is where he had lived when I met him. Everything was just as he had left it. I thought Bridget had said they'd changed things? I was glad they hadn't, and my spirits instantly lifted at the sight. The place was so *him*. Although he had not physically inhabited it for some time. His presence permeated the apartment in a way that it didn't at the penthouse. The thought caught me, and I tried to put my finger on the reason why this place felt so much different than the penthouse?

I guess I was tired, my addled brain was coming up with nothing. My thoughts preferred to drift, sifting through memories, like the first time he brought me here. The display of wealth had been intimidating. He was, and still is, the golden child of some of Vancouver's top socialites. Back then I was a nobody, broke and from the wrong side of the tracks.

I walked down the hall to his old bedroom. Everything was the same, a mausoleum to me. A room filled with him but covered with drawings and sketches of me. Many were drawn from before we met, using his imagination from Dan's description. Adam's drawings always caught aspects of me that I had never seen in photos. He was more interested in capturing my soul, my essence, versus an exact image. His first show had been packed to the rafters with works of art featuring me and, at first, I'd been very uncomfortable and sometimes still was, but, his work was powerful in its simplicity and everyone wanted to own a Northrop original. He and my brother Dan had become an overnight success.

Adam's older work of me showcased my impish grin and the slightly sardonic expression I often wore. The ever-present sparkle in my eyes. That sparkle was gone in his newer work. We could call that growing up, but a lot had happened since we first met and it showed in his work.

I took my time examining different drawings. I stopped, and my jaw dropped. All the drawings above his headboard were ripped or scribbled on. Some even said, *'die bitch'*. Oh my god, someone that wanted to harm me had been in

Adam's apartment. I turned to flee down the hall to the kitchen when the hair on my arms suddenly stood. I felt a presence, someone else had come in and it wasn't Geoff. I pretended to examine a painting while covertly glancing to the bay window hoping to see a reflection of who I was dealing with.

A bright light momentarily blinded me. When it passed, I saw it was a woman and for a brief horrifying moment wondered if it was Mercy. As she moved down the hall toward me, I realized it was Bridget the housekeeper. Remaining silent and acting oblivious to her presence I continued to watch her. Something was totally off, why would she send me here to see changes that never happened? Crap! Could she have meant the destroyed artwork in the bedroom?

Her angle shifted and I saw what she held in her hand. No. It couldn't be. She was so loyal to the Stanfords. Then I remembered the time that I found Adam entertaining Katya on my living room floor. They had left and later he had called to explain. When I'd finally cooled down and called him back. He hadn't been home, but I left a message with Bridget. Adam never got the message. When I resurfaced in his life, Bridget had looked upset.

I hadn't given it a second thought back then. Now I wondered if she had been in love with Adam this entire time. Some horrible female stalker movie had just come to life and was following me. My thoughts shifted. Maybe she had been hired to be an insider for the Asian gang Mercy was affiliated with? I ducked behind the kitchen counter and reached into a cupboard for a frying pan. If I could surprise her, then I could subdue her and run for help.

I snuck around the side of the counter, she went the other way. When she rounded the corner, I hit her hard and ran for the door. I flung it open, and hit a small wall. An Asian man dressed all in black was standing there. I screamed as loud as I could. He grabbed me by the hair and dragged me into the suite, shutting the door behind him.

He threw me against the back of Adam's couch. I tripped and fell over it, going through the glass coffee table on the other side. I was pulling myself upright, when my assailant reached down and grabbed a fistful of hair, dragging me to my feet. I glanced down, noticing a few of the glass shards had cut me. I was bleeding.

My assailant was facing the window. I assumed looking down to see if security had been alerted by the noise. Bridget staggered to her feet opposite me. Her back to the door, her gun shakily pointed at me. Holy shit! *Think, Montana*. My assailant spared a nod in Bridget's direction, but then let me go when something caught his attention down the hall. I'd heard it too and wondered if rescue was possible?

Bridget shifted her position and came closer to me. With the blood loss, I had collapsed to the ground, and now she stood over me with her gun pointed down at my forehead. Her usually calm demeanor was completely gone and in its place she wore a victorious grin.

"Now Adam will be all mine."

I spared a glance to the bay window in time to catch Geoff sneaking in and waiting by the hall for the assailant to come back down. Then he raised his gun at Bridget. The next moment was a blur. I heard the cocking of the guns. Bridget must have felt Geoff's presence or heard the second gun, because she looked away from me to him. I took my chance and kicked her hard in the knee cap, which was all I could reach from my position on the floor. As she staggered backwards, she dropped her gun. Falling to the ground, her vacant eyes stared at me, when the bay window exploded into a million pieces and fell around me like snow.

The assailant came barreling down the hallway into a waiting Geoff, who hit him on the head with the butt of his gun. All this was a blur, but also felt like I was watching it in slow motion. I reached out my hand to catch the falling snow and wondered vaguely if the house had blown up. I felt disconnected. Looking down I saw a lot of blood. Everything was blurry and my head felt so heavy.

"Montana, love, are you all right?" I saw the assailant stand up and point his gun at me. I pointed, and Geoff turned as the gun was fired. Charlie came bursting in, and his gun rang out almost simultaneously with that of the gunman.

The gunman went down and Geoff's bicep was bleeding. The bullet had nicked him on its way to catching me in the side. A distant part of my brain was computing that I'd been shot. My reality was one of fluff. I felt like I was not made of matter but of something thin and floaty. I had no balance, no stability.

I was slipping in and out of consciousness. Geoff was yelling at someone who had entered the room to have doctor Sun on alert at VGH. I heard something ripping, felt pressure around my leg and arm, then something painful pressed into my side. Geoff scooped me up and I opened my eyes and glanced down. For the briefest of moments, I wondered what had happened to my white silk nightie. Had I changed into a red one? My brain felt like it was operating on extra slow play on a VCR. It took my foggy brain time to register that it was the same nightie.

My two selves, conscious and subconscious, were having a conversation. They spoke to each other while still another part of me observed the conversation. Removed, I became a watcher from on high to the events unfolding around me. My subconscious self was connecting the sensations from my time in the hospital years ago when I was in a coma. I had been afloat then in a world filled with images. It had been a soul journey, a return to me. I'd had to go through my life, to the events leading up to my attempted suicide. At the end, nothing was left, but to decide to awaken and move on or let go and die.

Clearly, I had chosen life at the time. Now I felt like I had been ripped from life to a place of drifting. There had not been a choice this time, just circumstances.

Chapter 5

I was drifting through rooms filled with people I didn't know, looking for Adam. I knew he and Dan had parted ways in New York and he'd continued to Chicago from there to meet with Jean Pierre. I'd been a little annoyed that he was meeting with the rich, entitled man from France, as his family rubbed elbows with Katya's family. The woman had tortured me on her brief visit to Vancouver years earlier and slept with Adam on my living room rug. Somehow she managed to insert herself into our lives at the worst possible times, and had even refused to tell my brother Danny when I'd called him in Europe needing his advice, without which I had instigated a fight with Mercy where she had literally stabbed me in the back.

Before Adam left, he and I'd had an interesting conversation.

"I sometimes feel bad, princess."

Adam had often felt bad or guilty about a great many things. "Why, because you couldn't control the weather today, or something more mundane?" I'd teased.

"It's because of my need to paint you that your face is slowly filling the walls of rich men's estates all over the world."

"Eww, Adam! When you put it like that I feel violated. Gross!"

He smiled but it didn't reach his eyes. "I'm pretty sure Jean Pierre is going to buy my Montana Renaissance Collection."

"Oh?"

"Yeah, he's been charged with restoring one of their castles and it's you he wants hanging on his walls, no surprise."

I sidled closer and slid onto his lap, "And that bothers you?"

He sighed and slid down so we were eye level, "Our careers skyrocketed at the same time. You guys were in the news with the band, as were Dan and I, you and me... it's been a lot of upheaval and excitement. But as far as the art goes... everyone wants the cool rocker chick. I can barely keep up to the demands and yeah, sometimes that bothers me."

He sighed. "What I'm trying to say is, I feel responsible for a lot of what's happening to you. Yes, the band had a large following, but it grew a hundred times in size overnight, and I'm partly to blame, as well as Dan."

He'd never expressed regret before and I didn't know how to help him battle this particular demon.

"The problem is, any other girl and it probably wouldn't be a problem, but you're not any other girl, you're my girl—my muse—my brat—my goddess—my sun, moon, and stars. One day, you will be a legend worth millions of dollars."

I was missing the issue. "So? Why does all this add up to you feeling guilty?"

Before I could get an answer, I was sucked out of the huge building with the many rooms and into a hotel room. Adam was on the phone, frowning at whatever was being said. He quickly hung up and grabbed a remote for the television. He clicked on

CNN. I watched enthralled as a helicopter flew over his parents mansion.

"I wonder what happened?" I said it aloud but Adam didn't hear me. Was I dreaming?

Adam's eyes were glued to the T.V. "Please, let it be a simple burglary, and not Montana. Please, please don't let it be her." I was right here beside him, so clearly it wasn't me, but we watched the story unfold. His childhood home was swarming with police and reporters. We saw Charlie and then me, covered in blood, being carried from the house by his father.

Adam backed away from the images until his legs hit the bed and he fell down on his ass. The news showed Geoff handing me over to the paramedics and following us into the back of the ambulance, keeping his hand on my shoulder.

Adam slid from the bed to the floor, his face portraying utter shock, "So much blood." He rested his arms on his knees and with tears sliding down his handsome face, he continued to watch. The doors closed and the ambulance sped off, sirens blaring.

Following that scene, there were two body bags being removed from the house and a reporter talking to Liza, Adam's mother. Then the cameras panned to a news reporter saying that Montana Stanford had been shot while visiting her fiancés home and she was in the hospital in critical condition.

What the hell? How could that be when I was right here?

"Now in other news..."

"Other news? She is the only news!" Adam shouted at the screen. The phone rang and he climbed to his feet. "It's me," he said in a choked voice into the receiver. Whoever was on the other end was not getting a reaction from Adam. I heard yelling and recognized my brother, Dan's, voice. Something about a plane and to get to the airport.

"Yes. Okay." Adam dropped the phone in the cradle. He looked like a zombie as he threw items into his suitcase. I followed him in the elevator but when he exited and got into a cab, I seemed unable to follow. I closed my eyes and imagined an airplane. When I opened them, I was on the plane with Danny and Ace. They were watching the same footage Adam had been watching in the hospital.

Both my brothers wore expressions of grief as they watched, "Don't worry guys, I'll be fine, I'll get through this like I always do." They didn't hear me and I was beginning to suspect this was all just a bad dream or a hallucination.

"What happened tonight, Dan?"

"Mo was home with a few friends, and Alex and Allyson. Alex said Charlie came charging in and hustled Mo out of there. Other guards showed up and whisked everyone away to a safe place. Our sister went to Geoff's, as you had suggested."

The footage continued to play flashing to the body bags and to me covered in blood.

"That's a lot of blood, Dan. I got a bad feeling."

The plane landed and Adam boarded. He looked like death, they all did and hugged each other tight, bonded in grief.

"I watched the footage at the hotel and again in the hangar while I was waiting for the plane to arrive. Why was she at my parents' place? She should have been safe there," Adam sunk into a chair.

"I know Adam, I know," Dan soothed. "Just hang in there. The faster we arrive, the faster we can help."

That's right. Stop acting like I'm dead and think of a wonderful thought, any happy little thought. As kids, Alex and I loved Peter Pan and now seemed just as good a time as any to share Peter's advice.

"It's my fault."

Dan and Ace gave each other puzzled looks. "How can it be your fault, Adam? You weren't even there," Dan said.

"We did this, Dan, you and me, especially me. I was talking to Montana about this very thing right before I left. How much more vulnerable I've made her because I've painted, drawn, sculpted her, and then put her on display for the world to see."

"Adam, be that as it may, we really have no way of gauging if what you are saying is even relevant. Why don't we stick to the facts? I don't know anything but what I saw, same as you. Dan spoke with Alex and knows more." I marvelled at Ace's ability to be logical and to the point. Just a year ago he would have been losing his shit and threatening the pilots with death if they didn't hurry the hell up. He'd grown a lot since finishing college and joining Geoff's company.

"That's right, according to Alex, who was brought to the hospital from a safe house." Both men were about to interrupt Dan, who held up his hand. "Guys! I can only tell you what I got from my very brief conversation with him that he'd had with Geoff. Both Bridget and the Asian assailant were killed. Alex said that Eddy and Geoff are assuming this is the work of the Yakuza, but how Bridget is involved, I couldn't tell you. During the attack, Montana's brachial artery was cut in her forearm.

Your glass coffee table was shattered, Adam, so they're thinking it has something to do with that. Geoff said Montana managed to save him from getting shot in the back. The bullet grazed his bicep and went into her. Geoff said she'd been partying with her friends and consumed a lot of booze. Her blood was thin before the wounds. She's lost about five pints of blood and is in critical condition at VGH. The doctors do not expect her to make it through the night."

"What? But, I'm right here!" *I tried getting their attention.*

"I can picture Montana wandering around my old apartment. The smile she'd be wearing as she got lost in memories. I see her face the moment she realizes she isn't safe. Her survival skills would have kicked into overdrive. She must have fought to save herself. She's fierce, determined. There is no way she's dying tonight. Is Alex in the room with her?" *Adam had called it, that is exactly how it happened minus the being coaxed there to see the so-called changes that Bridget mentioned.*

"I have no idea." *Dan replied*

That was a good question. Alex wouldn't let me die. I knew he could keep me here. He'd done it before and he could do it again. I was about to say as much, when I got pulled out of the cabin, and stood in the emergency ward of VGH.

The place was pandemonium. There were cops stationed at every door, and a stressed-out Eddy was barking out orders. Geoff was sitting with Kristine and Allyson. Otter was leaning against a wall talking with Chrissie when Adam, Dan, and Ace walked through the door.

Kristine rose and rushed to Ace, holding him tightly in her arms. He finally let his guard down and quietly sobbed. Geoff excused himself to speak with Adam and Dan. I moved closer to hear what he had to say. He wrapped an arm around each of them.

"I know this is hard, but I need to update you, and then we need to vote."

"Vote, on what?" Adam asked, confused.

"Son, the doctors aren't holding out on much hope that Montana will make it. I say we get Alex in the room."

"Where is Alex?" Dan asked, looking around.

"Chapel. I'm assuming he told you about the blood loss? In transport, she went into organ failure and is now in a coma. I'm sorry the news isn't better."

Adam sagged in his father's arms, "It was worse than my worst imagining. Some part of me never believed that she wouldn't pull through."

"Gentlemen," the surgeon got our attention, "If you're going to say goodbye, now is the time."

Adam's eyes bulged with the incredulity of the situation, "Goodbye? I'm not saying goodbye! Where is Alex?" Adam's voice penetrated all the other noise combined in the waiting room and for a split second, all activity ceased.

"I'm here," Alex came around the corner.

"Listen, desperate times call for desperate measures. We are not saying goodbye. Alex is going in, right, Ace?"

I knew why Adam said that, technically as my guardian, Ace could veto the rest.

He nodded, "I Insist that Alex go for us all and be left unmolested."

The surgeon agreed. With a glance to the group, Alex took a big breath. He slowly exhaled, rubbing his hands together, and entered the room. While the remainder waited outside praying that the twin thing was enough, that God was listening and would help. That something would happen, and I would live.

As much as I wished to be in two places at once. I could feel Alex tugging at the edges of my consciousness and, this time, I wanted him to find me and bring me home.

Chapter 6

When you hover between two planes, the passage of time is different and there is no way to actually measure it. Despite the unmeasurable hours, I knew Alex had been with me a long time. Although not fully conscious, I felt the moment when my body moved from danger and my brother collapsed forward on my bed.

The door to my room opened and I heard him say, "She'll live." There were stumbling sounds and then a nurse's voice wanting Alex to be checked in. "There's nothing I have that medicine can help with, unfortunately. I just need to go home."

A gasp and then Allyson's voice—"Ace, can you carry him to the car? Otter and I can take it from there."

Footsteps in my room. A feminine energy at my side and slight tugging. The nurse checked my vitals.

"I was asked to give blood." That was Ace.

"You go ahead, brother. Adam and I are staying here."

I must have drifted off to sleep, because when Dan spoke I startled awake. "I still remember the day that my parents brought Mo and Alex home. I wanted to hold her so badly. When my parents sat me down on the couch and showed me how, she was placed in my arms. I gazed down into those three-day old blue eyes and fell in love. The intensity of her gaze pierced my heart. I thought I had never seen anything so small and fierce. And now look at her, Adam, so still and pale. I hate what you said on the plane, that we did this to her, but maybe you're right. Maybe our desire to share our muse with the world has helped to bring this down on her."

Interesting. I completely disagreed, but my ability to intercede wasn't there yet. Come on Adam, tell him he's wrong, I silently begged.

"I was wrong Dan. This had to be Mercy, and she hated Montana long before she was famous, long before the public had seen her. Mercy hated Montana right from the beginning. Maybe her popularity increased Mercy's hate, but I don't think we could have stopped that. Mo is famous in her own right, without us."

I couldn't see it, but imagined my brother nodding his head as he absorbed Adam's words. "Dan, have you noticed that Montana's anxiety is spiking with each traumatic experience? Each one breaking her spirit bit by bit. I remember what she was like when I first met her. My god, she was saucy and had an excuse for everything."

Danny laughed, "Yeah, she used to drive me nuts back in those days. The risks she took."

I imagined him shaking his head as he shared those memories.

"She was always watching out for us though, as funny as that sounds. Part of all this Mercy shit is Alex. Remember how she had played those games, wanting Alex just to piss Mo off. Those childhood games should have lost their steam with age. Maybe in her demented mind, she blames Mo for her actions and this is settling the score?"

"Maybe. How could she have known way back then that a little high school jealousy power play between her and Mercy would turn into a war."

A chair scraping and then Adam was holding my hand. More scraping and Dan took up residence on my other side, taking my right hand in his. "I don't know, Adam. She is the toughest girl I know, and she has lived through a lot, but not once did I ever feel it was something she wouldn't come back from. Even when Mercy stabbed her, I just knew she'd get her mobility back and because of you, she did. This though, a savage attack in your family home, with real guns. She must have been terrified."

Hours passed, maybe days and each time I woke it was to Adam's voice telling me a story or a joke. Sometimes he was begging me to wake up and I wanted to, I really did, but I was so tired.

"Adam, don't you think you're jumping the gun? We don't even know if she will wake up." Dan's voice startled me.

"I know, Dan, but today I woke up and felt hope in my heart. I don't know where it came from, but I have this feeling that she will be waking up soon."

"Even when she does wake up, she's going to need weeks of rest before flying anywhere and I'm assuming you've spoken with the record company and Alex? I imagine they'll be way behind on their next album release with Mo being out of commission for so long."

How long had I been asleep?

"I'll deal with all of that. I guess what I'm asking is if you'll be okay to hold down the fort for a couple of weeks?"

I spoke and was shocked when the whispered words weren't just thoughts, "Where are my boys off to now?" Just speaking exhausted me.

"Tell me you heard her speak, Dan, and that wasn't just my imagination."

"I heard her clearly, man."

I heard steps and the door opening. "She's awake!"

More footsteps and I managed to crack open one eye.

"You guys look like shit, did someone die or something?" My comment broke the tension. You would think I had been made of glass, with the way they hesitantly approached the bed. All except Alex, he climbed on my bed for a brotherly hug.

"Thank you, Alex. I never would have made it without you." He squeezed me a little tighter before letting me go.

"You're welcome. Don't do that again, you almost completely drained me in the process."

I received my share of hugs from the rest once Alex moved off the bed. Ace, Adam, and Dan congratulated Alex on saving me, like he had won an award. The idea of saving me being equivalent to a prize was amusing. I was sure he felt anything but. Alex took the compliments in stride, and his comments made me wonder what had really happened in my room while I was in a coma. Adam left to phone his parents with the good news, and Alex left to call Otter. That left me with Ace and Dan for a moment. My parents, I reflected. For as much as Ace had been like a father, Dan had really offered me the role of a mother in a lot of ways. I had never thought of it before nor made the connection until now. He offered the unconditional love, the encouragement, and the building up. Very much like I imagined our mother would have.

Gazing at these two very important men, their haggard looks aging them, I was struck by how truly lucky I really was.

"Thank you," I sighed. My voice hoarse from not being used for a few weeks, "for always being here for me. I never realized how much you have given me. I love you both so much."

"We love you too, Peanut, always." Ace leaned down and hugged me again. Then sat back in the chair and held one of my hands. Dan flopped himself down on my hospital bed and sighed. A deep sound of contentment.

"You know we had no idea if you were surviving this one. Should have known from the start you would pull through."

"If Alex hadn't been here, and didn't possess that gift of his, I may not have. I don't remember much, just a feeling." They nodded their heads in agreement, the three of us shared a moment of comfortable silence.

I was exhausted and said my good nights, but not before requesting they all go home. They left, and I drifted into a deep sleep.

My mother and I walked along a beautiful harbour. Occasionally, she would stop and cock her head as if she was listening or place her hand on something with her eyes closed. She inhaled deeply of the salt air and seemed to glory in the bountiful nature surrounding us.

"Mom, where are we?"

She smiled at me and her face was radiant. She glowed, and some part of my mind registered that this was no ordinary dream. This was a vision. Her radiance seemed to come from within, and as she took my hand, I felt her light throughout my being.

"Montana, my love, do you know when the phone is going to ring, before it does? Or, you think of someone and suddenly you see them?" I nodded. "This is your sixth sense, darling, your intuition. Alex has a very strong, well developed sense. Like everything he does, there is tremendous purpose and direction in Alex's choices. He has done what he needed to do with his gift, by saving your life."

She paused as if choosing her next words, "I don't have to tell you that Alex and you are very different." She eyed me meaningfully. I laughed out loud, my dream mom was giving me the stink eye. She joined me and her laugh was like chimes tinkling in the air.

"That is why you have chosen Adam. He is what you are not, all the qualities you lack to control yourself and your desires. But you are an amazing young woman, my daughter, a survivor, you are so strong and resilient. You're beautiful and soft in so many ways. We can't all be like your brother. Thankfully, as the world takes all sorts, Montana."

She sighed, this time gazing at me with pure love in her eyes, "You're here to give hope, Montana, to be that example of what's beautiful in this world. To bring awareness to those in need, to love the broken things. Even your Adam needs your particular brand of essence that comes through in his art.

You may find that your sixth sense is enhanced because of your deep connection with Alex. You will find out that you can tap into him as easily as he can tap into you. Open yourself up and listen to those déjà vu moments. Help the earth and its inhabitants. You've been given a voice, child. Now use it to lift others."

I nodded again. She smiled and pulled me in tight. I felt a timelessness in her embrace. When she pulled away, she handed me a shell.

"This is to remember, Montana, to give when you can, to help when you can. You have always stood up for others, it's in your blood, who you are. Now use it to make a difference to those you share the planet with."

She smiled and began to fade. I was rooted to the spot and watched until even the light that had surrounded and filled her had also gone.

When I woke, I opened my hand and there, lying on my palm, was the smallest mother of pearl I had ever seen. She had been here; my dream had happened. Hella! I was blown away. I wanted to share my vision with Adam, but when he showed up a short time later, I was being moved from the critical care ward and into a private room. I was rendered speechless by all the cards, flowers, and gifts that filled my room.

"Adam, what is all this?"

"Eddy did a press conference for us and let your fans know that you were out of critical care. Stuff has been pouring in since last night. Knowing you would be moved to a private room, the staff started filling it with gifts. You have the best smelling room in the entire hospital," I did, he was right. A full gurney pushed by a smiling nurse entered. At this rate I wouldn't get to my bed.

"Wait, please. Are there patients here that don't have flowers?"

"Of course," the nurse answered.

"Well then, I would like to share, please. I want every person on this floor to have as much as will fit comfortably, and then to the next floor with the deliveries." The nurse left with the gurney. I was exhausted just from being wheeled from one room to another. Adam helped me to settle, and then laid down beside me. Hours later, the rest of the gang found us asleep and in each other's arms.

I woke to see Alex staring at me. *Hello,* I spoke without the use of my mouth. Ha, Mom was right, my sixth sense had increased. *Yes, I'm different,* I spoke into his mind directly. He looked startled for a moment, and then we both laughed out loud, for the benefit of the rest of the room.

"It's that twin thing again," Ace said. Then we all laughed.

My family and the band had been cautious with the press, acting completely ignorant of the circumstances surrounding the attack. Eddy had felt that the less they said the better for us all. The fan mail and gifts had poured in, and despite sharing the flowers and plants with the entire hospital, I still required a van to bring the rest home. Two weeks later, Eddy created a police escort home as the fans were lining the streets for blocks.

I was so touched; I opened my window and told Charlie to slow down. The love and relief I saw opened my heart like a raw wound. My fingertips brushed over extended hands. Shouts of "we love you" and "we knew you could do it," filled the air. For the first time in my career, I felt completely connected to my fan base. I cried and laughed and sang with them on the slow drive home.

Exhausted, Adam put me to bed, and I slept deeply. I woke hours later feeling better, stronger and in a funny way, more alive than I ever had.

Chapter 7

A week later, Adam and I flew to the Cayman Islands. Geoff had made sure the island police, who knew him well, were aware of our presence. He also set up private security for us during our stay.

I was desperate to get in the water, or on, or above, whatever, as long as I could feel it. Between the tour, coming home to winter and the hospital stay, I still hadn't made it to the beach. That was a new record and one I wasn't happy about. The sparkling turquoise ocean and sandy beaches called to me like a siren. I was more than happy to listen to their call. I couldn't think of a better way to recuperate.

Our inter-island transport pulled into the harbor, I was out the door and walking as fast as my legs could carry me to the parasailing desk. Adam caught up with me and grabbed a hold of my arm to slow me down.

"Easy, Brat, or you'll end up back on bed rest."

"Oh come on, Adam, with you there it sounds more like a good thing than a punishment."

His eyes sparkled. "Careful, or we'll go straight to the house and directly to bed. What I meant was, if you overdo things you could end up on bed rest so slow down, okay?"

"I know what you meant. I was just teasing. I get it, I do, but I'm just super friggin' excited, okay. I mean look at this place, it's totally rad!"

Adam chuckled. "It is. Come on, let's go see if they can fit us in."

As if they wouldn't. Geoff and Liza had stayed here so often, I was sure the Northrop name had some pull and we'd be floating above the earth in no time. Ten minutes later, we were being strapped into our harnesses. I was a little uncomfortable at first, as it pressed against my still healing wounds, but that was replaced with elation when the wind swept us up and we ascended in seconds into the beautiful sky.

I was so caught up in the beauty of all that I saw and was snapping pictures like crazy. We'd made sure to hang our cameras around our necks for this very reason. I opened my arms to the sky, tilted my head back, and enjoyed the wind on my skin. I soaked in the sun, the salt air, and every moment felt like nature's embrace.

Beside me, I heard Adam's camera clicking away, and then I must have zoned out completely until we began our descent. My eyes snapped open to see we were close to the ground. Then it was over and we were helped out of our harnesses. The earth felt weird under my feet, and I was quite wobbly. Adam wrapped a supportive arm around me as we headed to our rental car.

I continued being clicker happy with my camera on the fifteen-minute ride to our island paradise. Adam would occasionally glance over at me. I knew this rather than saw him. "What? Did I catch some fly action while in the air and have dead bugs in my teeth?"

He laughed. "I just find it amazing to look at you, and know what you have been through, yet here you are. No one would ever know, by looking at you, that you had just been shot and almost died. Something is different about you, and I haven't put my finger on it yet."

I was silent, something was different. I could feel it too, but what?

We arrived at the house and I went exploring while Adam unpacked. Instantly, I was in love with the place. Despite all the glass walls that opened up to various patios, it was private and I didn't feel like a fish in a fishbowl like I'd assumed when we pulled up.

The pool outside was protected on all sides with a high wall. I glanced around and not seeing a soul, quickly stripped out of my clothing and jumped in the pool.

"Dang!" The pool was set at a very comfortable eighty-five degrees celsius. Not having to swim to stay warm was an added bonus. I lay back, closed my eyes, and floated. "Mmm, so good." My ears were under water and being this close to the ocean, I could hear it beneath the surface of the pool, and enthralled by the sound, I drifted. Visions of sea life danced in my vision.

Adam was cutting fruit when I entered through the sliding door carrying my clothes.

"Hey water goddess, enjoy the pool?" He'd seen me. Of course he had, Adam wouldn't let me out of his sight and who could blame him. It hadn't been long since my family was told to say goodbye. Adam aged while I laid in the hospital bed unconscious. By comparison, he looked happy, with way less tension in his shoulders since we'd arrived.

"Sorry I left you to do all the hard stuff. I just had to get in that pool. I love it here, Adam."

"Why don't you grab us towels, sunscreen, and uh, maybe put on a bikini? I'll bring the food and drinks and meet you outside on the beach."

"You got it, kitchen god," I strode away swinging my hips to draw his attention to my bare ass. In the huge walk-in, my clothing had been organized and stacked neatly away. My guy was the best. I grabbed a white bikini, as that was Adam's favourite colour for me, a couple of towels, sunscreen, and a baseball cap for each of us. I was so pale that even with lotion, I expected to burn, and I didn't want my face peeling, yuck!

Two comfortable loungers faced the ocean, I dropped the towels down and took a seat. Adam joined me a few minutes later with sandwiches, nibbles, and a jug of mojitos.

"Oh yeah, let's get this party started," Adam left and came back with two refrigerated glasses and poured us each a drink. "To us," I clicked Adam's glass with mine and took a deep drink of the cocktail. "Yummy. It sure was nice to have everything fully stocked. How did your dad manage that?"

"A very good property manager."

Adam put on his aviators and baseball cap and relaxed back on the lounge. Good. He needed to catch up on his rest, too. A pod of whales, outside of the bay, came into sight. Holy crap balls! I'd never seen a whale before, except at the Vancouver Aquarium.

This was an entire pod, I began counting, but I was too far away. I made my way down the beach and out into the water, and swam a ways out and continued counting. Wait until I told Alex about this, he'd be so jealous.

Then the strangest thing happened... I felt them. Even from this distance. I attempted to connect with the herd. Focusing on their pulse as a whole and sending them a greeting. *Hello beautiful friends.* I imparted through a picture I hoped they received. I got my answer when as one, the whales slowed down and looked at me. I mean directly at me. Holy cow bells! *Be well. Be free, my friends.* They studied me a moment longer before continuing on their journey.

I watched until the very last one was out of sight before returning to my lounge. I chugged my drink, put on my sunglasses and hat, and lay back intent on taking a nap. More like wanting silence to process the exchange that just happened. I remembered what my mother had said and the little pearl tucked in my pocket.

"Montana, did you happen to notice that pod of whales? They seemed to notice you, unless my eyes were playing a trick on me."

A lazy grin lifted the corners of my mouth. "Mhm... weren't they lovely... I really wanted to swim with them, but they were too far out for me." I sighed in contentment and drifted off.

A few days later we were lying around the pool, "Adam, how do you feel about inviting Alex and Allyson to come join us? I really think my bro would love this place. It has such an awesome vibe. The local culture, the music, I think they would love it." Alex and I had talked in the hospital, once I was on the mend. He'd said that I left my body, and he pulled me back. I knew all of that of course as I did visit places I wouldn't have otherwise, but the angst it had caused him reminded me how fragile life was, and how everyday should be celebrated instead of being taken for granted.

"Of course, and I agree, they would love it here."

"Thank you, Adam, you are the best f.i.t. ever."

"Fit?"

"Dur, fiancé in training," Adam laughed and then shook his head. I reached for his hand and intertwined his fingers with mine. We fell asleep in the afternoon sun. I woke up long before Adam. I suspected he hadn't slept much for weeks while I'd been in a coma and then recovering, and he was still catching up.

The setting sun cast beautiful red and orange beams over the pool. I stepped into the water which felt like liquid silk against my heated skin. I had always loved the beach, but since coming here, that shifted to needing the beach and the water. What changed? I couldn't say exactly, but for sure a shift had occurred inside of me. I removed my bikini and flung the wet garments onto the pool side. I'd never thought of myself as a skinny dipper, although I had done it once with my best friend, Chrissie, on a double dare. Then it had been cold, we'd been drunk and I was terrified of something in those gray depths biting me.

Weirdly enough, the water wasn't all I was feeling the need for. I gently floated on my back and hummed the first few bars to one of our newest songs, "In Your Eyes", and glanced at Adam to make sure he was still sleeping. I was not comfortable with my voice and although I'd sung for him once, I wasn't planning on having a witness, again, anytime soon.

His body hadn't changed, but unfortunately his aviators reflected so I couldn't say for sure that he was still sleeping. No one had ever heard me sing for reals. I mean, belting out Joan Jett in the shower didn't count. I didn't sing backup for the band, which is why Ann and Stella had been hired.

Stella had been giving me lessons, at Alex's request. He was hoping I would finally give in and do backups along with Ann, once Stella's contract ended. I wasn't really opposed to the idea, but I had an issue with me, a fear, which is why I'd never been comfortable being in the public eye and left all the hand shaking to Alex. He loved the attention both on and off the stage.

I preferred this right here. Being in the moment, being myself, the girl in the cut off jeans hanging out and having a few laughs. When I played drums, I lost myself in the music and it fed me in a kind of way that nothing else but dance had done when I used to take classes, but it wasn't who I was, I guess or what defined me. Mom had said in my dream that I was meant to help those I shared the planet with. I wasn't entirely sure what that meant or looked like but I had a feeling I would find out soon enough. In the meantime, I fully planned on laying back and enjoying our vacation.

It was dark and my grumbling tummy told me it was time for dinner. I reached for my towel and Adam tugged me on top of him.

"Eek! Adam! You scared the crap out of me." I straddled him, allowing my long legs to dangle on either side of his hips.

"How is my siren?" My tummy gurgled right on cue. Adam chuckled.

"Dinner it is," He lifted me off of him and smacked my ass. "Go shower and I'll take care of the rest."

I entered the dining room to see candles lit and wine poured.

"You take such good care of me, Adam." He placed a plate of linguine and clams in butter sauce in front of me. I inhaled, my mouth watering. "It smells delicious, but you're going to make me fat at this rate." A bubble of laughter broke loose from Adam's throat.

"Brat, you burn way more than you consume which is why it's hard for you to gain weight. I don't think an extra pat of butter is going to make you fat. Besides, no matter what, you always look perfect to me."

"And you always know the perfect thing to say. You really are the dream guy you know. Women everywhere would be jealous, if they knew how well you treated me."

"Well then, I guess it's lucky for you there is only one girl I want," Adam placed a bowl of salad between us and sat down.

"I'm so at peace here, I almost feel guilty."

Adam put his fork down. "What do you mean by guilty?" Adam was wearing that look that made me feel like he was looking right through me. Crap, why hadn't I kept my mouth shut? I put my fork down and took a swig of wine.

"Just that life has been so loud and busy for months now and this is like a total shut down, it's almost shocking. With all this time to think and relax, I feel kinda guilty, I guess."

"Really? You almost die and you feel guilty. I don't think so. What else is going on inside that head of yours?"

Ugh! Why did he have to take something so simple and turn it into problem solving. I picked up my fork and took a bite of food, deliberately taking my time before swallowing. "I don't know how or why, but somehow everything that is happening is my fault." I pulled off the bandaid and waited.

Adam studied me for a moment. Weighing my words. "I think that is a massive overstatement. It's funny," he continued with his all-seeing gaze gluing me in place, "all those times that Dan talked about his talented sister, he never mentioned you were a weight carrier. I thought that was Ace, but I'm starting to see that many of his traits have rubbed off on you."

I gulped. I hadn't thought about that before. Ace had carried the burden of taking care of me, Alex, and even Dan to an extent for years. He'd been the head of the household since high school, when our father was away working on the rigs. I'd always noted that in some ways my brother was Atlas, with the weight of the world on his shoulders, but hadn't noticed that same trait creeping up on me.

"You're right. I sound like a martyr. When did that start? But as you brought that up. I've been meaning to tell you something, an observation really."

A smile tugged at Adam's lips, "I can't wait."

"The night of the attack when I was at your parents, I did take a stroll through memory lane. Your early drawings of me showed a very different Montana. The impish grin and the eyes filled with excitement aren't in your more current work. Why is that?"

His expression hinted at sadness, "Because, Brat, it isn't there, and hasn't been since Dan and I left for our summer trip to Europe. Something inside of you shifted. I'm guessing it is the load of trauma you're carrying. It's weighing you down, Mo, that's why I wanted to bring you here. I want to see your soul in your eyes once again, not that hunted look that has been there for too long."

I nodded my head. "Yeah, I'd like to see that, too. Thanks for bringing me here and I can't wait for tomorrow. It's been a long time since I got to hang with my brother when it hasn't been business. You thought Ace was bad, Alex is like a force of nature driving us both forward. I'm still hanging onto his coattails but sometimes that's hard. I just want to let go and set myself free."

Adam nodded, "I'm sure Dan feels the same around me. What an interesting parallel. I'll take that as advice and check in with him more as my friend and not just as my business partner."

"I'm sure he'll love that. Now, forget about all that stuff. If you want to see my soul, I know a good place to start."

Adam's eyes glinted, "Do you? Let me guess, it begins with me sweeping you into my arms and carrying you to bed?"

I laughed, "Or you can just chase me," I jumped up from my chair and raced through the house for the bedroom. Adam caught me around the waist and swung over his shoulder.

"Adam!" I squealed.

He chuckled, "You're in for it now, Brat."

A zap of heat radiated to my belly. I knew he'd deliver, Adam never committed to anything he didn't follow through on.

Chapter 8

Adam and I stood at the private air strip waiting for Alex and Allyson to arrive. When Geoff's private jet landed and pulled into the hangar, I was practically bouncing. Beside me Adam chuckled, "You know you saw him six days ago."

"I know but it's not that I'm excited about but sharing the island with him and Allyson. This will be our first time having quality time with them and away from the studio." The steps dropped and Alex stepped out first and waved, with Allyson right on his heels.

He and Adam back-slapped and then we were hugging. "I've been having weird dreams."

"Oh?"

"Yeah, swimming in the ocean and being surrounded by dolphins. I've had it every night this week. I figured you were sending me a message. Needless to say, I couldn't wait to arrive. Thanks for the invite, sis."

I disengaged from our embrace to hug Allyson. "Well, I haven't seen many, but I did have a lovely interaction with a pod of whales," I laughed at Alex's raised brows.

Adam swiped Allyson's luggage, "She really did, I swear they stopped swimming just to look at her. Weird, right?"

"What are we doing first?" Alex tossed his luggage in the back beside Allyson's.

"Montana suggested we take you on a tour of the island first. How does that sound?" Adam asked and jumped into the driver's seat.

"Good, I'm dying for a little sun and culture," Alex leaned back, his hands behind his head. The top was off the jeep and, as soon as we pulled out of the hangar, we were enveloped in warm sun and salty air. I heard a moan from the back seat and turned to see both Allyson and Alex tilting their faces heavenward.

We stopped for lunch at a cafe that opened onto a square that provided loads of entertainment, including a band. We drank pina coladas and ate fried bananas.

"Mo, what do you think if our label signs some international artists? We could blend sounds, put their traditional sound with our newer one and create something new and original."

"I think it's brilliant," I answered dreamily.

"I can't remember ever seeing you this relaxed, sis."

"Mmm. I feel like a person here."

"Dare I ask what you mean by that?"

I opened my eyes and gazed at my brother. "I'm just me here. Not the baby sister, or even the twin, despite you being here too, and not the drummer or anything else, just me. Best gift I've ever gotten. I'm connecting with myself in ways I didn't realize I'd lost."

"Well said," Adam leaned over and kissed me. "I think we should head to the house. You'll want to rest up before we leave." Adam paid our bill and we left, but not before Alex gave one of his cards to the lead singer of the band that was playing in the courtyard.

We arrived at the luau, for lack of a better word. It was an outdoor pig roast feast with all the traditional dishes and entertainment. I was immediately impressed with the rich colours and beautiful textures that had been created. Adam, who always carried his camera and a sketch pad, started sketching the moment we were seated.

He closed it once the drinks arrived and snapped a few pictures. Allyson and I were dressed in traditional garb, while the guys wore shorts and t-shirts. We'd been tasting the local cuisine for about an hour when the band took a quick break. Alex took the opportunity and headed over to the group to introduce himself. The man was like a dog on a bone. I watched with interest as twelve dancers took the stage. Behind them were ceremonial drummers. They banged out a quick beat and the dance began. As soon as the drummers started I couldn't sit still. I bounced and studied the choreography at the same time. The women would do some intricate thumping as they swung their hips, they'd turn north and then work in a clockwise fashion. After a full round they would go in reverse. Then at each new interval, they would add in more steps and go faster than the last round. It was impressive. One of the dancers beckoned to me and Allyson, who had been happily bouncing beside me, to join them on stage.

They slowed down, giving us and a few others from the crowd time to learn the moves. The faster it got the more I lost myself in the rhythm. I hadn't danced like this in forever, the experience enhanced by the torches piercing the darkness and the salty sea air, turned me almost feral. I flung my body about, uncaring as to how it looked. The faster it went, the more I let go, until like playing the drums, the music used me.

At some point, Allyson dropped out, as did the other guests but they didn't leave, they joined the drummers clapping and chanting *ALALAHE*. I caught Alex watching me, wearing an indefinable expression. As the music built to a crescendo, the dancers blended in with the others and left the stage to me. The moon's light shone on me like a spotlight. I moved in a trancelike state at lightning speed through to the end of the drumming.

I was panting hard. To say I was out of shape would be fair, especially after my recent hospital stay. Allyson was all smiles as she hooked her arm through mine and we rejoined the men. I downed a glass of water and the remainder of my drink.

"Welcome back. That was quite the performance."

"Oh yeah?" I leaned over and gave Adam a kiss. We chatted a little about the music and the plans Alex was formulating and finally got up to leave when only a few stragglers were left. Adam asked one of the staff on our way out what *Alalahe* meant.

"Shining One, because your woman is infused with the light of the gods." I blushed but Adam nodded his head. "I have to agree." The drive home was incredibly quiet when compared with the wild drum dance I'd just taken part in. I was thinking about the look Alex had given me and wondered what it meant.

The next day we had a boat rented to go scuba diving. Adam was the only one certified, so our group headed to the resort first, for us three to get certified. Two hours later, we headed out to the sea, ready for our wildlife swim. At least, that is what we were hoping for.

Adam drove the boat and found a spot close to the reef. He brought an under-water camera and caught a hilarious photo of Alex being surprised by an eel that had been hiding in the coral he'd stopped to look at. Adam and I came to the surface and removed our masks.

"Did you see your brother's expression? Hilarious"

"I did. We'll have to blow that one up and put it in a frame so everyone can see it and have a laugh. Adam, look, a pod of dolphins," I was pointing at a fast approaching group. This is what we'd hoped for. Adam put his mask back on and used the transmitter to let Alex and Allyson know to come up to the surface.

The dolphins beelined for me and quickly surrounded me. They were friendly, chittering, and rolling over for a belly rub. This was better than I'd hoped for. When Alex surfaced some broke away from my circle and bumped him for rubs, too. His smile was infectious and my face felt ready to split in two with the enormous grin I had.

I cooed to them trying to communicate as I scratched and rubbed. Adam had climbed on board as the dolphins didn't seem to want his attention or Allyson's. Adam snapped away with his camera. Alex grabbed onto a dorsal fin, and the dolphin took off like a shot giving him a ride. I followed suit and we chased after the pair.

I shouted for Adam and Allyson to come back in. They dove in and dolphins offered each a ride. We sped around in the water chasing each other and had a blast. Allyson got creative and grabbed on to two, winning our little race. She swallowed water while giving her victory shout and sputtered as she laughed.

One dolphin kept pulling my attention, as it seemed way less happy than the rest. I did my best to comfort and soothe the dolphin until it was time for the pod to move on. We waved as they swam away before climbing into the boat. When we all finally got out of the water and onto the boat, we were trembling with exhaustion. We waved goodbye as the pod moved on.

"Bar none the coolest experience I've ever had," My brother was still grinning ear to ear. It was nice to see him so happy. We chatted on the ride back, about how their skin felt and the sensations we experienced while swimming with them.

Allyson and I drifted off into our own conversation as it was hard to hear over the motor. Alex and Adam sat in the front two seats, and when we turned toward shore, the wind changed direction and I picked up on their conversation.

"She died in the hospital."

Adam, was taking a swig of his beer and sputtered, "Pardon?" I knew the truth of what Alex was saying but I hadn't shared it with anyone. Alex was staring out at the water as he spoke, as if held by a vision, lost in his memories of the night in the hospital alone with me. I felt his pain and aloneness.

"She died and I had to pull her back, that's why I was so exhausted. Have you noticed she is different? Animals respond to her in a way they never did before. Almost like they know she died and came back. The after-life experts say that animals have a stronger sixth sense than us humans. I suppose that is why every animal within a mile radius seems drawn to her. You have noticed it, haven't you, Adam?"

He nodded in agreement, "Although, I'm not sure not with your thought process, Alex. But then again, I've never saved anyone."

"I've read first-hand accounts of people that have died and come back. Her world will never be the same. She will never be the same. I suspect she will do some amazing things with her life, as she can connect with the less tangible aspects more than most can." Alex continued.

Is that what this was? The whales and the dolphins, what my mother had shared, and if so, how did helping them play into all of this?

"But it explains this ethereal look she has sometimes that she didn't have before. When she exits the pool at the house, when parasailing, and again last night when the locals kept shouting *Alalahe,* she was different, illuminated is my best word for it."

"I saw it too," Alex added, "when she was dancing. It was like the moon held her in its glow and lit her up inside. I couldn't take my eyes off her."

That answered my question regarding why he'd been looking at me that way. I guess I kinda knew what they meant because in all those moments they both mentioned, I'd felt different. Connected to a higher something.

Suddenly the boat shifted, like it had hit a rock. I glanced over the edge and saw a very large turtle. I'd only ever seen those tiny things in the pet stores, but this turtle was easily the size of me. Before giving it a second thought, I was over the edge.

Adam cut the engine, "What is she doing?"

"She saw something beneath the water," Allyson offered with a shrug.

The sea turtle appeared bigger on the surface, I caught Alex's eye, sending him an unspoken communication to join me. He dove into the ocean, popping up beside me a moment later. We each took a side and maneuvered through the water with the turtle for a while. He was so different than the dolphins, equally fun but in a very different way. He reminded me of a grandfather indulging his children versus the playmate energy of the dolphins.

"How was it?" Allyson and Adam asked in unison. Alex and I laughed, as we fell, exhausted, into our seats.

"Fantastic, he's an old guy," Alex said which left a questioning look on Allyson's and Adam's faces. "He told us. Right, Mo?"

"Yeah, he did. The way he kept going on about his family history, and his social security number. He was lovely, wasn't he, Alex?" We laughed at their expense.

"Ah-dur, Adam, the spirals tell us their age," Alex dripped with sarcasm. We all burst out laughing at that.

"You two are both brats," Adam chided, his voice laced with amusement.

Once we docked, standing was a little difficult for me and Alex. We'd swam more in this outing than probably in our entire life put together and my legs felt like rubber. "You two, sit tight. I'll get a wheelbarrow," Adam said it like he was talking to little kids.

"As if," Alex said and wobbled back to his feet. "I just need my land legs. Right, Mo," he said, holding out his hand to pull me up.

"Right, bro."

After long, painful minutes, we arrived at the car, then drove a few blocks to a restaurant and sat outdoors on the patio. After ordering, Alex finally broke the spell.

"That was the best time I've ever had."

"Me too," I chimed in. "Alex, we never talked about what happened at the hospital. I saw you when you came into my room, but I don't think I was in my body. Does that sound weird? It was similar to the time I was in the coma, but different at the same time."

"Yes, it makes sense. I saw you, Mo, watching me holding your hands. I saw you there, and you were not you as you are now, it was your spirit. It's kinda hard to describe, but I didn't really see you with my eyes either. I knew you were hovering, I felt that. I pulled you back, obviously not physically as your body was lying in the bed. It wasn't like the time before the attack either when I climbed in your head. That was much easier. This was feeling you exclusively with my energy, imagining myself holding you, and placing you back in your form. I didn't know what I was doing, but somehow it worked. You, sister of mine, are a miracle."

I gazed at my brother, my heart full of gratitude. "No, brother, you are the miracle. I haven't shared with anyone, I wanted to tell you and Adam that day I was moved into my own room, but remember all those flowers and presents we had to deal with?"

"Oh yeah, the entire hospital smelled like a floral shop"

I nodded. "Right, so we were distracted, and I forgot about it until now. I had a dream about our mother. We were strolling on a boardwalk by a beautiful ocean. She talked about you, Alex, your *gift*, she called it, and said your sixth sense was highly developed, and I needed to work on mine. But ours were different. Yours, Alex, is meant to help me, exclusively. Which is probably why you learned to tune into me so long ago. But mine, it is to help the world, like the animals and people who need help. Basically, Mom said I should use my sixth sense to help others in need. Here's the weird part."

They all sat forward, eagerly awaiting the *weird part*, as if the dream I shared hadn't been weird enough. "At the end of the dream, Mom gave me a tiny, mother of pearl. When I woke up, it was in my hand." Of course, I'd been carrying it on my person since and I pulled it out of the pocket of my shorts and showed it to them. "Crazy, eh?" Their expressions confirmed my question.

"Did Mom have anything else to say?" Alex asked in a hopeful voice.

"Yeah, she said you got your shit together way better than me, but I think we all know that already."

Our group broke into amused laughter, effectively ending the awkward conversation. We moved on to other topics until our food arrived. Later, as we rested by the pool, Adam proposed an interesting idea. "Sweetheart, how do you feel about spearheading a charity? We could have a project manager put it together and run it for you. We can use some of my art to help raise awareness and funds, if you like. Maybe you and Alex could do something with your music also. I think you could do very well, and then it won't always fall to you, or us, to financially bail out animals and people that are in trouble, but it would be up to the organization."

"Adam, you're brilliant! Of course, that is exactly what I'll do, and I know just who to ask."

Chapter 9

Later that night, we had a clam bake out on our private beach, accompanied by pitchers of margaritas for us girls and beers for the guys. Alex, who never traveled without a guitar, sang while playing on his acoustic. Stuff that we never played on stage, songs from the sixties and seventies, that we'd grown up with that our parents had listened to.

The more we drank, the more eclectic his song choices became, and the more unguarded I became. I joined Alex in a few songs, more goofy stuff where we replaced the lyrics with their own. Adam and Allyson both spoke several languages and added to the hilarity of what we made up. The four of us laughed so much my face hurt, and I'm sure I wasn't the only one.

The longer it went on, the more bold I became until Alex asked me to sing a duet. A ballad he'd written for two but had only sung himself.

"Come on, Mo, sing it with me."

I knew the song, as I'd heard my brother sing it enough times, but I knew my mistake when Alex wore a wolfish grin.

He'd finally gotten me to sing with him and it was good, really, good. A part of my alcohol soaked brain understood that a shift had just happened, maybe Montana Stanford would no longer be able to hide behind her drums. Not because he'd make me sing but now that I'd accepted I could, only playing drums wouldn't be enough.

When we finished. Adam and Ally clapped enthusiastically. I performed a mock bow from my cross-legged position on the sand. After that, I sang the rest of the night, no matter what he threw at me. When Alex finally put the guitar down, we laid back and stared at the stars. Adam disappeared and came back with blankets, pillows, and bottles of water. We got comfortable, and within minutes I was out like a light, opening my eyes to the first rays of sunshine warming my face.

Seriously the best sleep I'd ever had. Up first, I headed into the kitchen to make coffee and brought out a tray laden with mugs and cookies just as the others woke up.

"Morning," I set the tray down and handed out the coffees.

Alex scrubbed his face before grabbing a hold of the mug, "I slept like the dead."

"Me too," Allyson added. "I've only slept outside once before and it was on a family trip. I'd snuck outside during the night and fell asleep in a hammock. This was more like a camp out or slumber party and way more fun though."

"Montana and I slept outside in her backyard once. It was nice gazing up at the stars and dreaming about our future."

"I remember that," I cut in. "Adam told me our future after I asked him if he'd marry me one day and we'd live in a white house with a picket fence."

"Oh, that sounds exciting, what did he say?" Allyson asked.

"He said no, because I'd want to be close to my brothers so we should get a palace in the sky and I guess that came true when Adam's parents gifted him the penthouse. But, he said one day we would own a castle in Scotland because that's what I really wanted."

"I like that. Alex, we need to discuss our plans."

Alex rolled his eyes at me, "Way to go sis, you just had to share didn't you?"

"Well it's not my fault my perfect man always knows exactly what to say." I pretended to be annoyed but my eyes were sparking with amusement. After a quick clean up, Allyson and Alex took the jeep to go and have some time sightseeing on their own, leaving me and Adam alone.

We were in the kitchen doing the dishes from the clambake, when I heard desperate chittering from outside.

"Adam, grab the gun," I yelled as I took off at a run for the beach.

"What gun?" He yelled back.

"Office, desk, top drawer. The key is on the bar."

Something was wrong with my new ocean friends. Conviction surged through me as I pumped my legs to get to the water as fast as I could. I saw several dolphins surrounding an injured dolphin and swimming around them trying to get to her was a shark. "Jesus," I muttered, and plunged into the center when I held the dolphin and whispered soothing words, while her pod pushed at the shark whenever it tried to dart inside their protective ring. Adam threw me the gun. "I'm calling the marina for help," he yelled and ran back to the house. The dolphins were tiring and the shark knew it, he was getting closer but I held him off when I shot at him. I didn't want him dead, just injured enough that he would hopefully swim away, but shooting at something that moved that fast wasn't easy and I'd never held a gun before.

Adam was back, he'd grabbed a hefty piece of driftwood from the beach and banged at the shark whenever he got too close. Thankfully, we didn't have long to wait. The marina physicians showed up with security in a boat and shot the shark with a tranquilizer gun.

Someone from the boat got in the water and steered the sleeping shark to the transportation apparatus in the back of the boat. The boat left and moved beyond the reef. A second boat came toward us and the dolphins made room for the team to examine the injured dolphin. Then he and his assistant moved over to the dolphins, they parted and made room. Adam stepped back, but I stayed with my arms around the dolphin, talking to it in soothing tones.

After it was checked and treated, the water team exited the ocean and joined the rest of the team on the beach that had arrived by land. It was then that I noticed the beach was full. A reporter was there and, what appeared to be, a whole bunch of tourists and local islanders. I heard "Alalahe" being chanted and watched as Adam sank to the sand, exhausted.

I felt the fatigue as the adrenaline wore off and sunk down in the low tide. Alex and Allyson came flying up in the jeep and ran down the beach.

I grinned at my brother. "Finally, they have been waiting for you."

"For me?" Alex asked.

"Well, us, this is the same pod we swam with yesterday. They have imprinted on me, now it's your turn. All four of us, not just me and Alex. Come on." We swam, rubbed, and sang with the pod. I could never put into words what that was like, the closest I could come to was magical. I hoped me and Alex could formulate this experience into a song and dedicate it to the new foundation I was going to start.

When we exited the water and said goodbye to our friends, I knew I'd never be the same. I felt alive in a way I'd never dreamed possible, connected to the earth in a way I didn't know existed. The four of us wore shit-eating grins, and I knew I wasn't the only one, that this miracle had been a shared experience.

I wondered if this is what it was like for those giants of the natural world, like Diane Fossey and Jane Goodall. They could arguably be the most connected humans to our supposed cousins, the apes. Incredible women with incredible love to save and cultivate the lives of gorillas.

Unlike me, I came to this connection by accident. While naturally an environmentalist, it had never been my calling like those amazing women. But now that I had it, being a famous musician would help propel the charity and hopefully bring awareness and help to our ocean friends.

"What do we do about all the people? They just witnessed the power of nature. It would be a good time to raise awareness for the dolphins." Alex said.

"You're right, Alex. Do you think you could get Otter to fly over, and we could put on a little impromptu concert on the beach tomorrow night, to raise money?"

He nodded. "I guess, raise money for?"

"Why, Friends of the Ocean, of course," Allyson answered. The four of us grinned like a bunch of loonies. Okay, we have a plan. I turned to address the crowd and the growing reporters.

"Can I have your attention? Tomorrow evening there will be a dinner and benefit concert to support our brand-new charity, Friends of the Ocean. Anyone can purchase a ticket. They will be two-hundred dollars per person. If you would like to be part of this event and cannot afford a ticket, show your support by volunteering. We would love for you to take part. The benefit will be held here on the beach; start time 7 pm, with dinner at 8 pm and the concert at 9 pm."

Allyson had run to the house to get paper and pens.

"Please list your skills and contact information on your paper and hand them to Allyson or Alex." I pointed them out to the crowd and the couple waved so the volunteers would know who to approach. "Thank you, and we look forward to tomorrow night," I finished.

"Adam, how can we pull off a dinner on such short notice," Alex asked.

"Easy," he laughed. "I'm calling my mom." Then the onslaught of volunteers had reached Alex and Allyson.

I heard him giving orders for two lines to be formed. Adam went to the house to call him mom, and I followed him. Before I entered, I turned to see Alex roping marina volunteers into helping him with the crowd and smiled.

"Mom, did you see the news?" I heard Adam say into the receiver. I couldn't hear her side but Adam smiled at whatever she'd said. "You'd make me a very happy son if you did. And can you bring Otter with you. I need him to play tomorrow night."

After whatever she said, Adam asked if his dad was home. Interesting, as he never asked for his dad when he called home.

"We're better than alright, Dad. We are about to give birth to an amazing charity called, Friends of the Ocean and Dad… can you get on the phone with the lawyers and set us up, please? Our first event is tomorrow night."

Through the phone I heard laughter and then the dial tone. "He's on it." Adam said, hanging the receiver back in the cradle. We headed back outside to help with the line. An hour later, the beach was clear. We hit the hot tub. I brought out drinks, water, and food. We sat around and discussed details.

As sunset hit, Alex and Allyson took the jeep and headed into town for a late dinner and to talk to some of the locals to see if they wanted to join us tomorrow night. I was ready for a shower and bed, despite still being on a high from earlier. When I exited the bathroom, Adam was sitting on the edge of the bed wearing a stern expression.

In all the excitement, I'd forgotten the gun. And as events played back, I also realized that jumping in the water to save a dolphin against a shark had probably been irresponsible of me in the grand scheme of things. I knew Adam would support me no matter what, but there was no way in hell he'd stand for me putting my life at risk willingly.

I could tell from his expression that a lecture to cement in those thoughts was about to happen. "We need to talk." Adam tugged me between his legs. "Clearly your safety, or lack of safety, needs to be addressed, Montana. You know I love you?" I nodded. "However, you made a deal, and you haven't been keeping up your end." I was about to interrupt, but he cut me off. "I have supported you without question, but today you put the dolphin's life before your own. You didn't even think about the consequences."

I let that sink in and wanted to argue with him. I shifted uncomfortably.

"In addition," he continued in the sternest voice I'd ever heard from him. "You had access to a gun. How did you know it was there, and why didn't you tell me?"

Now I was squirming. He knew how much I hated being held accountable for my actions. I'd always been like this and couldn't shuck the habit.

"Your dad told me it was there and where the key was. He said we should have it with us, in case something happened. We were having so much fun, I totally forgot about the gun. I only remembered when I saw the shark. I am sorry, Adam. I didn't keep it from you on purpose, I just forgot to tell you. I know it's lame, but I don't know what else to say."

"I have the responsibility of keeping you safe, right?"

"Yes," I squeaked.

"So, how do you think I should handle this situation, Montana?"

"How about a stern warning?" I asked hopefully. The intensity of his gaze didn't change and I found myself shifting uncomfortably from foot to foot.

"Consider this your only warning. I have told you before, the thought of losing you kills me inside, and I'm sure it's not just me. Don't put any life before your own, please. We can help lives, and hopefully save many, but not at the risk of your own. Understood?"

"Yes, completely."

He pulled me onto his lap and I wrapped my long legs around his waist. "I love you, my Greek god."

"I love you too, my goddess."

Chapter 10

Why? I questioned myself for the hundredth time that day, did I agree to sing? Alex had insisted I was ready, but how he could possibly think so was beyond me. This wasn't sitting on the beach and drunkenly carrying a tune, this was in front of the world because a shit-ton of news outlets were covering the event.

Thankfully, our first song was the one we'd sung together the night before. Looking out to the beach, I took in the busyness unfolding. Adam's parents had arrived late last night with Otter, Ace, and Dan in tow. Dan and Mom took over the planning of the event. Alex and Otter worked with the locals creating the stage and setting up the sound.

Allyson worked to organize the local talent coming in to perform with us. Geoff was still working on the final details for the charity with Ace's help, and Adam was the gofer for both his parents. I wandered from one group to the next, looking to help. But everything was running well, and I wasn't needed.

With added security in place I felt safe to wander on my own. I needed to ground myself. This entire idea had me feeling so overwhelmed. I was great with coming up with ideas, great with being inspired and taking on new challenges, but very few things held me for long.

I wandered away from the busyness and sat down in the sand. I closed my eyes and just breathed. I would need some booze if I was going to sing. How much could I have and keep my shit together. I didn't know, but I would find out.

With an hour to go, I went inside to get ready, and poured myself a very large rum and coke. I drank while I changed and did my makeup. Being an island performance, and outdoors under natural light, I wasn't concerned with stage makeup. In my week here, I'd gotten some color and only needed to highlight my eyes and lips.

My looks were the least of my concerns. Tonight's performance had to be seamless. Fans and friends from all over the world were attending, and some of those fans were huge in the music industry, and none of them had ever heard me sing, and just thinking about it made me want to puke.

The first hour was split between a few of the island bands. The next hour would be us. Alex was pleased with all of the performances so far and I knew he would be doing business with them in the future. Hopefully, we would play just as well as the warm-up bands.

I stepped up to the microphone and held it in one hand, while the other hand rubbed the necklace Ralph had given me as a gift all those years ago. I used it as my talisman, every time I performed, and tonight was especially important. I knew he was watching, and sent out a little prayer to him and my parents.

Alex started:

Dad, a man I never really knew, your death is sinking in, your skin like porcelain, cold and far away, time flew.

A man who could see me through, the worst and best of times.

The worst times, and the best times, and all that exists in-between.

You are a wise man, you are a good man, your love helps grow the parts in me. The parts I never let anyone see.

You taught me to be a man and fight for something, fight for something, fight for something.

It was my turn. I took a deep breath.

Dad, I remember when you dried my tears and bandaged my knee, and all the time you took care of me.

The worst of times, and the best of times, and all that exists in-between.

I was a walking disaster, your love for me, an ever after.

Dad, you were a man of vision, a man of love, you left too soon, still I cry and hope I don't fail, never give up, never give up.

Our duet: *Dad, a man I never really knew, you have passed and are gone, but your might, your teachings and your insights exist in all the places I still tread.*

You still exist in those lonely places in between, one day I will see you, I don't forget that you are the love that holds me, in those hard to reach places.

The worst of times and the best of times, we walk and see you in everything we do.

As we sang, mine and Alex's voices blended. Otter joined us in the chorus and his voice melded with ours, just like our instruments. It was magical, and the audience went crazy. Behind Blue Eyes had created another first, and it was a hit!

My fear evaporated. The duet was with strings only. So, for the rest of our performance I played and boldly sang. The weirdest part for me—we hadn't rehearsed, but intuitively I knew when to sing more than back-ups, and Alex knew when to give me the lead.

I could tell he was super charged from the new dynamic, as he played the shit out of his music. He didn't hold back, his enthusiasm propelled me and Otter to a new performance level. Being on the gorgeous beach, playing our hearts out, was the best. I hadn't had so much fun since our early days in practicing in the garage.

After our set, the three of us caught a moment together. "Stanford twins strike it rich with duet," Otter said, impersonating a newscaster. I couldn't help but grin.

"It was good, wasn't it? Did you feel that cool vibe in our voices, Alex, like our instruments?"

"Boy did I."

Otter nodded confirmation that he did too.

"I think everyone did, Mo. That was pretty powerful. How does it feel to be a singer?" I didn't know, and I certainly needed some time to process what I'd just done.

I joined Adam and Dan at their table.

"That was pretty impressive, my *Alalahe*," Adam whispered in my ear as he leaned in for a kiss.

"You guys thought it was good?" They both rolled their eyes in response.

"You three kicked it up like ten notches. Your band should be hitting superstardom any day now," Dan joked.

"I hate the thought of all those men ogling you at once," Adam sulked. I laughed.

"Really? Like they don't ogle me in the hotel in France that has pictures of me in most of the rooms?"

"Yes, well, the difference is, those were stills. Tonight, you were a gorgeous moving dream. Every person here fell in love with you. The new singing sensation, living art. Now they not only love you, but they want you."

Adam said it light heartedly with a twinkle in his eye, but it made me shiver. That was a good point. I had just made myself highly visual. In fact, that was all I had done this entire trip. I moaned inwardly and suddenly felt the need to hide. I didn't want to be noticed. Not as a female, not as art, not as a singer, not as anything that separated me from my safety net.

My euphoria instantly vaporized and was replaced with fear. Alex had joined us and was sitting quietly beside Dan listening. He picked up on my fear right away.

"What's wrong, Mo, you downshifted pretty fast."

"We may have just made a huge mistake, Alex. Making myself more conspicuous. With all the attacks, and now the animals and the singing. I feel like an idiot. I'm just setting myself up, don't you think this is the time for me to be more... conservative?"

He looked me straight in the eye. "Now you listen to me, sister. If Dad thought for a second that you were being less, doing less out of fear, what do you think he would say? 'You don't get to hide 'cause there are rotten people in the world. You celebrate who you are and what you do, and own it, girl, that's what living your best you is all about.'"

I looked at Dan and Adam, and they nodded in agreement. My euphoria was back.

The next morning, the locals who had helped came back to assist us with clean-up, which was super cool and generous of them. When we were done, Alex and Allyson took advantage of their remaining time on the island by getting some contracts signed.

Geoff, Ace, Adam, and Dan discussed future plans, including security and how to incorporate art ideas for fundraising. I had asked Liza if she would spearhead my new non-profit organization. She had accepted.

Phone calls were pouring in. Marinas around the world wanted me to visit their dolphins, animal activists, marine groups, you name it. They called, and I was feeling excited, but overwhelmed by all the sudden changes.

After our little impromptu concert, the studio wanted a meeting with us.

"They'll be looking for a new contract with "singer" being added to your role as drummer," Adam commented.

"I know." I sighed, "but we've come too far with our own company to stop and change things now. Alex and I have no interest in being under contract any longer than we have to.

Atlantic Records gave us a great opportunity, but we were pretty clear about our direction as a group and a company."

I needed a time out, and the stillness of the beach was calling me. I headed for the sliding doors and made eye contact with Adam, who returned my head nudge with a smile.

With coffee in hand, my notebook and a pen, I walked down to the water to breathe. Staring out at the sea, feeling the warm sand beneath me, I was in my happy place. I smiled, all those trips to Second Beach and English Bay throughout my childhood and teens, had created this need within me.

Like my drums, the beach and ocean resonated through me. I realized I needed the sea like I needed air, food, and water. The beach would always be my first bliss.

Two days later, we flew home. I was sorry to go. The connection I'd felt with the place and the people was truly transformational. In two weeks, I had saved a dolphin and came out of the closet as a singer, altering my career and our band.

"Thank you, Adam." I cozied up to him on the plane ride home. "Thanks for taking me there. It was a life changing trip for me, and I loved it. I hope we can go back."

"You're welcome. We can go anytime. Now that you have been, and know the island, you can go for some down time. Maybe if you and Alex need a break during or after touring and I can't get away. Mo, you can use it anytime is what I'm getting at. It belongs to us all and would be a great place for you to spearhead your Friends of the Ocean engagements.

Use it as a hub, if you will. That will make it a nice write-off for Mom and Dad." He laughed.

"Good point. I'll make sure to let Alex know. I'm sure he'll love that."

Chapter 11

Two days later, the boys and I were back in Atlantic Studios at 8 am to fulfill our contractual obligation. Walking out of there with our final cheques in hand felt amazing.

I received my promised bonus for every song I'd written for our albums while under contract. Back in the old days when we started, I had been the only writer. Alex caught on and in the past few years, even Otter wrote a few that were recorded. Still, over half the songs were mine, and since my singing debut, I was getting requests as a songwriter for other musicians. I couldn't wrap my brain around that. Why wouldn't they write their own songs? When I asked Alex, he laughed at my stupidity.

"Come on, sis. Most bands these days are front bands. They don't write their own music like the old bands did. The industry is changing, bands are collaborating, writers are writers, and you are an amazing writer, easily one of the best."

"You're shitting me? Come on, one of the best? I doubt it."

"My god, woman, sometimes you have a thick head. You never see it, do you, how good you are?"

"Ummm, I guess not. I never think of myself as a separate artist from you. I always think *us*. Must be a twin thing."

He studied me before he answered. "I don't think so, Mo. I think you have always undervalued yourself. As your brother, I have always seen your talent, and as your partner, I make sure everyone else does, too. You are the only one who has never seen that you are an amazing writer, and could easily start a writing career and never perform again. Maybe take some of those offers to write. You're really good."

I was shocked. I was an artist. Why didn't I see that? Why did I never see myself as one? Good question. Some alone time with wine and time to process was needed to answer that question.

On one of our lazy days by the pool in the Caymans, Adam had suggested that I find a personal assistant. On our return home, I placed a call to Chrissie and asked her if she was interested. She was super excited because she was tired of the minimum wage jobs she'd been stuck with since grad.

With the album finished, I had time on my hands and decided to pursue one of the offers to write for a hot new rock band that had a female lead singer. I had met her on our European tour. She was Australian and had a single that bloomed into a platinum album. Chrissie's first job for me would be handling all the logistics.

In the meantime, I worked on a hobby I hadn't had time for in the past two years, organizing my thousands of photos. Adam and Dan had taken some of my work, mainly photos of the band, and blown them up and framed them. Since their big opening, their gallery has become a popular place for Vancouervites to shop.

Local artists had been given their own section. Most of the work featured was of Stanley Park and the beaches. Mine were of the band, all of which had sold, and it was time to add some more.

The news story from the night of the shooting had skyrocketed sales of art that had anything to do with me or Behind Blue Eyes. With me safe, for now, Adam was back at it and his days in the studio were long which provided me with plenty of time to work on personal projects. Shifting through boxes, I found an old shoe box containing photos I'd taken long before I met Adam and had a decent camera.

A smile lit my face as I found a picture of Alex with Ralph, the original drummer and my bro's best friend, and Otter. They were dressed in black and white and staring at the camera with tough guy expressions. In the next one, they were cracking up. I loved the innocence I saw. We'd been about twelve at the time. Babies, in comparison to now but thought we knew everything.

It made me feel wistful for the past. Then I found a bunch from the Halloween dance. Mercy, me, and Chrissie posing for the camera. My heart hardened looking at her. She'd really taken me and my family for a ride and I wore the battle scars to prove it.

I tore the photo into tiny pieces. My focus was broken by the ringing of the phone.

"How is my darling almost daughter-in-law?"

"Hi Liza. Fine, just going through some old photos. How are you doing?"

"I'm in a quandary, darling. I have people from all over the world calling me and begging for you to come to their marinas and take a look at the dolphins and other marine life. Their health and habitat seem to be the primary concern. They're looking for feedback from you regarding their facilities and rehabilitation processes."

Ugh, what did I know of their rehabilitation processes? I couldn't just ask the animals how tank life was treating them. I think the news media had grossly exaggerated my abilities. Chrissie was supposed to run interference with the studio and my schedule, Alex and our new label, and now Liza and the charity. For Liza to call me instead of Chrissie, told me that she was wanting a solution immediately.

"Hang on, Mom. Let me go talk to Adam, and I will call you right back." It had taken me a long time to call Liza, mom, but she really had been like a mother hen and not just for me, but for my brothers as well. I walked down the hall and gently knocked on the studio door. "Adam. I need to speak with you for a moment."

"I'll meet you in the living room in five." I pictured him with a paintbrush in his mouth, and giggled at the image. Deciding he needed an actual break, I grabbed a bottle of water and a beer for each of us. Realizing he would be hungry, I also grabbed a veggie and cheese tray to snack on. I brought it all into the living room, just as he was sitting down on the couch.

He was barefoot and bare chested. His only clothing, the jeans I loved. I couldn't take my eyes off him, as always, hunger for him was my visceral reaction.

"What's up?" He either didn't notice the look of hunger on my face or was deliberately ignoring it. Fine, I would put it aside and get down to business. I handed him a beer.

"Your mom called. Her phone won't stop ringing. Marinas are begging for the dolphin girl." I didn't like the title, so when I called myself that it was with extreme sarcasm. Which wasn't lost on Adam, who wore an amused grin on his face.

"Anyway, I was wondering how you felt about me going away for a few weeks. You're busy here... I'm not. So how would you feel about Chrissie and I and a bodyguard or two hitting a few of these marinas?"

Adam regarded me with one of those all-seeing looks, straight through me, and like every other time, I squirmed. What did he see, I always wondered? One day I would get up the guts to ask him.

"Montana, do you trust me?"

That wasn't what I was expecting. "Of course I trust you, one hundred percent. Why?"

"This is what I propose. I hire the bodyguards of my choice, and make all the arrangements with Mom, and Chrissie, who will facilitate the arrangements and handle all the logistics. Do you agree?"

I didn't want to miss out on the opportunity by questioning it and readily agreed. I hadn't been out of his sight since surviving the attack at his parents home, but who could blame him for the close watch?

He went to his office to return his mom's call. When he was done, he announced he had to go out for a bit.

"Can I come with you?"

He picked me up and held me for a moment. I breathed in his scent which always caused a tightening in my belly.

"I have to go," he steadied me on my feet.

"What about a shower?"

"Later. Want to see if Ace and Kristine want to get together for dinner? I can make a reservation for the Panorama Roof."

"Okay, when are you back?" I asked, feeling suddenly lost.

"Give me two hours, and then I'll need time to clean up. See if they can meet at six."

I nodded, and he went to the bedroom, grabbed a shirt, threw on his boat shoes and a jacket and was gone. I wondered why the urgency, it was the end of January and not warm. He should have put on something more weather-appropriate. I laughed to myself for sounding just like him.

I went to have a shower, and when I got out gave my big bro a call.

"Ace Stanford here."

I giggled. "Hello Mr. Important, this is your favourite sister."

He chuckled. "You mean my only sister."

"Right, so I have no competition, therefore, I must be your favourite."

"Does my favourite sister have a reason for calling?"

"Yes, if you and Kris don't have for plans tonight, then Adam and I request your esteemed company at the Panorama Roof at 6 pm."

"Sounds like fun. Let me check with her. I'll call you back."

Ten minutes later the phone rang.

"Montana Stanford here, how can I direct your call?"

No one responded, just some heavy breathing and then they hung up. A moment later the phone rang again.

I answered, "Look, whoever you are, piss off!"

"Montana, it's Ace. What's going on?"

"I thought you just called but it was some pranker doing heavy breathing."

"Is Adam home?"

"No."

"Hang up and hide, NOW! I'm on my way."

I hung up the phone and went to the closet where I had hidden from Adam the first time he brought sushi home for dinner. It seemed the best spot, as no one knew it was there. Just as I pulled the ceiling tile shut, I heard the elevator open. I was going to call out. But I hesitated, there was no way Ace could have gotten here so fast.

A chill swept through me, leaving a trail of goosebumps and a feeling of panic. I froze in place. My instincts told me to live, I mustn't move. I had a feeling of déjà vu. This wasn't the first time I'd hidden from someone after me in my own home. The footsteps coming down the hall acted like a trigger, and I began to shake.

I was trying to get my breathing under control. But I felt faint and knew a panic attack was on its way. Shit, I needed some self-talk. *Come on, Montana, you got this, girl.* My eyes were closed, and I was trying to go to my happy place as the footsteps drew closer. Shit, shit, shit. The words, *I'm going to die,* rose unbidden into my consciousness. My mind was replaying the night in Adam's apartment. I'd had the very same thought when Bridget stood with the gun pointed at me.

I couldn't die now. Survival called me to its lucid embrace. I melded into my hiding spot and began my anti-anxiety breathing; in for a count of three and hold my breath for a count of seven and slowly exhale for a count of eight.

I could hear whoever was in our home looking for me. They were thorough. I heard every door and cupboard open and close in the hallway where I was hiding. *Stillness,* I kept repeating to myself. As the footsteps approached my hiding spot, the door opened. I pretended I wasn't there, just part of the ceiling. A moment later, the door closed, and the footsteps continued down the hall. I released a small sigh of relief.

The footsteps were coming back down the hallway toward me, and then past my hiding spot. I heard the elevator door ping. *Shit, it's Ace, and I'm stuck in a damn closet!* Ace was calling my name. I envisioned Ace being taken by surprise, and shot, laying in a pool of blood on my floor.

I couldn't deal with that vision and had to do something. I let myself down from the ceiling, grabbed Adam's baseball bat and snuck down the hall. The assailant was approaching the elevator. Ace was nowhere in sight. I figured he must have gone around to the other side from the living room. I walked stealthily toward the assailant and saw Ace walking down the other wing, towards the guest room. He picked up the pace, and I followed both men. As Ace rounded the corner into the guest room, I hit the intruder with the bat.

Ace's face registered shock for the briefest of moments. "Give me the bat. Call Eddy, then see if you can find some rope."

I did as he asked and came back with rope, and within minutes Eddy, Adam, and additional cops arrived.

"How did he get past security?" Ace asked, his question spoken to the collective.

"I found both guards knocked out at the bottom of the stairwell. This guy wasn't here alone, but whoever helped him is long gone." Adam replied. Eddy pulled two of the cops away, and a minute later they left. The one remaining cop had the assailant handcuffed, he and Eddy dragging him up to his feet. The guy looked about twenty years old, he glared at me, and then spit in my direction. On his way out, he muttered in Chinese.

Adam led me to the kitchen. "Mo, are you injured?"

"No, I'm fine." But I wasn't. My heart was racing, and my blood felt like it was pumping too fast through my veins. Being ever aware of my swings, Adam poured me water and handed me the glass.

"Breathe, honey, just breathe, it's okay now." He spoke soothingly, and my blood pressure began to lower.

"How did you manage to drop him?" Eddy had just come into the kitchen and was speaking. I felt as if I was moving in slow motion as I answered him.

"He was only a few feet away from me when the elevator doors opened. We both heard Ace get off and call out to me." I hesitated. Did I share the image I had of Ace being shot and the horrific feeling I had following that image? I raced to the bathroom and threw up. A few minutes later Adam was knocking.

"Montana, are you okay? If you don't answer me, I'm calling an ambulance."

"You can come in, Adam." He entered to find me huddled on the floor shaking. He squatted and pulled me into his arms. I began to sob. I was terrified, and I didn't know why.

"Shhhh, baby, it's okay. Tell me what's bothering you. I've never seen you so upset, is it because of Ace?"

I nodded, as I hiccupped and tried to get my breathing under control. "Adam, I had a vision. I saw the intruder shoot my brother. I knew if I didn't do something Ace would have been shot. And that isn't all. As I hid in the ceiling panel in the hall closet and heard the footsteps coming toward me, I totally panicked. I felt that same feeling when Bridget stood over me with the gun. I was going to die. The footsteps and the gun, they were a trigger I think, does that make sense?"

Adam pulled me into his chest. "Of course it does, and we need to address that for sure. But right now, I think we need to finish the report with Eddy, so everyone can leave. Are you okay to come back to the kitchen?"

I nodded and rose on shaky legs. Adam held me tight as we walked back into the kitchen. Ace's eyebrows rose when he saw me so disheveled, but before he could speak, Adam shook his head. They would discuss me later when I wasn't around. Normally that would bother me, but right now, I didn't care. I clung to Adam like he was my only life line.

He sat down and pulled my trembling body onto his lap. "Okay, Mo, continue."

"I knew the intruder would surprise Ace. When Ace called out my name, the intruder headed down toward the elevator. I lowered myself down from my hiding spot in the closet and grabbed Adam's bat. I snuck up behind him and hit him over the head as Ace turned and realized the guy was right behind him. He dropped so hard I was afraid I'd killed him."

Eddy tried not to smile. "I'm sure you scrambled his eggs for a while. Nicely done." He winked so that only I could see.

A sigh of relief escaped my lips. If Eddy was okay with what I did, then I must have done good.

He had helped the band and worked as a doorman while going to the police academy. He became a cop and then a detective for the drug squad, and he was the toughest guy I knew. He had never been beaten in our 'hood by anyone. I think even Ace, had they not been friends, would have steered clear of Eddy.

"Eddy, do you know what that guy said?"

Eddy glanced at Ace and Adam before answering. When he met with no resistance, he told me. "You will die, white demon bitch, you will die." As the message sunk in, I buried my face in Adam's shoulder.

"Eddy, do you think this is Mercy?" I didn't know what I wanted more. For him to say yes or for him to say no. At least if it was Mercy, I could rule out foul play from unknown threats. Being an icon definitely had a cost associated with it.

Her entire time in jail seemed completely dedicated to taking me down, killing me. It was not nice, but it was not brilliant either. Someone else, an unknown enemy that wanted me dead that badly was super creepy. I shuddered in Adam's arms.

"I'm sure this one will remain as silent as the last one we caught. That's the problem with these gang members, they would rather stay silent and go to jail than risk being killed by their crime bosses. I have my opinion, but no evidence, Mo."

"See you tomorrow," Adam said to Eddy, who nodded in return.

Ace looked suspiciously at me, but said nothing, then added, "How about dinner at our house? You bring the wine, say seven-thirty? Give you some time to explain to my *little sister* that her much older and much larger brother doesn't need her protection. Especially when it conflicts with her own safety."

Adam said nothing, only nodded his head.

Adam was done seeing everyone out and securing the place, "I'm glad you're unharmed." He sighed as he sat on the couch and pulled me close.

"Yes, perfectly," I lied.

"You know when you do stuff like that, I want to take you over my knee and spank you." He was impersonating Ace. Instead of me laughing as he had intended, I began to shake.

"Mo, honey, I was kidding. It's okay, you're okay... maybe you aren't. What is going on with you?"

"I don't know." I sobbed, "I feel so shaken, and I don't know why, except the vision of my brother laying in a pool of blood on our floor caused me to have a full on panic attack. I couldn't let it happen Adam. It would have been like losing Dad, all over again."

"You're probably suffering from PTSD. It is completely normal to have triggers after all the crazy stuff you have been put through. Maybe we should check in with your doctor that you had sessions with before, what do you think?"

I hesitated. I hated talking about my feelings, but if it helped get me over this irrational reaction, I was all for it.

"Sure, Adam, if you think it will help." He held me until the world turned right side up. A few hours later, we were ready for dinner. I dressed casually in wide-legged white pants, with a matching turtleneck. At my hips, I wore a wide pink leather belt, and on my feet, matching shoes.

Adam gave me an appraising look, and I knew the white would earn me brownie points for later. I was feeling much better. The earlier shock had worn off. I think the plan of going to my childhood home for a family dinner had helped settle the roiling feelings from earlier.

Adam threw on a navy shirt and khakis. He looked like some rich boat owner. He grabbed a bottle of wine and called security to say we were ready for our escort. With what had happened today, Eddy had sent over two plainclothes detectives. They had gone to Ace's to make sure everything was safe there first. We would have four people to watch our backs, and I was okay with that.

I pulled down the visor in the Porsche. "Adam, do I look rich? You always look perfectly put together, and ooze wealth. What do I look like?"

"A beautiful brat," he answered, laughing.

"Seriously, Adam, what do people see when they look at us?"

"A highly successful power couple. And yes, you look as wealthy as I do. You wear the mantle of success well and always look amazing. But then, I thought you were amazing to look at when you were barely fifteen, wearing shorts with your hair crazy and no makeup on."

I smiled. I had been such a wild child. Freedom called me and keeping me in class, school, or inside period, had been a real challenge when I was growing up. I was always at the beach or out on an adventure.

Now I could never just go out. I was suddenly feeling depressed. I was rich, young and so very *not* free. I wanted a nice family dinner with my bro, without having to worry about being kidnapped or shot, but that no longer seemed possible.

I kept thinking that one day, Alex, Otter and I would be older, we wouldn't command the media like we did right now. Then it would be possible to lighten up on security measures. Who knew how long that would be? But the truth was, being a famous drummer was not why I was in danger. I had done that all on my own and long before I had become famous.

It was weird seeing Kris open the door to my family home. She gave me a hug, and handed me a large glass of wine. I laughed.

"You sure know me, don't you?"

She winked, "I thought it was the doctor's orders."

Ace was in the kitchen, so we popped in to say hi. I gave him a hug, a long, uncharacteristic hug, one I hoped imparted how much I loved him. He hesitated at the point that a regular hug would have ended. He held me tight, and then kissed my forehead.

"Kris has been dying to show off the few renovations we have managed to get done with our tight schedule and budget." Kris giggled and then led us to the master suite, the one that had belonged to my parents. I was almost scared to look. Ace had never changed anything, just moved into it when dad had died. She opened the door, and I opened my eyes.

"Wow," Adam and I both said, "this looks fantastic." The bathroom and bedroom were completely new and one big space. With the walls down between the bathroom and bedroom, it looked almost twice its original size.

"Well done, Kris, this is wonderful," I said.

"Are you sure, Montana? I didn't want you to feel like I was destroying your childhood home."

"I'd rather you make it yours, than someone we don't know buying and living in it. Besides, Ace has lived here the longest. He, and you, deserve to make it yours. I'm thrilled for you both."

She seemed happy with my response. "Well if that's how you feel, then come and see your old room." Oh no, she had me now. I didn't want to see it. I was surprised when she opened the door, and it looked the same as the day I moved out, including the security system on the window.

"Huh? But it's the same."

Ace joined us. He and Kris had a good chuckle at my expense.

"We kept it for you, Peanut, in case you ever want to be in your old room. Besides," he added when he saw my tears, "Kris and I are going to give tours of your room for extra money."

We four broke out into laughter. "That's a good one, bro."

Dinner was amazing. When Kris brought out dessert, I was ready to broach a subject I'd been entertaining since the concert in the Caymans.

"I've been waiting for the right time to bring up an important matter. I would like the floor for a moment, if you please. Friends of the Ocean is a rapidly growing charity. In a few short weeks, Liza has created a little group of volunteers that she depends on, but the growth is too much for the team. Alex and I are too busy for me to be much help. She needs someone to fulfill the role of an accountant/administrator."

I paused and saw three sets of blank eyes looking at me for further explanation.

"I like to keep my family close. Both Adam and I do, as you know. With that in mind, I would like to offer you, Kristine, that position. I know you have a job already, but I was hoping to persuade you to join our team. I know money isn't everything. You must do what you love, but it does pay well, so, um, maybe you could renovate Dan's room."

They chuckled, and I continued, "Your title and responsibilities will grow, but only if you would like them to. I need someone I can trust that also understands me, and the spirit in which this project has been created. I need that person to help make those critical choices of where and how to support and spend funds. This is our chance to make a difference." My eyes grew blurry as my words brought up an image of Dad.

"I think Dad would have loved this project; he had a special place in his heart for all sea life. Remember, Ace, when he would come home and share all those wonderful stories. He would tell us about what he saw."

He nodded in agreement and Kris leaned toward me. "Of course, I want in. I was hoping you would ask. I was so envious when you started the charity with Liza. I wanted to ask you if I could join the team, but it didn't seem appropriate. Thanks, Montana, I would love to help spearhead this amazing project and work with Liza."

I jumped up and gave her a hug. "Yay! I'm so excited you said yes. I feel better knowing you will be part of the team and running such an important department, Kris, you are perfect for this."

Ace pulled a bottle of champagne out of the fridge. When it was poured Adam held up his glass. "Here's to Friends of the Ocean."

"To Friends," we chimed. We left after that and headed to the West Side, to the marina where we parked our boat, *The Brat*. Adam sent the bodyguards ahead to secure the boat for the night, as he wanted to take the boat into the bay and spend the night, which sounded fabulous to me. Although it was cold, it was a beautiful clear night, and I knew the stars would be amazing.

Adam went to change, and I climbed up onto the railing which had transformed into a balance beam before my slightly inebriated eyes. Had I not been drinking, I'm sure the railing would have remained as it was. The ocean was very smooth, and I would be fine, I justified.

Until a wave came, and I lost my balance. I was about to tumble into the water, when I felt arms around my waist. Adam had grabbed me just in time.

"I can't watch you every minute of the day. Can't you just behave for five minutes?" he scolded, pinching my butt for emphasis.

"Where would the fun be in that?" Another wave pushed me off balance and deeper into his embrace. I was tipsy, more than I had realized. The boat was rocking and keeping my feet beneath me was proving difficult.

"I want to talk to you about your marina tours. But I think you're a little drunk."

I gave him a sloppy kiss. "If you weren't holding me up, I think I would be on my ass on the deck. Can we talk over breakfast?"

In answer to my question, he scooped me up and carried me down to our room. Soon I was naked beneath the sheets, with Adam behind me, his arms wrapped around me. We were gently rocked into a deep sleep by the gentle lapping of the sea.

Chapter 12

I rolled over, slowly waking. The gentle movement of my cozy bed reminded me that we'd slept on *The Brat*. Adam's spot was empty, so presumably, he was on deck. I yawned, stretched, and got dressed. Climbing the few steps up, I saw my man at the helm. He was wearing a cream cable knit sweater, his loafers, and a pair of navy pants that were rolled to just above his ankles.

I stopped to admire him, he was a sexy man. Perpetually tanned, never looked run-down, his skin literally was flawless. I called him my Greek god right from the first time we met. He was that and more; brilliant, thoughtful, considerate, and loving. Sometimes I took it for granted. This moment was not one of those times.

I stepped out, coffee in hand. "Good morning, *Adonis*." He grinned, pulling me into his side.

"Good morning, *Alalahe*."

"Really, Adam, the shining one? Couldn't the islanders have come up with something sexier." I laughed.

"The shining one is more a description of the actual title. *Alalahe* is the Polynesian oceanic goddess of love. I guess we're both rating pretty high this morning."

I giggled. Tucked into his side, drinking my hot coffee, with the cool ocean around us, felt blissful. It was a good time to count my blessings.

"Where are we headed, handsome?"

"Sechelt, to check on the foundation that was poured for our family compound. I want you to see how big it's going to be, and make sure everything is ready for the next stage of construction." He adjusted his grip, both on the helm and me. "We need to talk about your travel schedule, Mo."

I sat down, and he kept his eyes on the sea.

"Let's begin with security. I have spoken with Eddy. I was at the police station, having a chat with him, when the call came in about the intruder. The speed in which they entered the penthouse showed me you are constantly being surveilled."

I stared down into my half empty cup of coffee. Yes, I realized, and I felt it, a sense of foreboding like something inevitable was going to happen. Being in the Caymans, taking a step back from the day to day onslaught had been the best thing for me. I was able to move away from the emotions that these attacks ignited. The step back had allowed me to see the inevitable. Somehow, someway, whoever they were exactly, would get me. I knew it. The only question that remained was, would I survive?

"They like to strike when I'm out of the picture, so I must be being watched as closely as you are, but probably for intel purposes. At least that's what Eddy thinks. I've spent hours replaying your attacks, right from the time you were stabbed in the back when you were sixteen years old. Every incident from that time occurred when I was away from you. I've been entertaining the thought that maybe these attacks are not directed at you, but at me."

That brought me up short. I never considered the possibility that Adam was the victim of the attacks. Coffee forgotten. I left my half full cup on the bench and pressed myself under his right arm, while he continued to steer with the left. The salty wool smell and his natural scent was soothing.

"How would I feel if, through my negligence, something happened to you, Mo? As you know, for I've said it dozens of times, it would kill me. I am also the only child of my father's empire. I considered the possibility that these attacks are aimed at him. There are so many possibilities, but it doesn't change the fact that you are the recipient, and your safety is our greatest concern." He tightened his hold as if by doing so, he was reassuring himself that I was safe.

Maybe there was more to these attacks than any of us had realized, a twofer. Take me down and destroy one of Vancouver's favourite sons, in one swoop.

"Adam, we should cross reference my childhood connections and yours. Maybe there is something we are missing. I never considered the attacks being directed at you, or our relationship. You're right, it is always when you're out of the picture. I've never considered the larger implications."

"I think that is the purpose, Mo, to keep us away from figuring this out. Keeping our eye on you, and not, as you say, on the bigger picture. Eddy is already working on the tenuous connections. The only solid connection between you and me is Dan. But they've shown no interest in him at all. It's all so strange. Maybe it *is* you, and we're reading more into this than we should. Getting paranoid with all the cloak and dagger shit."

His thoughts on the attacks provoked deeper questions for me. What if this was older? If Adam was really the victim in all this, that would mean that maybe it was Geoff that was being targeted. He was pretty silent on what had happened with Bridget and why she'd turned on the family. Did he know more than he was letting on?

"Eddy volunteered to be your personal security, begged his boss to let him go. He figures they will come after you while you're away, and he wants the chance to catch them. I'd say you're the bait, and he is the fisherman, and I don't like it. He's worried, Mo, and so am I."

He paused, and I saw it etched in his beautiful face, in the lines around his eyes that had not been there a few months ago. Whoever they were, and whatever they wanted, it was affecting Adam. The strain of not knowing was hurting him, and I wished, in that moment, that I could take it away. I wished if it was simply me they wanted, that I could leave, and he would be okay. But this wasn't simple, he loved me, he would never leave me, and me leaving him would solve nothing.

"Adam, maybe I shouldn't be going. I mean, I know I have been called to be of assistance. But I don't like what this is doing to you, to us. I don't like any of it, and I don't know what the right thing to do is. Please help me to do the right thing."

Adam was quiet and unreadable for a few moments. I began to wonder if he was going to answer me.

"Montana, what Alex said to you in the Caymans is right. Don't let these guys win. Don't quit what you're doing from fear. We are doing what we can to ensure that things go smoothly. All you have to do is never be alone while in public, not even in an elevator. Can you do that?"

I stood and pressed my face against his chest, breathing him in, feeling his strength. I don't know what I had expected, but what he did say, lessened my anxiety considerably. "Yes."

He continued, "I am still ironing out details with Mom. I don't want the schedule to strain you. So only a few, okay, to get your feet wet and see what's what, sound good?"

I nodded my head absently. "Montana, look me in the eye. Yes?"

I pulled back slightly to connect my gaze with his. "Yes, I won't go anywhere without another person, and yes, I am good with what you are setting up with your mother for my schedule."

He tucked me back to his side, and we stayed that way until he needed both hands to steer the boat toward the landing. Two bodyguards had made the trip with us, inconspicuously staying at the other end of the boat to give us privacy. Now one went ahead, and one stayed behind to keep the boat protected for our journey home.

We followed the path uphill from the landing to the property Adam had purchased a few years earlier. The boat and the land he'd bought at the same time and had used the same boat to sail my brothers and I here for the first time to show us his plans. In the end, we decided to put our energies into one big family compound. Maybe down the road, when we all started having children, there would be a need for private residences, but we weren't there yet. For now, we could come here together, and enjoy the riches of the land and sea in peace.

The concrete had been poured for the foundation and the pool. When the project was complete, the pool deck would be level with the entertainment level. This level would include a movie theater, rehearsal room, pinball machines, virtual golf and whatever else the guys thought of.

The main level would have a large common area with a see-through fireplace dead center of an open floor plan. A large state of the art kitchen would be in the centre, and then down the two sides would be wings. Each wing would have three suites and be angled in such a way that they would have glass doors that would lead out to the wrap-around veranda. We gazed at what would be a monstrous family home. I tried picturing Dan and Alex here with a gaggle of kids. I couldn't do it without laughing.

"What's so funny?"

"I was trying to picture our family years down the road, specifically Dan and Alex with kids. The picture was very funny."

Adam smiled. "They will both make excellent fathers, I think, and Ace of course," he finished with a laugh. "Maybe you can give your nieces and nephews ideas on how to escape out of their bedroom windows without being detected."

I punched him in the arm playfully. "Don't tempt me. This place looks bigger than I imagined. How much is it going to cost to run?"

As he answered, we headed back down the path towards the boat launch. "I have no idea, but with the size of it, we decided on solar and wind power. Being up on the cliffs, when the wind comes it's very strong. We will try and operate eighty percent of this place naturally, not only because of the potential costs that would be incurred, but also because it's environmentally better."

That made me happy, anything that helped rather than hurt the planet was right up my alley.

"We're doing a weekend building party when you're back. Everyone has already booked it off."

"Who is everyone?"

"Us, Alex and Allyson, Ace and Kris, my folks, and Dan. Maybe Eddy and Chrissie, and a team of security." Of course, Dan was mentioned solo, no date or girlfriend. His single status had been bothering me for a while, it just didn't make sense.

"Adam, why do you think Dan is still single? The guy is gorgeous, kind, talented and rich. He should have a gaggle of girls hanging off him all the time, instead of being Vancouver's most eligible bachelor."

"I don't think you will like the answer." I waited for him to continue and prayed this had nothing to do with Jaimie, his one and only true love who had gotten Dan addicted to coke just as he was becoming a well-recognized artist.

"I think he is still in love with Jaimie."

He was right, I didn't like the answer. Dan never spoke about her, at least never around me. Was I holding him back? I hated what she had done to him, and I totally blamed her for Dan spiraling downward into drugs.

"Do you know, or are you guessing?"

He ran a hand through his hair and looked like he was deliberating with himself. "Why do you want to know? Why now?"

"Because, Adam, I can't be the one holding him back from happiness, despite my very strong feelings about that woman. That's unfair to my brother."

"He told me he was but asked me not to tell you."

I pondered the idea of Jaimie back in our lives. Could we trust her? Could I trust her? Did it matter, if in the end he was miserable without her? It had been a couple of years since Dan's deep slide into drugs, more than enough time to get over her and move on, unless he was truly in love with her.

I was silent on the trip home, my thoughts buried in Jaimie and Danny's predicament. I'd heard through the grapevine that she'd gotten clean not long after Dan, but could she be trusted?

We were only home a few moments when Eddy arrived. I left him and Adam to talk, and went to the kitchen to make coffee. With those two discussing plans, I slipped away to the office to call Jaimie. I decided that if my brother was still in love with her, then I must find out if she was still in love with him, and if so, play cupid.

I was beginning to see what the guys were always harping on about. Despite professing my want and need for relaxation time and privacy, I was always getting in their business. I rationalized that as the only girl in the family, it was my job. I suddenly saw how alike Ace and I were, and wasn't a fan of that realization.

Ugh! I was that annoying sibling now. I promised myself that after this time, I would behave myself and focus on me, Adam and my career. I told myself that, and then tried to believe myself and ended up laughing out loud at my feeble attempts to match my mind-set with my new outlook. *Like whatever, Montana, you are what you are, girl, a sister who fiercely protects her brood.*

"Jaimie?" No response. "This is Montana… Dan's sister… hello?"

"I know who you are, Montana. Why are you calling?"

"I have a proposal, and I want to discuss it in person with you. Is there a chance you could fit in lunch at my place today, say one?"

She hesitated as if weighing out her answer. "I promise you, this is not vindictive. I just have something to discuss."

"Okay, I'll be at your place at one." I gave her my address and she hung up the phone. Adam went out to do some errands and made sure that the penthouse was secure before he left. Once he was gone, I whipped up some appetizers. When Jaimie arrived, I took her into my meditation spot in the condo and served us some relaxing tea. I wanted her in a place where I could read her clearly.

"It seems like you're living in Fort Knox these days, Montana. I've been following you and the band in the paper. You've had quite a time of it. Being famous can be challenging in ways most people never imagine."

I agreed, and we went on to discuss general topics, including art, but not her work or Dan. We drank our tea and carefully caught up, neither of us addressing the elephant in the room. We parlayed back and forth, and it was refreshing. I had forgotten how smart she was and astute at reading people. Jaimie, like Kristine and Adam, came from money. They were brought up in business and very much cut from a similar cloth.

I realized my probing was not getting me anywhere and it was time to change tactics. We moved to the dining room. She gazed out at our ocean view, while I went to the kitchen for the appetizers and a bottle of Jaime's favourite wine. When I returned, I poured her a generous amount.

She had a few sips and seemed to visibly relax. I decided to spring. "Jaimie, do you still have feelings for Dan?" She choked on her wine. I smiled at finally catching her off guard. She should have expected that frontal attack from me, if for no other reason the the warning I'd given her when she and Danny had first started dating—hurt him and deal with me.

"Yes," she croaked, then cleared her voice. "I fell in love with him the moment I met him, and it has never gone away. Dan is the man I wish I could have lived my life with."

I smiled, satisfied, her words were exactly what I wanted to hear. It was what I needed to hear to play cupid, but I still had reservations about her.

"This is good news," I said solemnly, not wanting to give too much away.

"It is?" She was thoroughly taken back and not sure how to react.

"Yes, Jaimie, wonderful news because he feels the same about you." She seemed flabbergasted at first, then she perked up.

"He does?"

"I told you when we first met that Dan is my hero, I would do anything for him. You took him down a dark path, and he almost died. If we hadn't forced him to the hospital that night, he would have died from an overdose."

This was news to her, and she looked down at the floor in silence. "I'm sorry. Truly sorry for what happened with Dan, and I ask your forgiveness, Montana. It was awful, and I would take it back if I could. I've gone through rehab as well and have been clean for almost ever since. What happened that night was a wake up call. Dan is a lucky man to have a family that cares so much for him."

I felt her truth. I saw it in her usually carefully guarded eyes. She had hurt, and she had lost too. We stood and hugged. Through my embrace I tried to communicate love and strength, and forgiveness. When she pulled back, she had tears in her eyes.

"Thank you, Montana. Thank you for being the bigger person and initiating this meeting." It was at that moment that Adam walked into the room. His eyebrows lifted at seeing Jaimie, but his only comment was, "Are you girls enjoying yourselves?"

We nodded, and he prudently left the room. "Jaimie, go home and get cleaned up. Be back at six-thirty."

"Tonight?" she squeaked, fear in her voice.

"Yes, tonight. I leave tomorrow to go on tour, and I want to see you two back together before I go. You never know how long or short life can be. Seize it and ride the wave for as long as you can." She laughed and hugged me at the elevator, before stepping in and waving goodbye, a huge grin on her face. I went to find Adam.

"What time is Danny expected over for dinner?"

"Six, does that give you enough time to manipulate everything to your liking? Really, Montana, you are full of surprises." His voice sounded amused, like a man tolerating the shenanigans of a child.

"I'm not manipulating. Okay, maybe a little. Come on, Adam, can you help me get these two lovebirds back together?" Before he could answer I added, "I have to call Dan and tell him what to wear."

Adam rolled his eyes and went back to his paperwork. I took a deep breath and then called my brother. "Dan, it's Mo, you're still coming for dinner, right?"

"Yes, I hadn't heard different. What time do you want me there?"

"How about sixish. I need to talk to you about something before I leave tomorrow, and it's kind of important. I was hoping you would wear your buffalo jeans with your white shirt."

"Montana Stanford, what are you up to?"

I flinched. "Don't be so paranoid. I am leaving tomorrow, and you never know, Danny, what can happen. Can't you just make your favourite sister happy and wear the outfit?"

He chuckled, "You're my only sister."

"Exactly, so, your favourite. See you at six." I hung up the phone. Whew, this matchmaking stuff was intense. I felt like I needed a long shower, but changed my mind and chose the double soaker tub. A few minutes later, I thankfully sank into its hot, bubbly embrace. My body relaxed but my mind was racing with all the things I could do to make tonight perfect.

Dan showed up just after six with a bottle of wine and wearing the specified outfit. His all-year tanned skin looked amazing in his light blue jeans and white shirt. Adam was still getting ready, so I uncorked the wine and placed it on the table to have with dinner. We made small talk over a couple of beers, and I steered us out to the heated patio.

"Are you excited about your trip?" he asked, taking a swig of beer.

"Not entirely. Um, yes and no, feeling unsure about a lot of things right now. But as excited as I can be."

"What's the problem? I heard that Eddy is coming along on the trip. He and Chrissie are an item now. Is that bothering you?"

"Not at all. I'm glad they are together. My two best friends being an item makes my life easier. Eddy coming is easing Adam's stress and that works for me. I just have a bad feeling.

You know, Eddy thinks this may be about more than me. He has a theory that maybe you, and/or Adam, are the actual targets."

He sputtered the swig of beer he'd just taken. "Me? I have nothing to do with Mercy. Why would I be the target?"

"Well, you are the only connection so far between Adam's family and our family. The attacks happen whenever you guys are away. What if they are getting at you through me?" I could see the wheels turning, just as they had for me when Adam suggested the idea. Silent, he drank his beer, processing my words.

"Remember when Mercy first came on the scene, Dan? She was sneaky, more than I gave her credit for. But I was there to watch her, to witness what she was doing, and to keep her away from Alex." He nodded. "The notes, they're not really her style, not even something I could picture her saying. She'd be more like, *'hey bitch, I'm going to fuck you up!'*" I imitated her.

Danny outright laughed, "You do her well, sis."

"Whatever those notes are about, I can't control it. I don't like it when my choices are taken from me, Dan. That makes me feel like my life is messy. Traditionally, that's when all hell breaks loose because I hate being a victim. It's the worst feeling ever."

He grunted an affirmation, while he took a swig of his beer. "What else?"

"What do you mean, what else? Isn't that enough?"

"I meant, why am I here? Why am I wearing this, and where is Adam?"

My turn for a swig, more like two big swigs. "I have a confession."

"I figured, and it must be something big because you're squirming like you did as a kid when you got caught doing something bad."

I ignored his remark. "Dan, are you still in love with Jaimie?"

Ha! Now he was squirming, and I grinned at his discomfort.

"Did Adam say something? Is that why he isn't here? Is he hiding?"

"Don't be ridiculous, of course he isn't hiding. I asked him why you weren't dating and why you came to all the family events alone. It's been long enough, Dan, for you to mourn and move on. Fall in love all over again. I didn't understand why you didn't have girls hanging off your arms all the time. Adam mentioned that you may still have feelings for Jaimie... is it true?"

He sighed and sank into the lounger.

"It's okay if you are. I've come to terms with you two still having affection for each other."

He gave me a look, "What do you mean, you two?"

I quickly covered up by saying I was assuming she may feel the same way, and perhaps it was worth exploring.

"You're full of surprises, sis. I haven't spoken to her in almost two years, Montana. I don't really know how to answer that, except to say yes, I have feelings for her. But, if there can be more, I have no idea."

"I do," I whispered.

"Pardon me?"

"I spoke with her, Dan."

"When?"

"Today."

"Damn it, Montana! I knew you were up to something." Dan stood up and headed for the elevator. He was going to bail on dinner and the reunion with Jaimie. Adam was walking down the hallway right then and was about to join us, when the buzzer sounded. Adam answered it, and I endured the stony look from my brother.

"Just trust me, Dan. It's going to be an awesome evening," He was muttering under his breath about pesky younger sisters, when the elevator door opened, and she stepped out. I watched Dan's face, he was struck all over again. She had dressed carefully and looked like a million bucks.

I took the few steps forward that was between them and embraced her. "It's all up to you now. Go and get him. He's all yours, he just needs you to say that you are all his."

Dan retreated to the deck, and Jaimie followed him. Adam and I stayed in the kitchen to give them privacy. I turned on a walkie talkie—the other one was hidden in the plants on the deck. Adam gave me a look of disapproval and held out his hand for me to give it up. I pouted but handed it over.

A few minutes later, Dan and Jaimie came inside. "Everything okay?"

"Everything is great. We need to delay dinner an hour, we have things to discuss." Then Dan proceeded to take Jaimie down the hallway to the guest room.

"What is that about?"

"Oh, well, I prepared the guest room in case they wanted make up sex."

"You did what?" Adam asked, looking astounded.

"Well, I filled up the bathtub with bubble bath, sprinkled in roses and left a bottle of champagne chilling with two glasses. I sprinkled more rose petals on the bed. Dan does better in private. I expect he's showing her right now, just how much he missed her."

Adam shook his head in wonderment and then began to laugh. I blushed, I really was a brat. With Dan and Jaimie working out their *problems*, that left me and Adam alone. He looked like a man on a mission, as he pulled me in and grabbed my ass.

"I think my brat needs some attention." He squeezed and kneaded my ass.

"Uh-huh," was all I could get out, as I closed my eyes and gave myself over to the pleasure I was feeling. About a half hour later Dan and Jaimie returned, and my brother was all smiles for the rest of the evening.

Chapter 13

The marina tour was going wonderfully. An entire week had passed with no threats, notes, bombs, or snipers, basically a smooth trip. What the trip did highlight were the needs of both animals and wildlife marinas that were currently falling through the cracks of government and protection agencies.

A vicious loop was evident in the rehabilitation and release cycle. Every marina I visited so far had a host of marine life that had been cut by motor blades, and damaged in fishermen's nets. It was the human error that was responsible for almost one hundred percent of the animals I visited. How do we change an issue that affects the entire planet?

I was quickly discovering that my charity was a bandage, a much-needed bandage, but a bandage all the same. Fixing the problem would require more than being a first aid charity, we needed to get to the root of the problem and develop a prevention strategy. One that was a multi-dimensional solution for us, but also for those activists and groups we partnered with.

The boards that handled many of these places I visited were all about numbers and percentages. There wasn't a lot of humanness, no happy medium to be found. For the most part. If I had my way, the ocean would be patrolled and protected. Countries would not get away with some of the things they did. I heard that Norway, under the guise of scientific research, was killing thousands of Minke whales yearly, when they were only allowed a dozen.

The Saint Lawrence River was so tainted that scientists were discovering three-eyed fish and extra, or not enough, fins. Our ecosystem was out of control, and I wished it was just the big companies that we could blame. In a way, they were certainly the precursor to all the damage. They made or imported the crappy products that we the consumers purchased and threw away. Studies were showing that plastic was the worst culprit of them all. Garbage and illegal dumping were out of control. The trip was proving most educational and way beyond checking out some tanks.

I was ripped open, my compassion outweighing logic. To keep me grounded, I made sure I spent time in the tanks with the beautiful animals I was supposed to be helping. I didn't need to. What could they possibly tell me? I didn't speak animal, but it gave me the excuse to be immersed in a world that was far beyond the human condition. Tank time awoke the poet in me, the lover in me, the survivor in me. I felt akin to these beautiful animals, and knew, once touched by their magic, that I could never ignore the call to be with them.

We arrived in Hawaii where we'd be spending most of our second week. I was excited to see the marinas here.

Aesthetically, they'd done an amazing job with space by accessing the coast and utilizing the bays. Although the tanks were big and set in the natural surrounding ocean, I couldn't help but feel like the bays were giant traps, gobbling up unsuspecting sea life.

The inkling of connection I'd felt in the Cayman Islands was much stronger here in Hawaii. Stress and anxiety was moving through me in waves causing me severe agitation.

"Mo, what's wrong?" Eddy was running a security check in my room.

I sunk to the floor. "Help me." I buried my head in my hands.

"Mo, what is it? What's wrong?" Eddy said, kneeling in front of me, taking my hands.

"Eddy, I feel so much distress! There's a very unhappy pod of dolphins nearby, and I have no idea what's wrong or how to fix it."

I ran to the bathroom and threw up and staggered out. "Eddy, fuck protocol. I need to get down to that wildlife park thingy we passed on the way in. I think that's where it is coming from. This sound or feeling started when we were passing it. Tell Liza and Chrissie we're going now, without the press."

He nodded. "Get ready, Mo. We'll leave in ten minutes." He left to make the arrangements. I needed to get myself under control and tried to still my racing mind with deep breathing. I changed my clothes and sat down, focusing on Alex.

Alex, can you hear me? I need you. I need some back up, bro. Moments passed until a sense of calm infiltrated my being. Now I could take some deep breaths and feel myself relax. When Eddy and the rest of our little group showed up, I had calmed down substantially. We left for the marina, dressed plainly so as not to attract any unwanted attention.

On the drive over, I focused on my purpose, happy that I wasn't alone. Alex's unswerving tenacity was feeding me. His entire mechanism, how he operated as a person, was so different from mine. He reminded me of Adam a bit. Unwavering in all they did. I was nothing like that. My energy was like shattered glass.

We entered the marina and headed directly for the dolphin tank. The noise was deafening, but it wasn't coming from the area before me. It was coming from behind in the holding pen not open to the public. I nodded to Eddy. When no one was watching, I slid past their single security guard and made my way around to the back-holding pen. I jumped in and swam over to the dolphins. There were several, while only two were for viewing in the front. They circled me and allowed me to touch them. I felt fear, and wrongness. I couldn't speak to them, and I didn't really know how much they understood, but I talked to them all the same, just like I had in the Caymans. They seemed to understand that I was there for them.

I got out of the pen and slipped through a door that led into the facility. I found an examination room with medical equipment and files. I started flipping through the files on the dolphins. The records didn't make sense. Not only were the numbers in the files not reflecting what was in the tanks, but the medical reasons themselves didn't either.

The shipping receipts were the most disturbing of all. The sanction of illegal transportation didn't seem to apply to this marina. They were separating pods and sending them all over the world. The group in the holding tank, which apparently didn't exist as far as the number of animals tagged, was being sent to three different labs in China. Holy shit! This was a sale for experimentation, not for rehabilitation where they would play with friends and loved ones. I felt sick, no wonder this place felt wrong.

The dolphins were to be shipped out today, and my scheduled visit was for tomorrow. They were getting rid of the evidence before I arrived. Those bastards! I rounded the corner to where Eddy stood guard. I don't think he'd ever seen me so mad. His eyes instantly shifted and mirrored mine.

"Eddy, these assholes are illegally selling wildlife for experimentation all over the world. I saw the paperwork. I'm going back in the tank, as their departure is imminent, and they won't take them if there are witnesses. Tell Liza, she knows what we need to do, send her to talk to the marina owner. The owner may have no idea what is happening, but then again, he might. Either way, the only place these animals are going is back home."

He came back moments later. "She's on it."

He stayed by me as I swam and sang and talked to the dolphins. I tried to make them feel safe and impart hope. I had no idea what I was doing, but I was following what my mother had said, my sixth sense.

It wasn't a long wait for Liza and Chrissie to return with the owner, who was also the majority shareholder. Eddy helped me out of the tank, and we went to speak with Jon Kim. The release was arranged for the evening, just before sunset.

Jon Kim had the marine veterinarian fired, and the police were called. Management had been suspicious of him for some time, the shareholders had just been waiting for him to be caught so they could get rid of him.

"What I don't understand is why? What was the gain for him?" Jon Kim asked.

"He has been dealing with poachers, ocean pirates and using your marina as a holding bay." I answered. "Then selling off what he bought to other countries that either want them for experimentation, or food. Either way, it is completely illegal, and I'm sure that not only will authorities throw him in jail, but Friends of the Ocean and other wildlife organizations will press charges."

That was a shock to him, which spoke volumes to me. "We have to make sure that you had no knowledge or involvement, and that this was done against the marina and not part of a bigger illegal enterprise. We are making sure the vet isn't your fall guy."

His eyes widened, and his jaw dropped a bit. Good, cocky S.O.B. needs a little shaking up to throw him off his game. Whatever his next move was would reveal his true nature.

"Do the dolphins know how long this has been going on," he asked.

I snorted at his ignorance. "Jon Kim, despite what the news says about me, I do not talk to animals. I simply can feel when they are happy or not. Their distress is what brought me here a day early. But based on factual evidence, the paperwork in the lab, five years."

"Five years?" He seemed stunned. "I will have my people phone every location that has received sea life from us over the past 5 years. If they are still living, I will arrange to have them brought back."

And there it was, what I'd been looking for all afternoon, that he was a good guy. "Eliza Northrop, whom you have met, will help oversee the contacting and release of the animals. They didn't go to the marinas, Mr. Kim. They went to other, less savoury places. She has come to learn the heads of many of these *places*, and can help."

He seemed grateful, and together, they went inside to begin the process. I had another hour in the tank with the dolphins. They seemed calmer, almost like they understood. I was thrilled to be part of the release back to the ocean for the tank dolphins. Based on location, all the marina had to do was open a gigantic gate in the sea. I was with the dolphins when the gates opened, and we swam out.

The joy was indescribable. I hung on to two of the dolphins, and once we were out of the bay, I let go and they continued. Eddy and Jon Kim, along with a pilot, picked me up in a boat. We stayed in the bay until they disappeared from sight. The boat turned to head back to the marina, and that's when I saw the crowd on the beach.

Cheering rang out across the water, reaching our ears. When we pulled up and jumped out of the boat, flashes went off, many reporters took pictures and fired questions at me faster than a speeding bullet. Jon Kim removed the attention from me to him, when he gave a small speech. At the end, he held up my hand like a champion who had just won a fight.

It was a victory for the marina, and they would use it. I was cool with that. We all had a living to make, and marinas were very expensive places to run. Before we left, I told Jon Kim that I expected to only hear good things regarding his marina. That our group would be checking in to make sure the marina stayed ethical.

I was exhausted, my energy from Alex long since used up. The four of us went back to the hotel. More reporters and paparazzi were waiting for us. I did my best to be respectful of the onslaught of questions, but I felt myself fading and excused myself to use the washroom.

Chrissie came with me. She used the facilities, but I just sunk forward resting my elbows on the counter and splashing cold water on my face. As I stood to wipe myself off, two Asian women walked into the bathroom. Just as Chrissie exited her stall, one of the Asian women grabbed my arm and twisted it behind my back. The other approached with a knife.

Chrissie screamed and ran for the door. I heard her screaming for Eddy. I waited until the woman in front got closer and leaned back into the assailant behind me and kicked the woman with the knife in the face. She fell back crashing into the counter and sprawling on the floor.

The one behind me let go and stepped back pulling a gun from her waistband as Eddy came barreling through the door. His distraction gave me the chance to kick her in the knee and she went down, but the gun fired. The bullet ricocheted off the porcelain sink and just missed my head.

Eddy grabbed her and had her face down and in cuffs in seconds. The gun fire alerted security, and guards came pouring in. The other Asian woman was cuffed and they were dragged to their feet and out the door. Additional security made their way to our suite to make sure everything was in order. A police officer followed me and Eddy up to our room to take my statement.

It was a good thing that we had extra security, and they had gone ahead, as there was a package in my room, with another note, same message as all the others. Eddy was furious, determined to find out who the hell had let this happen. He pulled us out of the hotel and moved us to an undisclosed location. Once we were safe inside, I headed to the shower. I was freezing, as I had been in wet clothes for hours.

Screw the shower, I needed a bath. I could hear Eddy on the phone with someone, Adam maybe. I was too tired to care. When I was done, I crawled out of the bathroom and into bed. Eddy was done on the phone and asked me if I needed anything.

"Eddy, would you please stay? I'm afraid and I'm missing Adam. I don't want to be alone."

"I was planning to, Mo. Don't you worry about anything. Just sleep, I will watch out for you. I'm sorry, I should have swept the bathroom before you went in." My eyes were closed and felt too heavy to open. I managed to pat his arm in comfort.

"It wouldn't have mattered, they came in after me."

I was beginning to drift when he said, "Don't worry, just go to sleep, and when you wake up, we'll get you dinner. Just sleep." He rubbed my back just like he had many times in the past when I would crash in his parents' spare room and within seconds I was out.

The next day we headed back to Vancouver, cutting our Hawaii trip short. With the breach in security, and the attack, we decided it was best to head home. Eddy had security at the elevator, the lobby, and our awaiting transportation.

He wasn't taking any chances for the trip home. As I ducked my head to get into the waiting vehicle, I stopped to gaze at a woman who was standing back in the crowd. She wore sunglasses, but I knew it had to be Katya, Dan and Adam's art friend from Paris. In the car, the door closed behind me and I looked out the back window, but she had already disappeared.

Why was she here, and why would she be at my hotel? We had been moved to an undisclosed location the night before, but somehow everyone in Hawaii knew where I was the next day. Somewhere there was a leak, or maybe hotel staff sold our location for a few bucks. I didn't know, but it sure felt like Eddy and Adam's theory could be true. Maybe the notes were not from Mercy, maybe there was another player in this sinister game, and Katya had something to do with it.

I thought about Katya on the plane ride home. She was a nasty little narcissist. I pissed her off when I scooped up Adam for myself. She had done everything to distract him from me when she had visited Vancouver for several weeks, back when I was fifteen. She had contributed to my being stabbed when she wouldn't let me speak with Danny when he and Adam were in Italy. She'd sabotaged me every opportunity she had. Despite all of that, I'd never considered her a real threat. But, she had been to Adam's enough times back in the early days that she could have met Bridget the housecleaner at the Northop estate. Maybe she wanted to finish what she had started all those years ago with Adam and have him for herself.

They would have made a beautiful couple, with their dark hair and green eyes. She was a tiny, petite French woman, with connections all over France. Her family were old world money and major art collectors. Adam knew her through the family, and Dan had met her when he had his art scholarship.

When she first came to stay, I was blown away by her looks. I felt like an ugly duckling around that woman. Back then, Dan thought Katya was the most amazing woman he'd ever met, but it was more like worship than actual attraction. She was the treasure he could never have. Her very feminine

French ways caught the attention of Ace, who subsequently broke things off with Kris around the same time. Of course, they got back together with some scheming on my part.

Katya had an effect on every man except Eddy. I hadn't mentioned to him about seeing Katya outside of the hotel as I wanted to speak with Adam first. I was still lost in thoughts of the past when we landed safe and sound back in Vancouver, B.C..

Chapter 14

I was first off the plane and looking for Adam. When my gaze landed on his, joy warmed my heart. I raced ahead and jumped into his arms, wrapping my legs around his waist.

"Adam! I missed you so much. I wished so many times that you had been with me. This stuff is so much bigger than I could have imagined, and you would have been a huge asset, but your mom was a good fill in. Did you see me on television?"

He laughed. "You mean riding out to sea with a couple of dolphins, yeah I saw. I was getting worried and thought you might ditch me for a handsome single dolphin."

I snuggled against him, kissing his neck, "I thought about it, but the fish smell was too strong."

He laughed again and set me down, when the rest of the group caught up.

On our way out, I paused at a newsstand that had several magazines featuring me on the cover. The Rolling Stone Magazine had the entire band, and an article on Allyson's reporting career before working exclusively for Twin Spin

Records. There was a little blurb in there on the new record label, and it included the type of artists we were attracting.

I read about how the Stanford twins were making their mark on the world. The article said every little girl in the world who wanted to be a superstar has photos of Montana Stanford pinned on their walls.

Business Weekly had Ace and Geoff on the cover shaking hands. It seemed our families were taking a lot of space in the media world. National Geographic had an amazing photo on the cover. "Look Adam, that looks a little like your work."

He studied it. "It does, but as I'm in the photo, it's definitely not mine." The photo was of Adam, Alex, Ally and I swimming with the school of dolphins after the shark attack. Whoever took it had captured the magic beautifully. Inside was an interview with Liza about Friends of the Ocean, and a few more pictures. One of Adam with his arm around me for support as we waded to shore.

The bullet hole in my shoulder was evident and it wasn't the first time it had been captured by someone's lens and published for the world to see. The results of that almost fatal night still gave me the shivers. It had been a close call, too close.

The man at the newsstand gave us a quizzical look. Like a buy or get out kinda stare. Adam held up the magazine and the man's frown lifted to a smile, "Can I have an autograph?"

Adam purchased all the magazines he had with us on the covers. We signed one of the National Geographics and handed it to him. At the car, Eddy and our security swept the vehicle.

"I should get an update from you, Eddy. Why don't you and Chris get settled, and then come over for dinner. It would be nice to catch up."

Eddy looked at Chrissie, who enthusiastically nodded her head. "Thank you, Adam, we'll see you around six."

Chrissie hugged me goodbye and the couple headed to their car. Eddy scanned for bombs or bugs before letting Chrissie get in the passenger seat. Eddy had always watched my back growing up and had treated me with respect. I knew he'd treat Chrissie like a princess, which is what she'd always wanted.

What I wasn't sure of was how their arrangement would work for him. Eddy had always wanted a big family. Growing up with my brothers and me, he'd seen first hand what a loud boisterous family was like and for some reason that was his hot button. I wasn't so sure that was hers. Chrissie had a way older half-sister who had moved out when she was six years old, so she basically grew up the same way as Eddie, as an only child. But their perspectives couldn't be more different.

I got in our car, impatient to get home and have Adam to myself. He was speaking with his mother, wearing a look of consternation. I let the window down a bit so I could listen in.

"How was she?"

"Amazing, a lot of what they wanted from her was way beyond what I would have considered in her scope. Adam, watch out for that girl of yours. She has such a wide open, sensitive heart. This world can be a nasty place; people like

Montana can easily get swallowed up. Much like the animals she is trying to protect."

"I know, Mom, she is special. I will remain vigilant." She gave him a hug and a kiss and said, "see you for dinner on Sunday." Adam got in the driver's seat and I waited until we were on the road before laying into him.

"You know, if you have questions about me, you can always ask, you don't need to check in with your mommy on how I'm doing." I was pissed, I hated when people talked about me as if I was some sort of victim, "I'm a bad-ass or have you forgotten."

His face remained passive, but his eyes darkened. "At it already, Brat? I was simply asking my mother," he enunciated the word Mo-th-er, "not my mommy, as you called her, how you had been as you are the only one that matters to me. She may have seen or heard things related to you that were not discussed with you and that is what I was asking, Miss Snoop."

Well now I felt stupid, but still pissed, and no way would I let him off the hook so easily.

"So now Liza is your spy? That's bullcrap, Adam, and if that's what you're up to, then I will fire her from the project."

Adam pulled into our spot in the underground. He didn't say a word but I could tell he was furious. Unlike Ace, who when angry had cultivated a look that imparted mess-with-me-if-you-dare, or Danny whose jaw would tick, Adam's eyes would go so dark they were almost black. It rarely happened and it had never been because of me, until now. I was being bitchy and unfair, but I didn't care. I was having a full on brat attack and I wasn't done.

"Oh, and by the way, I saw your girlfriend in Hawaii."

"What girlfriend do I have besides you?"

"Katya," I practically spat. "That bitch was skulking outside of my hotel trying to blend into the background, but I could feel her evil energy and spotted her. Did you send her to spy on me too?" I got out of the Porsche and slammed the door. "Because, I saw her in Hawaii." Security had already taken the luggage and was sweeping the house when Adam slid into the elevator before the door closed.

"Katya in Hawaii at the same time as you can't be a coincidence."

"Maybe she was there hoping to see you." I pouted.

Our elevator dinged open into our personal foyer, and we continued the discussion, "I know you don't want to talk about it, Adam, but what if she wants to finish what she started with you? Maybe I am just collateral damage. With me out of the way, she could swoop in, and be your grieving friend. I imagine with the hopes of winning you over." The more I talked the more idiotic I sounded. Why was I so pissed? My irritation had gone way off course.

"I doubt it, but I'll mention it to Eddy tonight and have him investigate her reasons for being there. Now listen to me, Brat, I want you in a hot bubble bath, and then our bed in one hour. I want to ravish every part of your body."

The spell was broken and I took off down the hallway, letting out a squeak of surprise when Adam playfully smacked my ass. A few minutes later, I was bent over the tub checking the temperature.

"I'll never get tired of that view."

I gasped and turned around. "Looking is all you're going to get if you keep scaring me like that, Mr. Northrop."

"My apologies, princess. I've come to serve you wine," He placed it in between the candles and held my hand while I stepped down into the deep soaker tub.

"Would you like to join me?"

"I would, but if I did, then we would be ordering take out. I'll see you in about forty-five minutes."

"Yes, sir," I did a mock salute. After my soak, Adam and I had a lot of catching up to do and we'd run out of time. While Adam made the call for our order and answered the buzzer to let Eddy and Chrissie in, I stood in my closet in a white thong, while debating what to wear. I didn't hear him come up behind me, until he smacked my ass. "Adam! Stop sneaking up on me and smacking my ass."

"I can't help it, you have an amazing ass and I love smacking it. What's the hold-up, Brat. It's just Eddy and Chris, you can wear anything you want."

"Ugh, I just don't know what to wear. I know it sounds dumb, but for the life of me, I just can't decide."

"Let me," Adam always enjoyed choosing my outfits for me, so I let him. I'm glad I did. He chose ultra soft pastel balloon pants with a satin chemise top with spaghetti straps. I quickly dressed and admired the way the silky material clung to me like a second skin.

Adam grabbed a pair of ballet flats and had me lean on him while he slid them onto my feet. "Thanks, Adam, I feel like Cinderella. I really don't know why getting dressed is so hard sometimes."

"I do," he said as we walked down the hall to the dining room.

"Why?"

"Because, darling, you are an emotional everything; dresser, eater, drinker. Completely impulsive, right Eddy?" We'd entered the dining room, Eddy and Chrissie were sitting with the drinks Adam must have poured before coming to see what had taken me so long.

"Absolutely, and you've always been that way. I've known you as long as your brothers, and I agree with Adam, you're an emotional everything."

Chrissie was laughing.

"You agree with these guys?" I asked accusingly.

She nodded her head and broke into peals of laughter. I tried not to join in but their humour was contagious. The sound of the buzzer cut in. Chrissie and I set plates outside on the deck table, while Eddy and Adam unpacked the food and brought it out.

We sat and enjoyed twilight, indulging in fantastic French cuisine and funny stories from the three of us who had just returned. Some funny, and some not so funny. I talked about the scope of work that was required to get the protection agencies to do what they advertised.

Chrissie went over the bathroom incident at the hotel. "I don't know why they let me go, I guess they didn't realize I was with Mo. Otherwise, I can't imagine they would have let me leave the bathroom."

"I think they thought they could kill me before anyone could come to my rescue. That, or as you say, they must not have noticed that you were with me."

Eddy nodded his head. "I hate to admit my negligence, but I agree. Without Chrissie's warning, you may have not made it out of the bathroom."

"Ugh, is there a worse way to die?" I joked. "I mean, really. Famous twin, Montana Stanford, dies in a hotel bathroom. That's terrible." We all laughed despite the seriousness of the situation.

"And then all those reporters the next day, any idea who leaked that information to the press, Eddy?"

He sighed, "They all deny it, but for sure, someone in the hotel. When I talked to the news crews, they said they had all received an anonymous tip in an email at the exact same time as each other. The thing I find weird is, the Chinatown connection isn't in Hawaii. It feels like an act they wouldn't perform, which goes back to the theory that Mercy is not responsible for the notes."

I eyed Adam and he nodded his head, affirming I should share my thoughts. "Eddy, I have a theory about the note writer. This morning when we were leaving the hotel, I saw Katya in the crowd. She was wearing dark glasses, and she had her hair pulled back, but I recognised her right away."

"Katya?" both Chrissie and Eddy said in unison.

I shared my thoughts and the possible connections. Then Adam took over.

"I spoke with my father when we arrived home. He said the family owned a large hotel chain. I was unaware of that. I only knew they were old money and have accrued a massive collection of art. They bought out the chain that owns the second hotel you checked into in Hawaii, Eddy. I think Mo is right."

Eddy let go of a whoosh of air and sat back in his chair.

"Well, that gives an entirely new take on the notes, doesn't it? Clearly, she is referencing you, Adam. I remember those days, she had her claws in you so deep. Me and Mo steered clear of all of you while she was here. In fact, Mo spent many nights at my house.

"He's right, and I'd been meaning to confirm with you Adam, did she ever meet your housekeeper, Bridget?" Adam looked thoughtful.

"Yes, I believe they did meet when I brought Katya in to say hi to my parents. She would have met Bridget for sure."

"Oh—my—god! I just put it together. Adam, that is how these attacks have been one step ahead of us this entire time. Bridget would have had access to your father's notes and been able to overhear conversations. She could have told anyone, the Chinatown gang, Katya, anyone."

"Adam," Eddy caught my attention. "Who is the new housekeeper at your folks house now?"

"Let me give my father a call."

"No," Eddy said. "Don't call, in case she is working with someone and hears the conversation. I think it's safe to say that the information is coming from your father's house. I will do some digging and talk to him at his office tomorrow."

"Wait," I interrupted, "there is one thing that doesn't get explained. If Bridget was responsible for the intel, how would an informant for the Yakuza be connected to Katya?"

Adam scrubbed his face. His voice held a deep sadness when he spoke. "Katya knew when you called that night in Europe, Montana. She knew Mercy stabbed you in the back, and she met Mercy. Why wouldn't she use Bridget, or whoever else she could to brainwash her into helping.

"They are a rich, powerful family," I shuddered, "and to think she used Bridget for intel. The night in your apartment, she probably communicated with the Chinatown gang's leader and offered them whatever information Bridget had in exchange for the attack. That is Katya, the most manipulative woman I have ever met." We were all silent, digesting my words.

"If that's true," Eddy spoke, "then it would make sense on another level. The mastermind. I'm sorry, but Mercy is a narcissistic manipulator, she doesn't have the brains to spearhead something of this magnitude. And maybe the Chinatown gang is being spoon fed intel and money to do the bidding of Katya, and Mercy has been the connection between the two all along. Maybe Mercy is Katya's puppet and was set up to be the fall guy."

The idea was so sensible. Why hadn't any of us thought of it before? "So, what's our plan, Eddy?"

"I think we should act as if we are none the wiser. Adam, if you can do some digging on Katya's family. Don't talk to your father about it, unless you are not at his home or on the home line. We have to assume his office has been bugged, possibly his phone as well. I'll get a printout from the telephone company and check the outgoing calls. We have a lot to work with that we didn't have an hour ago, Montana. Well done."

I gave Eddy a small smile. The implications were overwhelming and I was quickly becoming exhausted from my emotions going into overdrive. The guys were right, I was an *emotional everything*. We had dessert and called it an early night. I fell asleep quickly but was plagued with nightmares.

Chapter 15

Our work weekend at the property had arrived. We chose to take our boat and brought Chrissie and Eddy with us. After our intense dinner conversation a few nights earlier, we had much to discuss.

My theory regarding Katya being in league with Mercy, and the Yakuza, was still being investigated, but Eddy felt we were on the right track. I think we all took a deep breath knowing that we maybe had a modicum of control for the first time since Mercy's last well laid plot to get me removed from the band.

The boat trip over proved to be more relaxed, even than I'd hoped for. I made a *friend* with an adorable seal and named her Bubbles. I fed Bubbles sandwiches, and in turn, Bubbles did tricks for us, a very entertaining seal.

Adam handed the wheel over to Eddy for a bit so he could take pictures we could later use for Friends of the Ocean. The rest of our work party and half a dozen bodyguards met up with us shortly after arriving at the site. Eddy divided his team into sets of two, doing a thorough sweep of the grounds. When we were cleared to work, we broke into groups.

Adam wore a grin from ear to ear. His dad had started his mega empire as a construction guy and, as a young teenager, Adam had worked with his dad on breaks from school. This was probably the first time in twelve years they would be hammering side by side. I imagined Adam doing this with our children one day. He was so patient, I knew he'd be able to pass on a lot of skills and knowledge to them.

Geoff, Adam, and Ace had designed the family home with little input from me. I didn't want the responsibility. That would change when we worked on the lighthouse because it would be the first thing beside my bedroom back home that would be all mine.

Adam handed me a hammer. My favorite mundane task other than interior painting was hammering. Hours of enjoyment with nothing to occupy my mind. No one else in my family liked to do it and they were happy to leave me alone with the hammer and bucket of nails.

Dan, Ace, and Adam worked with Geoff on the outer wall and I followed behind them. They offered me a nail gun, but it wasn't nearly as fun as pounding a nail into wood, so I declined.

Alex had the music blaring, as he worked on measuring and sawing the lumber. Chrissie and Allyson oversaw the food and drinks. Having zero experience holding a tool, they said they weren't going to start now.

When Ace said he needed a bathroom break we took one as well. Everyone seemed to be having fun, and that was what this was about. In one of the philosophy books my therapist had me reading, it discussed life is the *journey*, not the destination. To always be straining or yearning for what's next took you away from living in the present. Standing here and witnessing that very thing all around me was exactly what the book meant.

From the corner of my eye, I caught Ace darting behind the structure we were working on with a huge super soaker in hand. A huge grin split my face. I ducked away and went to his vehicle to find the other three in the back seat. He'd premeditated a water gun war. I loved that! I grabbed two and went and filled them up. Just as I was capping Alex's gun, Ace came barreling around the corner, "Got you!" He pumped out water so fast, I was soaked before I could make my escape. I was laughing as I came skidding up to Alex and said, "Water fight!" And tossed him his loaded soaker.

I ran behind the next car, Ace barreled past me but when I left my spot he grabbed me around the waist. I pushed off the car with my feet and Ace tumbled back on the dirt with me on top. I pushed off him and pumped out water, soaking him in seconds.

Alex joined me, but Ace swept out his leg and tripped me. I lost my grip on the soaker and he pinned me down with one of his huge hands and soaked me again. Alex tackled Ace and the three of us were drenched and laughing so hard, we could barely breathe. I spared a glance for where I'd seen Adam last to see he was still there and standing beside him was Liza, both were laughing at our shenanigans.

Ace stood up, and held out his hand to Alex. Pulling him to his feet he put him in a headlock for a noogie. Dan must have found the remaining gun in the car and shot at Ace until he let Alex go. I was out of water, and grabbed Alex's fallen soaker and my own and raced off to fill them, leaving Dan to face off against Ace.

An evil grin split Ace's face, and you could see Dan realize he was in trouble. Ace tackled him to the ground. Dan called for help just as Ace tackled him to the ground. Back with the guns, we soaked Ace and the ground and found ourselves slipping in the mud. Down on the ground now, our water fight shifted to a mud wrestling match, with the three of us against Ace. I was laughing so hard I could barely breathe.

Ace was trying to crawl out of the mud hole but we wouldn't let him out. We were all laughing so hard our wrestling became more of a crabs in the bucket routine—each time one of us tried to crawl out, the other three would pull them back.

"Lunch in half an hour." Allyson yelled.

That was all the motivation we needed to crawl out of the mud pit and make our way down to the boat to shower and change. I fell behind my brothers a bit and watched as they playfully shoved each other on the way to the boat. I was reminded of the book, *The Outsiders*. My three brothers were like those guys in some respects.

The next day, us ladies decided to go to town for supplies. Adam had purchased a truck from a farmer on a neighboring property, who also stored it for us. When Adam had alerted him to our weekend party, he'd dropped it off for us to use while we were here. This would be my first opportunity to drive it.

"I know, don't speed, stop reminding me," I looked at Adam trying my best not to roll my eyes, but I was anxious to get behind the wheel. I almost never drove Baby these days. My cute VW Cabriolet spent more time in the underground of our apartment back home than on the streets of Vancouver. With security, Eddy or Adam driving me everywhere, my opportunities had been limited.

"Montana," he growled, his eye color darkening, "Promise me, you will never be alone." We were walking toward the truck, I turned around to give him a hug. "I promise," and walked backward toward the truck making goofy faces at Adam. A loud boom and I was being propelled through the air toward Adam, landing where he'd once stood.

My head felt like it was exploding, and my hands moved instinctively to my ears. I opened an eye to see Adam about a dozen feet in front of me, lying still. I was overcome with dizziness. My guts couldn't hold their contents, and I was puking and screaming from the pain the movement caused my head.

Ace was at my side, rolling me onto my front. and holding me still. He may have spoken, but I couldn't hear anything, just the horrible ringing in my ears. Through the ringing, I could make out the sound of wailing, an ambulance? I closed my eyes, the light was too much. Now blind and deaf, I had nothing to stabilize consciousness, and let myself go to the dark.

I floated in and out of consciousness. At some point I knew I was on a gurney, a part of me was hovering like I had before but a part of me also knew I was still very much in my body. Whatever had happened, I wouldn't die. Had that come from Alex? I tried to speak with him but the pounding and pain acted like a blocker. I'd have to be satisfied with the belief that my brother was here with me like he always was when I needed him most.

In more lucid moments, I would try and open my eyes. I'd be overcome by the sensation of being upside down. I would force myself back into darkness to keep from throwing up. I felt a hand, heard a voice but it sounded like it was spoken from the other end of a mile long tunnel.

Where was Adam? The last time I'd seen him, he'd been unconscious on the ground ahead of me. I'd been closer to the explosion and hoped that meant he was okay but why he wasn't with me was a concern.

I heard a sound that woke me from my sleep. It sounded very far away. But I heard it. The voice said, "If you can hear me, blink." I blinked. Then darkness, maybe I'd dreamt the voice. I didn't know, but the next time I woke up, I heard voices a little more clearly than last time. They sounded closer, like the next room instead of a block away.

"Hello?" I cleared my throat and tried again. "Hello?"

"Montana. Thank goodness you're awake."

"Adam? You can hear me."

I felt his hands gently grip mine. "Yes, I can hear you." I breathed in a voice that didn't sound like me. It was scratchy and old sounding.

"I need water."

Adam held a straw to my lips but only let me have a little. "I'll get the nurse to check on you before I give you more," he removed the straw. I tried moving my head, and it seemed okay. I didn't feel like I needed to vomit, but it made the ringing a little louder. The explosion, it all came back to me in a flash.

"The others?"

"Everyone is fine."

"I was so worried about you, Adam, when I saw you on the ground knocked out but I couldn't do anything to help."

"Just a few bumps and scratches and a little whiplash, nothing to worry about. You took the worst of it. When the truck exploded, glass shattered and embedded into the back of your body. They induced a temporary coma to get all the glass out."

"Where are we?"

"Scotland. I'll explain everything, just let me get Nurse Campbell first and then I'll tell you what we know so far." He went out the door, and I was left to stare at the ornate ceiling in a very large bedroom, at least what I could see of it.

Adam came back in with a short woman who was talking with such a thick Scottish accent, I had to strain my ears to understand all she said, which sent my neck and head into spasms.

"There, there, now, lass," she tutted as she moved my pillows and gave me a little more water. "You've been out for quite some time, you must be still while I see to your vitals."

Adam stood behind her, watching intently.

"How long have I been out?"

Adam's focus moved from the actions of the nurse to me.

"Two and a half weeks, as of yesterday." I shook my head, and pain shot up through my skull.

"You're still suffering from whiplash. Don't bend your head forward or back, just gentle lifts, aye, and limit the side to side motion. Relax now, lass. I'll see to some nourishing soup for you." Mrs. Campbell tutted and left the room.

"I feel like I'm in an alternate universe. Why does this place look like a 15th century castle?"

Adam chuckled. "Because it is a 15th century castle, and Mrs. Campbell is the custodian. She is also a nurse and local healer whose family has been a part of the castle for over five hundred years."

Adam held the straw to my lips for a few more sips of water.

"I'm ready, tell me everything, Adam."

"Katya."

I closed my eyes. I had been right, she was connected, probably the note sender, and all for what? 'Cause she wanted to fuck my fiancé?

"It turns out Bridget was working for Katya, and so was the new housekeeper, Olga, who we found out is also Bridget's sister. That's why the notes often preceded you to locations and why the Asian gang was always one step ahead, because they knew our plans."

"Does that mean Katya is the note writer?"

Adam nodded. "She is, and she convinced Olga that you were responsible for Bridget's death, so getting her to agree to pose as a housekeeper was easy. Then she placed bugs throughout the house, but mostly in my father's office and on his phone. Katya is also responsible for the bomb explosion in England that almost claimed your life."

Holy hell! This was too much. I leaned over the bed and hurled into a bucket. Adam held my hair out of the way and helped me back into a comfortable position.

"Katya was arrested on several counts of assault, and two counts of aggravated assault. With her no longer able to spoon feed the Chinatown gang information, we should all be safe, at least long enough, for you to heal. Mercy and the Chinatown gang will be hung out to dry if Katya decides to throw them under the bus, but Eddy doesn't think she will. He thinks she'll hold out on the hope the gang will finish you off without her help. Until someone talks, we can't tie the gang and Katya together with a nice neat bow. That's why we are still in danger."

Adam fell silent. I felt like I had been thrust off a cliff into a deep chasm that I didn't wish to visit. Adam squeezed my hand.

"Montana, I've been trying to think of a good reason for you to not leave me. Half the shit that has happened has been because of a love-sick psychopath. I'd completely understand. I'm to blame, I did this to you." I went to shake my head then remembered Mrs. Campbell's warning and sighed instead.

"Don't you see it? Mercy would never have gotten as far as she did if not for Katya. She has the money and resources. The joke? Eddy is convinced Mercy doesn't know who has been feeding intel to the gang. She's so greedy, she doesn't care, and it enabled Katya to use Mercy's hate and resources to get at you. It's totally over the top. I'm still reeling from the information."

How Adam could think this was his fault was beyond my comprehension. Who could have predicted Katya, or that Mercy would be willing to go so far in annihilating me. They're both lunatics.

"Adam, this is not your fault, but I know you'll blame yourself anyway. I bet Ace is right now too, and he had nothing to do with any of this. I need you. I want you. I am completely in love with you. Regardless of all the craziness that has surrounded us since the beginning of our relationship. Not Katya, Mercy, or the Yakuza can change that."

"I love you, too."

I'd healed while I'd slept but wasn't looking forward to seeing the damage done from the explosion. Until my eyes saw the truth, I could pretend everything was fine. Adam slid onto the bed beside me until we were in a gentle spoon position. His hand clasped mine as we slowly drifted off to sleep.

Chapter 16

We woke to the tuttings of Mrs. C, and sunlight streaming through the huge windows.

"Well, hallo," she said with her fabulous Scottish accent, which was much easier to understand today. "Glad you're awake, I need to check your bandages." She chatted away. not needing me to chime in as she moved me this way and that, unwrapping my bandages and clucking her tongue.

With Adam's help, she bathed me and despite the discomfort, and having an almost complete stranger see me naked, I couldn't hold back the smile. There was just something about Mrs. Campbell that put me at ease. I imagined her as a farmyard hen clucking all the rabble into place at feeding time. She had a power of persuasion about her that spoke to me. She was a safe person for me, and I liked her.

After bathing me, she had me lie on my front, incessantly talking about anything and everything all the while. She re-bandaged me where it was needed. So instead of looking like a mummy, I resembled a patchwork quilt that got hung on the back of a sofa. I certainly felt like I'd been hung out to dry.

Despite the chill of the castle, I requested she dress me in shorts and a t-shirt, instead of the loose pajamas she had chosen. I needed to feel air on my skin. Adam had gone ahead to say that I would be attending lunch with the group, and to get another place set for me.

"Listen, lass, you will be going through rehabilitation. Don't expect to be able to just get up and walk. Your fine and gross motor skills have been asleep for a while. The swelling on your brain at the time of the explosion forced the doctors to put you in a temporary coma. This entire last week you could have come out of it at any time, but I guess you needed the extra healing time."

"Okay," I said. Here goes nothing, and I used my spindly arms to try and push myself up. I couldn't.

"I daresay, lass, your laddie couldn't either, and he was only down for a week. Let me go and seek some assistance for ye, aye? Then you'll be as right as rain."

Before I could answer, she was gone out the door. I could see what she meant. I couldn't even pick up my arms and put them up in the air. Fingers were okay, but, other than fingers and toes, my body felt like lead. Ace came into the room wearing a gigantic grin.

"Peanut," he enthused. "Am I glad to see you awake, at last."

Mrs. Campbell followed right behind him and gave him instructions on where to avoid putting pressure, not that Ace needed much guidance, he'd carried me through so many injuries, albeit there were a lot of spots to stay clear of. When I was finally in his arms, I almost wanted to tell him to put me back in bed, because of an overwhelming feeling of inadequacy. I didn't want to disrupt the dining room, or see expressions of pity.

"Uh, is this a good idea?" I asked hoping they would both say no.

"Alright, missy, this is a good start. This strapping lad won't let anything happen to ye and yer with family and friends. What could be bad about that?" She continued chattering all the way to the dining room. Ace followed, and I hid my face in his broad chest.

"Peanut, don't worry. Adam is sitting right beside you and will help you eat. You've been out for a few weeks, remember. I'm excited you're willing to join us, and I know everyone else will be, too."

We arrived, and I steeled myself for the looks. But I was surprised when all the faces lit up with smiles. They seemed thrilled, and one by one came over to give me a kiss, or a very gentle hug. Except one old lady I did not recognize who sat beside Geoff. She gazed at me, and there seemed to be something so familiar about her. The eyes, they reminded me of mine and Alex's.

Ace still held me in his arms, and I felt safe and protected. With my confidence bolstered from the positive reception, I nodded to Ace that I was ready to be delivered to my chair. He sat me down and placed a blanket around my legs and feet for extra warmth, then he joined Kris opposite me.

Once I was seated, Geoff held up his glass, "I think I speak for everyone here, Montana, when I say that we are very, very happy to see you up and about." I was rooted to the spot, what do I do? "To Montana, an all-around amazing human being."

Everyone toasted, including myself, as Adam had given me a glass of something to cheer with. Thoroughly embarrassed, I sunk down in my chair and waited for lunch to arrive.

"Who is that woman who keeps staring at me?" I whispered to Adam.

"This is going to sound crazy. Remember I told you about Kate and Charlie?"

"The lady from the plane that you cheated on me with." I winked.

He laughed. "Exactly, well, that is her.

"What? How can that be?"

"She told me that, after she visited Japan, she would be coming to visit her great-niece in Scotland. It turns out Mrs. Campbell is the great-niece she was speaking of."

"Holy shit, that's crazy."

"I know, and it gets weirder. Look at her eyes. Who do they remind you of?"

"Well, I was thinking of myself, at first, but I'm thinking more like my mother's. Why?"

"Because, Montana, she is related to your mother, her great-aunt."

The hair on my back stood on end, like a ghost had run its hand up my spine causing a frisson of electricity.

"Adam, I want to talk to her. But privately, later, can you bring her to our room?"

"I can, she wanted to meet you anyway."

This is all so surreal. What were the chances that Adam would be on a plane with a relative of mine that I'd never met? A million to one? Kate was busy listening to Geoff, but her eyes were on me and held secrets I wondered if I wanted to know.

I pulled my eyes away from hers to look at Ace. He was watching me. He knew something. Maybe Kate had shared some stories about our mother with him. I couldn't shake the feeling that this trip, us in Scotland, was meant to be. It was bizarre, but what wasn't in my life?

Lunch arrived, and I was lost in trying to feed myself. After several attempts with a spoon, Adam fed me. Not like a nurse feeds a patient. But like a man who was taking care of a woman. He was so romantic, and it wasn't lost on anyone else who got to share in our intimacy. When he was done, he picked up my linen napkin and gently wiped my face. He leaned in and kissed my lips. I felt his love in that kiss. I returned it and delved into his mouth with my tongue. Witnesses be damned.

"I love you," I said in a husky voice, as I pulled away to gaze into his beautiful eyes.

"I love you, Montana, always and forever." Our magic moment ended when we realized that every set of eyes in the dining room was staring at us. Alex held up his coffee cup, "to my sister and her man." He toasted.

"To Montana and Adam," the group returned.

And just like that, I felt the veil that had haunted me since I woke up yesterday, lift. We were going to be okay, together we were stronger. After lunch, Ace carried me back to mine and Adam's room. He didn't want Adam to strain, as he was still on the mend as well. He helped me get propped up in bed.

"Ace, have you spoken to this Kate person?"

"Yes, I have."

"Who is she, Ace? Is she really our mother's great aunt, like Adam says she is?"

"What do you remember of our mother, Mo? Did you know she moved away from the Maritimes right after high school?"

"No. I didn't"

He continued, "She left and came to British Columbia. She met our father not long after she arrived. I have never met anyone from her side, just a few close friends she considers family that she met on her trip west. I'm kinda named after one of those friends, Deuce."

"I didn't know that." Suddenly everything I felt I knew about my family felt small at best.

"Dad worked offshore in the Maritimes, and he had letters from Kate in his box of correspondence. As far as I can tell, this is our grandmother's sister."

That was a lot to process, "Ace, do you think this is all a coincidence? I mean, what are the chances?"

He laughed, "It is pretty strange, but Geoff has been looking into her, and he said she's the real deal. I'd say it is serendipitous."

"Okay, but if she is Mrs. C's great aunt, and our mother's great aunt, how does that work?"

"Good question. Our mother's great great great, not sure how many greats, grandmother was born in this castle. Mrs. Campbell's family has been here for as many generations. Somewhere back in the data, Mrs. C is descended from the last laird of the castle. He slept around apparently, and liked them young. He had sex with Matty Campbell, the daughter of a kitchen servant, who produced Mrs. C's line. The laird was married at the time to a McGregor that prudently changed her name to Campbell."

I had questions about why that was prudent but didn't want to interrupt because I was having a hard time following.

"Our mother's line is descended from that union. So, way back our generations began with the same father, but different mothers. The connection is tenuous now, but imagine back then, our mother's ancestor was half-sisters with Matty Campbell."

I was stunned. How did all of this come about? "Ace, how did you find all of this out?"

He snorted, "My boss, of course. Geoff started researching safe houses in case we ever needed one. When he found this place and did some research, he found enough information to make him dig deeper. He's pulled all the public records on our connection to Scotland to keep us safe."

I wondered briefly if that was his only reason. Something about all of this felt too coincidental, but I couldn't put my finger on anything specific. It was more of a feeling at this point. But I promised myself, I would be alert and see if there was a mystery afoot.

"This is weird, I feel like I never really knew my family, and now I feel that more strongly. I wonder why our mother left the Maritimes at such a young age and alone? What was going on in her life that she took a journey away from her family?"

Ace shook his head, "I have no idea, maybe Kate does."

We heard a knock at the door and Kate McGregor herself entered my room, with Adam on her heels. Ace excused himself. Adam got her a chair and set it up beside my bed so we could visit.

"I'll fetch some tea," he said and then left. Tea, this was so weird, a rum and coke would be more appropriate or maybe Scotch. What a Scottish thing to want. It was here, it was in my genes all along, and I'd never known. Never met anyone from my mother's side of the family. She never actually said they were dead, I just assumed they were.

Kate stared into my eyes, a small smile on her lips, "Hello, Montana. I am very happy to finally meet you, my dear."

I saw what Adam meant about her face, it was a wonderful face, so full of a life well lived. Her eyes sparkled with mischief. Like Mrs. C, I found myself liking her instantly. "Hello Kate. It is so surreal to meet you. I mean, how did this come to be? Was meeting Adam a fluke?"

Her eyes lit up even more if that were possible.

"Yes, but I like to believe it was serendipitous."

So that's where Ace got that description from. I wasn't so sure she was telling the truth.

"But?"

She laughed. "Oh, you are a sharp one, aren't you, dear? I have kept tabs on your family since your mother left Nova Scotia in 1960 to escape a relationship being forced on her by her parents. Your grandmother was heartbroken when Maggie left, but then again she'd never been very supportive." It was weird hearing my mother's first name being used by someone I'd never met before.

"I have read about you, of course, before I met your young Adonis."

Adonis, ha! She thought of a Greek god too, when she looked at Adam.

"I played ignorant with him because there seemed no point in connecting our lives, if we were only ever meant to meet on an airplane. But when the entire clan came here, well, that is entirely different. That is serendipity giving us our marching orders."

She was a witty old lady, lots of spunk like Adam had said about her in Japan. He arrived with tea, and we spent the next two hours enjoying each other's company immensely. She told stories about my mother that I never heard before. She talked a little more about the circumstances surrounding her leaving.

By the end of our visit, I felt as if I'd found a piece of myself that I didn't know was missing. What I'd said to Ace earlier about feeling like I didn't know my family was gone. I felt like I had gained so much by meeting Kate. As she departed my room with a promise to talk more the next day. She left me with a cryptic thought, "Things aren't always as they seem, Montana, watch out for those closest to you and trust your intuition first, always."

Those closest to me? Was she telling me that there was someone here who wanted to do me harm? Regardless of what she said, I couldn't imagine anyone in our inner circle wanting to hurt me. Maybe it wasn't who I was closest to, but who was closest in proximity to me. I noticed Charlie wasn't among the security team and when I questioned Ace on the way back to my room, he'd said Charlie had opted to head the Vancouver team and ensure homes and businesses remained intact.

Kate passed away that night, peacefully in her sleep. That was why she'd come to Scotland, Adam had said. But she had seemed so vibrant, so alive. We were all shocked by the suddenness of her departure. The next day, we held a celebration of her life. Geoff arranged for her body to be flown back home to Nova Scotia where she wanted to be buried. The day after that, my rehabilitation process began.

Chapter 17

Eddy and Mrs. Campbell were in cahoots, and as much as I appreciated their attention to every detail of my health, it pissed me off. The only saving grace was my irritation, it propelled me forward to recovery. The faster I could get some peace, the better. I wanted to swim in the ocean, take photos, and dance. That was my spiritual retreat, what made me feel my best. Not nasty tinctures, walking the halls of the castle, and resistance training. On top of it all, the stitches itched like hell and I wanted to scratch all the time. The image in the mirror was just as bad, a mottled pattern of varying colors as the bruising healed.

It was one of those healing processes where I was very aware of every single step forward. Where was the magic wand? Adam did his best to keep me sane during this arduous process, but there was quite a bit of whining on my part. The past five years I'd been the victim so many times. Everyone was always rescuing me instead of me rescuing them, and that's what pissed me off the most. I was tired of the damsel in distress routine, I wanted to save myself. These thoughts and feelings played in a loop most days.

Mrs. Campbell's concoction was beyond gross, and I almost hurled it back up the first time. I tried to elude her when she would come calling with her putrid drinks, but she always found me.

"Oh, lass," she would say, "this one here is to help with bruising," and, "Oh, lass this one is to help with tissue repair," and, "I've done the same for my laddie many times." She never said who her laddie was, but I instantly felt sorry for him. How many times had he endured her drinks, I wondered?

I was *lassed* out, but I did notice that every day I woke up, I felt better and better so the drinks were doing their job. A few weeks into my recovery their strategy shifted to strengthening and resilience. Eddy put me through my paces and she fed me a lot of protein and vegetables. What I wouldn't give for a pizza.

After a few weeks of walking the castle with Eddy, I was ready to graduate to jogging. We started before breakfast each day. After breakfast Allyson taught me tai chi and the element of breath and movement through chi gong. I found the chi gong most challenging as it required a stillness that I'd never had. But I saw the benefit of the control it taught and worked hard to achieve it.

After lunch, Eddy taught karate and Thai boxing. My life quickly began to revolve around food and working out. The afternoons were for the band. I started slowly making notes of current songs and singing backup. As I got stronger, I added in the drums. If there was time, before dinner, I'd go exploring the nooks and crannies of the castle.

In many ways, I became healthier and more focused than I'd ever been at home. Being isolated from the distractions of the outside world made my routine that much easier to follow. Despite the positives, of everyone I loved being in one place, I was struggling. The isolation was having both positive and negative effects on everyone, because of that, I didn't share my feelings with anyone on this matter.

I'd always considered myself to be a cool person living right on the edge of my culture. I loved my time with a passion and the West End was the heart of the cultural revolution. I missed the vibe from my downtown home, but I was discovering a bigger part of me enjoyed just being alive, being able to hear my thoughts and take the time to follow them. Not being rushed or pushed all the time by the world's agenda.

Despite the gains I was making physically, and energetically, I was plagued with nightmares that often left me screaming and panicking. Adam would wake me up, and we would eventually go back to sleep. I woke each morning with a haunted feeling that would alleviate as I got lost in my daily routine. One morning, after several weeks of the same nightmare, I knew something needed to be done and on one of our morning runs, I shared an idea.

"Eddy, I wake up screaming every night."

He slowed down the pace so we could talk, "I know, Mo. I heard you in Hawaii, and I can only imagine it's gotten worse."

"Yeah, they have but this past week it's been the same every night and I don't know how many more times I can witness myself and those I love being blown up. I need to heal in ways that running and tinctures can't help me."

Eddy came to a complete stop, "What do you need?" I felt my shoulders drop. He'd always listened to me and now, more than ever, I was grateful for him being such a good friend to me my entire life.

"I know there's a marina about forty minutes from here. It's on my list to visit. I want to know if you can arrange a private, off the books, tour for me. I know it sounds weird, but the dolphins help me feel grounded."

I could see Eddy weighing out the pros and cons. Finally deciding, he nodded and said he'd see what he could do. Hours later he found me exactly where he had left me. At my favourite spot in the castle on the turret that faced the far-off distant sea.

When I first started moving around the castle, I sat here for hours every day content to smell the sea and look out at the surrounding fields that spread around the castle. My surroundings were tranquil, almost perfect. Eddy sat down beside me.

"I have spoken with Geoff and Mrs. Campbell. There are too many variables, Montana. I am sorry, but I have another idea."

My disappointment changed to interest, wondering where this was going.

"This castle sits on a massive parcel of land. And has its own magic pools."

He was grinning as he watched me process this. "Magic pools?"

"Well, I don't know that myself. I'm taking Mrs. Campbell's word for it." He winked. I laughed.

"Okay, I'll bite, where is this magic pool?" I asked, warming up to the idea.

"About an hour walk. Want to give it a try?"

"Hell yeah, I'll give it a try."

"Tomorrow, after breakfast, we'll go on foot, in lieu of our workout, and whoever wants to join can. I'll be able to maintain the security this way and not alert anyone to our whereabouts. Hope it helps, Mo."

I sighed in relief that we had a plan. I'd read about magic pools, where the fairies apparently lived and imparted their magic. When Adam took me to Europe one summer, just after the band got signed, I'd seen a lot of advertising about magical places all across Europe.

As promised, after breakfast, Eddy, Adam, Alex, me, and two of our bodyguards headed out the back of the castle. Mrs. Campbell had drawn a map for us and we found the winding path from the map through the heather. It led us to a small river that eventually deposited in the fairy pool. Although it was only a mile and a half away, the pathway was rough for most of the walk.

Eventually, it levelled out to a dense copse of Scottish pines. On the other side was a burbling brook, several small gentle waterfalls poured over jetting rocks and shone like a brilliant treasure in the afternoon light.

Wildflowers bursting with colour and strange water plants were abundant, and in the bottom of the pool were coloured stones. The air was heavy with the mist from the falling water, and I felt like I'd entered a magical place.

I was taken aback and rooted to the spot, as I took it all in. My senses absorbed the environment, processing the abundance and the peace it offered my soul. Adam had his camera out and was taking pictures at record speed. I saw Alex looking as spellbound as myself. He stepped over to me. Hand in hand, we headed to the edge of the pool.

I took off my outer layer of clothing, as did Alex, and stepped gingerly into the cool water. I heard small plops, like the sound little fish make when popping up their heads above the water line and then diving for the bottom. I stilled, allowing them time to get used to us invading their space. I wished only to share their water, not take it over.

I stood with my arms open and my hands just below the surface, eyes closed, and face raised to the sky. I could feel the energy in the water as the soles of my feet sank into the rocky bottom. For the first time in what felt like forever, I breathed a deep sigh of relief.

Adam joined us and we moved a little deeper. We floated and swam for a long time, not getting out until the sun had moved far along the horizon and our lovely haven was plunged into shadow. Goosebumps erupted on my skin when I exited the pools. Adam wrapped me in a huge towel and helped to dry me off. I went behind a boulder to change out of my wet clothing.

I was feeling happy and grateful, at ease and unhurried. When I was done, I joined the guys, and we moved to the entry side of our watery paradise and relaxed in the sun. I fell asleep and woke when Adam gently spoke my name.

I opened my eyes and felt the light within them, within me and graced him with a smile that reflected how I was feeling. He smiled in return and leaned down and kissed me. Then helping me to stand, we slowly made our way back to the castle.

Chapter 18

Eddy's co-worker, who had been specifically chosen by him and Geoff to penetrate the Chinatown gang, hadn't been heard from in a week. We all hoped that he was so deep, that he just hadn't found a way to contact his superiors. But when another week passed our hopes dropped; something was wrong. A week or so later, we heard his body had been found, killed execution style, with a shot to the back of the head.

With our connection to Chinatown severed, we had no way of knowing when they would be coming for us. Eddy stepped up security watches. I felt anxious. They would come for me. That was the reality. I wanted to be ready for them, I wanted a plan and was frustrated with what I felt was the lack of one. Eddy and Geoff's thoughts were that we should be cautious, and with enough people to protect us we'd be safe.

I didn't agree. My gut told me we needed to be better prepared than that.

I spoke with Mrs. Campbell about the castle she knew so well. I wanted to know if there were secret passageways and if the castle had plans that I could look at. I thought at least we could have options for escape routes.

Her eyes twinkled when she told stories about the secret passageways below. She gave me hints where to begin my search. With my journal and pen in hand, I went exploring. The size of the castle was hard to comprehend based on the exterior. The twists and turns, hidden doorways and secret levels created a web of illusion meant to keep its inhabitants safe.

I entered the first level through a stairway behind the kitchen that Mrs. C showed me. As soon as the secret door opened the smell of rank earth filled my nostrils. Yuck, did I really want to go down into what smelled like the bowels of hell?

I shined my flashlight on the stone steps. They were slick with moisture and algae. I wondered if this led to the dungeon. It had to have a dungeon, every castle did. I tried to imagine how long someone could survive down here. It was beyond depressing.

The long corridor I was walking along took an abrupt turn, and then I had to choose. Either continue straight or take a doorway on the left-hand side. I chose the left and was again descending a set of stairs. The air became thicker. I questioned the intelligence of my choice. Maybe I should go back upstairs and finish with the first level. I was about to turn back when I caught sight of iron up ahead. Set in the floor was a wooden door with an iron ring; this is what my flashlight had caught. I pulled on the iron ring. This trap door had not been opened in some time. I couldn't get it open, so I went back up to the ancient pantry and grabbed a crowbar that Mrs. C kept on hand.

I was excited, I don't know why. I guess the idea of not letting the door win. Really, Montana, my thoughts mocked me. I crammed the crowbar under the edge of the trap door and wrenched it back and forth until it came loose. Then I did the same thing eight more times, all around the wood. I grabbed the iron ring and pulled.

This time it pulled apart with a disgusting suction sound. The wood must have swelled with the dankness, and that was why I couldn't open it. The only light I had was the flashlight, and it was completely black below me. I almost had a panic attack gazing down; my claustrophobia wasn't looking forward to the descent into darkness. I kept thinking I would be lowering myself into a small space.

When I finally convinced myself I would be okay, I took the fifteen stairs to the next level, and there it was, a scene from a horror movie, the torture chamber, and off behind it, the cells. I was overwhelmed by the smell that was reminiscent of thousand years of piss and filth.

There weren't many devices of torture laying around, but an iron and wood slab stood at the center of the chamber. It was covered in dark stains that had to be blood. I almost hurled my lunch. I couldn't believe that human beings were ever kept in such conditions.

Dizzy with the smell and the images assaulting my senses, I made my way through as quickly as possible. At the end of the hallway was another trap door. Oh, good heavens, another level? Could it be any worse? Again, I used my crowbar to pry open the door and quickly made my way down.

This level smelled of water, stagnant pond water. I followed its earthen hallway to the end and found a door. I used my crowbar to wedge into the cracks and pulled and pushed like I had with the trap doors. This one was way more stubborn. Fifteen minutes later, I was about to give up when I got some movement. I managed to manhandle the three-inch thick door open wide enough for me to squeeze through.

All around the door from the outside was overgrowth and brambles. Beyond that were beautiful fields. I hadn't seen these before. I must be on a different side of the castle. Maybe this was the side with the turrets I loved so much.

I stepped about a hundred feet out into the field and looked up to see what I could of the castle. Sure enough, this was neither the front nor the back, and judging from the position of the sun, I figured this was the east wing of the castle. Looking at the structure, I wondered if it had been added in later years as it had a different quality to the stone than the rest. I would need to question Mrs. Campbell about this new discovery.

I drew the tunnel and the entrance and made some notes for later. Then I turned back and gazed out to the fields. They were flat with cliffs off in the distance and a copse of trees below. That could possibly be a good hiding spot as well. I pulled out my notebook again and made more notes.

When I shut the book and looked up. I saw him. A man was out in the fields, probably a mile from where I stood. I could have easily turned and gone back inside to safety, but my curiosity won. He was stripped to the waist and swinging around a large sword with incredible agility.

I wanted to get closer. Slowly, I made my way toward him. I noticed he was wearing a ragtag tartan that hung low on his hips. His skin was pale and his dark hair tied back. I could see now that the sword he wielded was a broadsword. I knew from reading about them that they could weigh up to one hundred pounds, and yet he moved like it weighed nothing. His muscles rippled as he moved through some type of intricate fighting choreography.

I witnessed the moment he knew he wasn't alone. A very subtle shift in his energy and a stiffening of his muscles. He was working himself in a circle in my direction. His movements so well-spaced and timed, had I not been paying attention I may have missed his intent. He wanted to see me without me being aware that he knew I was there.

Smart man, accessing the threat. He was definitely a warrior. I watched the slight tension in his shoulders as he moved closer. This man had seen action and had the scars to prove it. Maybe he did this for only fitness purposes now, but at some point, he'd needed it. I wondered what fool would have taken on this giant of a Scot.

He danced with the sword like he hadn't a care in the world, but I knew better. I smiled. This was turning out to be an entertaining discovery. He was Ace's height, but where my bro had the bulky football build, this guy was bulging muscles. He could be Conan the Barbarian.

He made his final turn, his sword extended, and stopped only inches from my face. If he had hoped to intimidate me, it didn't work. A lazy smile filled my face at the shock reaction on his.

He had a strong chiseled face with deep brown eyes and about two days of beard growth. He placed his sword tip down into the ground between us and sized me up as openly as I was sizing him.

"What are ye doing, Sassenach? Aren't ye supposed to have yer arse in that wee castle there yonder?" He put one hand on his hip and gave me a haughty look.

I laughed, I couldn't help myself, I felt like I was in a historical movie and played along. "I'd skelp yer wee mouth if you werna' so bloody entertaining, but as I'm in nae danger from the likes of ye, I'm fine, thanks," I switched from an accent that matched his to Canadian English. I waited, head cocked for his response, and instead he picked up his sword and started off down a hill I'd not noticed. Hmmm, not very much fun. I followed him, and again he must have sensed me, and turned around.

"Ye'd be Montana, then?"

Was that a question or a statement? Why did he know who I was? Who was he? Now my back was up, maybe this was a trap?

I traded my Scottish accent for my West End cool, "Maybe, what's it to ya, eh? Who are you anyway?"

He grinned, his face lit with amusement that traveled from his eyes and filled his entire persona. He reminded me of my brother, Dan. Where the latter was radiant, the former held a hint of mischievousness. I couldn't help myself. I let down my defences and returned his grin with a lopsided minx grin. He laughed and I joined in. The tension flowing from my body. I had nothing to fear from this man.

"Yer mouth isn't so smart now that ye may be in danger, eh lass?" Before I could answer he continued, "I'd be Mrs. Campbell's son, Declan Campbell. I am aware of ye because me ma has told me of what has happened." He studied me for a moment. "Ye look good, recover quickly."

I nodded. "So you're the wee lad she keeps referring to. Not so wee if you ask me." He laughed. "Your ma, as you call her, has been a big help feeding me disgusting tinctures. It's been worth it just to hear her incessant tutting and stories. She is the most entertaining."

"Och, aye, I know the taste of her bleedin' tinctures. Bad enough to kill a man, I say, but still, she is me ma and has always been able to fix what ails me."

I reached forward to shake his hand, "Nice to meet you, Declan Campbell." He had a warm strong hand shake, although rough and calloused. The type that knew hard work, not painting, and reminded me of my dad's hands. I felt a ping in my belly, a familiarity. I felt as if we had met before although logically, I knew this wasn't the case.

Wait a second, generations ago we would have been half siblings. Ha, maybe my genetics were what recognized him. Still, it was like meeting Mrs. C and Kate, I liked him as immediately as I did both the women.

Eddy would like him too, which gave me an idea. "Declan, would you be interested in doing some training with that sword? We have been working out and doing martial arts, but we are in danger, as you know, from a very aggressive gang with a long reach. We could use some weapons training, if you're interested in helping us out?"

He hesitated, "At least come and meet Eddy. He's a detective from Vancouver, Canada, and one of my best friends. I think you and he would have a lot in common. Besides, we all love Mrs. Campbell, the rest of the gang would love to meet her son."

He smiled and nodded in assent. We made our way back to the castle, and he took us through a hidden passage that I hadn't found yet and which was a more direct route from the door I'd wedged open. That took us to a bailey that overlooked the field where we had just been. What a vantage point, I thought. I sighed at the immense rugged beauty that Scotland had to offer.

There were these alcoves every few feet that were followed by projections, thrust out from the bailey wall. The projections were about four feet by two feet. I figured they had been protection hives for archers at some point. They offered me the opportunity to climb atop and spread my arms wide. Something about this side of the castle felt magical, and I wanted to be embraced by it.

I stood on the edge feeling the energy of the space, Declan briefly forgotten, my purpose in returning to the castle forgotten, even the notebook at my feet, forgotten. I was alive, and I could feel the oldness in the stones beneath my feet and the ground spread out below me. There was nothing like this in Canada. It was like candy, and I couldn't get enough.

The rustling of the tall grasses below sounded like whispering, thousands of voices lifted towards me. A familiar tug again on my lower extremities. Adam had told me, when he was helping me rehabilitate, that your feeling center is in your second chakra, which is the reproduction organs. That made sense, and maybe why when people fell in love, they thought it was a gut instinct that they had found the right person to fall in love with, but maybe it was just the feeling center within waking up.

When the moment passed, I jumped down, and we made our way to the castle entry. Declan talked about the history of the castle. It had seen plenty of action, as it was over five hundred years old. He'd played in the castle as a child and knew it like the back of his hand. We came up from the bowels of the dungeon and opened a door behind a tapestry in a hallway adjacent to the kitchen.

As I came out from behind the tapestry Adam and Dan happened to be walking by, and their eyes bugged out like they'd seen a ghost. I laughed, and then Declan appeared behind me, a sweaty highlander with a sword, and they must have thought they were seeing things.

I made the introductions and went off to find Eddy. Declan hung back and talked with Dan and Adam. As I rounded a corner that would take me out of sight, I stopped to look at the three men. They made an interesting sight. Dan and Adam shared the Greek god look, both with tanned skin and slim muscular builds, while Dan had light brown, tawny, hair with blue eyes, Adam had the darker hair with green eyes. Declan had shoulder length dark auburn hair, with deep brown eyes, and much paler skin.

All very different looks, but there was something about the three of them. Together they created some type of symmetry. I found Eddy in the castle gardens talking with Mrs. Campbell. They stopped when I entered. Mrs. C's expression said she knew what I was about to say.

"So, you met my wee laddie then." Hmmph, again not a question but a statement. He must have gotten his communication skills from his mother.

"Yes, I did, and I brought him back with me for Eddy to meet. He's talking to Dan and Adam right now. I think he could give us some weapons training that could come in handy. Maybe not in Canada, but definitely here."

We left a chuckling Mrs. Campbell in the garden and headed into the castle. I told Eddy about the secret passageways and how I had been mapping them. I explained the advantage of the new passageway that Declan had shown me and the door behind the tapestry, along with the dungeons and the back door to the outlying fields.

He seemed very interested. Tomorrow he and I would go exploring with Declan, if he was willing, and see what else we could find. Knowledge was power and may come in handy if we found ourselves under attack. I made the introductions between Eddy and Declan and left them to their conversation, and before they were out of sight, I saw Declan nodding his head to something Eddy was saying. They disappeared in the direction of Geoff's temporary office space. Good, if he was introducing him to Geoff, then he saw what I saw, and maybe Declan would be added to the security detail as well. Certainly, no one knew the lay of the land like he did.

The next day, all the men, plus me, and Allyson, arrived for weapons training. Declan had set up a medieval courtyard, and I was giddy with excitement. I say medieval because he had a large circle made from stones and a smaller circle also made from stones.

He set up targets running parallel with the long courtyard. Two, at each fifty paces, until we had six sets. Training started in the larger ring with simple wooden swords and we learned how to thrust and parry. Once we'd perfected that, we began basic combinations. As we grew, our weapons changed. In week three, we were fighting with blunted swords in mock one-on-one battles.

We learned Declan was a master craftsman, and as a gift, Adam had commissioned him to make real swords that they designed together. I loved my sword. It was light and had my mother's family crest of the McGregors embossed on the hilt, the infinity symbol, and the initials M.N. for Montana Northrop, cleverly engraved into the cross piece or guard.

After receiving them, we trained with them. Our skills increased so that we were able to do full fight sequences in twos and groups. Declan and Eddy were always trying to prepare us for a surprise hit. Some days we had an audience.

Every day was loads of fun. Hard, sweaty, arduous fun. Adam and I fell into bed every night, too tired for anything but sleep.

We'd been in Scotland for the entire spring, and now we were on the verge of summer, and there seemed no change to our circumstances. At least, it hadn't been discussed yet as to when we might go home. Personally, as selfish as I knew it sounded, I didn't care. I was happy, and my pace of living was one I could control for a change.

I'd been avoiding alone time with Alex because I knew he didn't feel the same way. He was anxious to further our studio and while I was more relaxed than ever, he was almost a ticking time bomb. I knew he didn't blame me, but I also knew he felt that despite the price on his head, I was still the main target, and he felt he was relatively safe and should maybe return home. These words were never shared between us, but they didn't have to be for me to receive the message loud and clear.

It was another two weeks of bow training and hand to hand combat with dirks, what we call knives, that Eddy received news. The Yakuza were in Ireland making a gun deal. That made us a little nervous, as Ireland was very close.

That evening, during one of our games nights in the entertainment room, Eddy announced Declan's responsibilities were shifting to my personal bodyguard.

"Wouldn't it make more sense for us to go home?" I'd asked, annoyed with Eddy for attaching the giant Scotsman to me like that. Not that I minded his company, as we got on well, but he was intense. Like if you put Eddy, Ace, and Adam together in one human, you'd get Declan. Besides, using his immense skills to watch over me seemed like overkill.

"With a possible attack being imminent," Eddy replied, "it makes more sense for us to stay put. Back in Canada, with all of us spread out, we're easier to pick off. We'd never see them coming. Here, the enemy would be hard pressed to take us by surprise."

That was the end of that discussion. The next week passed with no new updates, and the threat we'd anticipated seemed to have passed. We relaxed a little and Declan continued to expand my knowledge of the castle by helping me discover its hidden places.

"Where does this passage lead?" I asked as we spiraled down toward the dungeons.

"I don't know, lass, always thought maybe a cellar. Let's check."

We opened a door at the end of the hall. There were more stairs here, and the air became thick, dank and wet-very wet.

"I wonder if it leads to the burn," he said, and we followed the path out to a grate that was about three feet in diameter and looked like it opened into a cave in a hillside. Declan smiled, "Aye, I know what this is, lass, the escape hatch for the castle inhabitants. In case the castle was to get overrun, and the women and children needed a route to get out."

The cave was quite deep, and there were signs that someone had hidden here a very long time ago. Further into the cave mouth, I saw a fresh fire recently dampened.

"Declan, this is fresh," I said as he made his way over to see the remnants of a fire recently put out. Instantly on alarm, we ran to the ledge and peered at the castle. Off in the distance we could see people moving up the eastern slope of the ground toward castle, where I had first met Declan. I was about to ask if he knew who they were, when I got that very creepy feeling. I knew we were under attack, and now we needed the quickest way back, to warn the others.

Chapter 19

From this distance, we watched bodies scramble over the walls and into the castle. My heart rate increased, and my breath became heavier. I was poised for action, but still pondered the right course of action. I was hanging over the cliff edge, trying to figure out my chances of not breaking my legs if I made the approximate 30-foot drop to the rough landscape below. I knew it was ridiculous, but I had to get us moving before there was no one left to save.

"Come on, lass, we have to go and warn the others."

I followed Declan as he took us in the opposite direction, through a copse of woodland trees to the right of the cave. Then we quickly wound our way down the hillside from there and moved with stealth speed toward the castle.

He was eerily calm and if I'd had the time, I would have asked if this was what he was like before one of the death matches he'd participated in, but now wasn't the time to think about anything but saving my family. Likely, whoever it was wouldn't hurt them, but hold them hostage, until I arrived. I would do whatever it took to make sure they are safe.

"Lass, I know what you're thinking, but you will not go in there and sacrifice yourself for anyone, no matter what you see. Once they have you, they'll kill you and all of us anyway. You have to stay alive."

"I'm not some newb. I get it." The closer we got, the more determination flowed through me. We were finally at the end of an almost five year scheme and I wanted it over and had every intention of winning.

"Lass. I see your ferocity and iron will in every move of your body, but are ye ready for what's to come? Some may be dead already, you must keep a clear head. Do you understand?"

I nodded, not trusting myself to speak. We were almost to the castle, my imagination fancied I could hear the tall grass whisper, "Yes, victory is yours." Through a secret door, we snuck inside to the dungeon to gather our weapons from an ancient armory room.

I grabbed two sets of bows with extra arrows and a few knives. Declan grabbed his broadsword and three smaller swords, and a few knives which he tucked into the waistband of his trousers, then led us up the staircase that would take us out the door behind the tapestry in the hallway close to the kitchen.

"Montana, lass, If I didn't need your help, I would never allow ye to be in the heart of the danger. Stay silent, stay hidden when you can. You have the courage and the training for this, but dinnae be unnecessarily brave. If they catch you, lass, then we are all dead. They will kill us all in front of ye to make ye suffer, then they will kill you last. I repeat, doona let them get you."

"I'm not afraid to get hurt, but I promise, I won't let them get me. I'm not a victim anymore, Dec, and I'm done sacrificing."

He nodded. We listened at the door but didn't hear sounds of panic, no voices raised. Things were quiet, too quiet.

Declan cracked the door enough to peek through. With no one in sight, we stepped through, and I followed him down the hallway, duplicating the stealth I'd used sneaking out my bedroom window with no-one the wiser.

This was different. It wasn't about me and not getting caught. It was about me and not getting those I loved killed. My nerves were wound so tight. We heard shuffling and yelling coming from a passageway off the dining room. Declan gave me the sign to continue in the opposite direction of the noise. Then he disappeared down the other corridor and out of sight. Jesus bloody Christ help me, I silently begged, don't let me screw up.

I peeked around the next corner to find Allyson, Chrissie, Kristine and Liza on the floor, their hands tied. Allyson was bleeding from a cut to her forehead. She was probably the only one that had put up a fight. Before them stood a guard with a gun in his hand, but as all the ladies were tied, his body position seemed more bored than alert.

I caught Allyson's attention and signaled her to run interference. She was my sparring partner, and as we had practiced this move many times, I knew she could do it. She nodded and swept her leg hard right under her assailant's feet. I shot him through the arm. He yelped as he dropped his weapon. I shot again as he reached for it, this time pinning him through the leg.

With him incapacitated, I ran over and ripped his shirt, tying it gag style around his mouth. I untied Allyson and used her bindings on him. She untied the rest of the ladies while I dragged the assailant out of the way, so no one would be the wiser.

The five of us hugged, and then I led them back down the secret passage and gave Allyson instructions, as well as told her where the extra weapons were stored. She started to protest about not helping me, but the others needed protecting. She was the only one in the group with any weapons training. She finally conceded, and made their way down the stairs, I quietly spoke her name. She turned towards me, eyes raised.

"Ally, if I come across anyone else, I will send them down to you. Listen for our whistle." She nodded and then disappeared into the dark, with the rest behind her. I left them once I knew they were safely down in the dungeon and moved the tapestry back in place. I continued back down the same hall where I had found the ladies. I peeked inside the great room and saw Ace cornered by three assailants. They had done a number on him. I didn't doubt he would have fought like a bear before being subdued and left on the floor with his wrists and ankles tied.

The third was holding a gun aimed at my brother's head. I shot that one in the back and he dropped like a rock. Ace took advantage of the distraction and kicked both his legs at the one closest. An audible crack said that Ace had broken one or both of the guys knees. I shot the third before he could reach for one of his fallen comrades' guns.

I quickly untied Ace who knocked them unconscious. We tied and gagged all three and pulled them out of view. I gave him one of my knives, but kept both the bows, in case I ran into Alex, who was an excellent shot.

"Nice shooting, little sister."

"Thanks, bro. Are you well enough to help me, or would you like me to stow you safely away with the ladies?" He gave me his look, and I giggled. I needed the stress release by being silly for a moment. I was relieved to see him still ready to fight despite all his cuts and scrapes.

"How did you not get caught?"

"Declan and I were across the field in a secret cave. We saw those guys enter the castle. Once we were inside, we heard yelling and a scuffle down another hallway, so we split up. Don't worry, Kris is fine. Her, Liza, Chrissie, and Allyson were the first ones I found."

He sighed in relief. We moved on then, creeping down the next hallway. We saw two assailants on the ground in a pool of blood. No sign of anyone else. A bit further on we found one of Eddy's men on the floor; he'd been shot.

"Damn, poor Amin." Ace stopped to check for a pulse. Nothing, he was dead. We kept moving down toward Jaimie and Dan's room. Behind their door, we heard fighting going on. Ace and I crept up. I motioned to him that I would go through another door that would take me into a secret passageway and right behind Jaimie and Dan's bed.

Ace nodded, and when he saw that I was in place, I signaled him to let me take out the guy who was holding a knife to Jaimie's throat to avoid her being accidentally killed. The door silently slid enough for me to get my nocked arrow through the slit sized opening and I nailed the guy right between the eyes.

Ace barged in and charged the two guys beating the crap out of our brother. Dan slid to the floor bleeding and in obvious need of stitches. Jaimie was so relieved, she flew into Dan's arms sobbing.

Ace had picked up a gun from the dead assailant, and said he'd continue down the next corridor. I felt panic ripping through me. I'd killed a man, possibly two. That was wrong, so wrong. I wanted to sit down and cry, but I remembered Declan's words. At least half of our group was still missing, this was not time to give in to a morality crisis.

With Dan in no shape to fight, I led them down the corridors to the hidden tapestry door. I helped Jaimie get Dan down that first flight of stairs, doing the bird-call, so Allyson wouldn't shoot. She bird-called back and materialized out of the dark taking over helping Dan the rest of the way. He turned before he was out of sight. He wiped his bloody mouth and gave me a lopsided grin.

"Thanks, sis, and be careful. Don't give yourself up, they will kill us all once they have their hands on you."

"I know. I love you, Dan." Tears glittered in my eyes, maybe this would be the last time I ever saw him. What if I didn't make it? This could be my last chance to see him. Seeing my distress, he said, "Montana, you're the one to win this. You can do it, don't give up."

I strengthened my resolve knowing he was right, and I had to win. I climbed back up the first flight, opened the panel, and slipped out into the hallway. I was feeling disturbed by Dan's words. He had nailed what I had been considering. If I was the key, then the rest would be free, clearly my thinking was wrong.

I was deciding on the fork in the hallway. Which way should I go? Follow Ace or continue towards mine and Adam's room? Something told me to go left to our wing. I was surprised to see Ace slumped over, unconscious, at the door to my room. He'd said he was going right, something either alerted him to come this way or something happened down the right wing that prevented him from continuing.

I took a breath and strengthened myself for the possibility that he was dead. But he wasn't, only unconscious with hands tied. I decided to leave him, but with hands unbound. He couldn't help me, so I moved on.

It was at my next turn that things were truly out of hand. Adam, Declan, and Geoff were corralled in a tight circle with five assailants around them. Damn, too many for me. Maybe without guns, I would have gone for it, but three of the five did. I couldn't possibly shoot all of them before they got off a shot, and who would they shoot?

I decided to look for help. With Declan and Adam caught, that only left Alex and Eddy with any training. Where were they? I snuck down to the end of the hall, I heard rooms being rifled through, obviously looking for me. I snuck to the band room and there was the rest of the group. They must have been playing when the attack started. Tim, Otter, Stella, Ann, Cole, and Otter's mom were there hiding and safe for the moment, but with the ransackers coming this way, I needed to get them out of here.

"Where's Alex?"

They didn't know, just before the castle fell under attack he had left. I pondered my next move. I couldn't leave them here. They were sitting targets.

"Come on, I'll take you to a safe hiding spot. Otter, you know the whistle, right?" He nodded. "As soon as I get you through a secret passage, you go down a curving staircase. It takes you to a slanting walkway to the left and then down one more set of stairs. When you get to the end of that first hall, before the second set of stairs, do the whistle. Allyson is down there guarding the others. She will come and get you, okay?"

He seemed to be in shock, "Otter, do you understand me?" His mother stepped up to his side.

"I do, Montana. I will make sure we follow your instructions," With that, I led them down the hall and into a small office. Behind a tapestry was a sliding panel. I opened it for them, and once they were through, I closed it and made sure the tapestry was perfect and still.

Now what? I needed a plan. I wanted Adam, Declan and Geoff free, but how? And where was my brother? I was shaking with the strain of holding and using the bow, and the results that using the bow had created. I had never killed anything in my life beyond a common house spider. I knew I would need to process that when this was all over.

Suddenly, I knew what to do. I sat down and focused on Alex, I showed him my view, let him see where I was. Five minutes later he and Eddy arrived.

"Mo, do you know where everyone is?" Eddy asked.

"Yes, well, I'm not sure about all your security, but I know Amin is dead. I'm sorry, Eddy," I guess I wouldn't be the only one processing all this death. "The rest are downstairs in the dungeons. Except, I left Ace unconscious in front of my bedroom door, and Declan, Adam and Geoff are being held by five men, three of which have guns. That's why I came looking for you, I need help."

"Dungeon?" Eddy asked.

I nodded.

"What do we do, Eddy?" Neither one answered.

"They want me, so let's use me as bait." Alex and Eddy didn't say anything, but I knew it would be the best way to separate the assailants, and once divided they would be easier to take down.

"Okay," Eddy said, "but if you go running in, they will assume someone they have not found yet is backing you up, so we have to lure them out instead." The three of us thought for a moment.

"What if I walk by the doorway where they are keeping them? Look stunned and take off at a run. They will leave one or two behind to guard the guys. You and Alex can take them out. I'll head down to the dining room. There's a door behind the fireplace. They'll give chase, but they won't find me."

"Then what? We still have whoever takes off after you to contend with, as well as any others we may not have seen yet." Alex seemed unconvinced of my plan.

"Don't worry, Alex. I'm sure between you and Eddy, you can come up with something," I handed him his bow and arrows and gave Eddy my set. I gave each of them a knife. That left me one, tucked into my ankle. "Besides, if this works, you will have three more to help. I'm sure Declan can think of something. Seriously, this isn't the time to have all our ducks in a row."

Before hesitating, I headed down the hallway where the men were being held. Eddy and Alex stayed in the passageway, so as not to be seen. And like we'd hoped, they gave chase the moment they saw me. I had four on my tail. Leaving only one for Eddy and Alex to dispose of.

I ran as fast as I could. Having the advantage of where to hide was only good if I could get there and through the door without them seeing where I went. I'd almost made it, when a shot rang out. My shoulder exploded with pain, and I fell onto the hard stone floor, just feet away from from safety.

Damn, I had screwed up again. How many lives could one girl get? A foot roughly pushed me onto my back and looking down was a face from my past, Mercy. How fitting, I thought, last time I had seen her, she had put a knife through my back and now a bullet through my shoulder.

She wore a triumphant look. Her eyes glittered darkly. She reminded me of a predator, maybe an Anaconda, something large enough to swallow a person whole. I wasn't about to give her any satisfaction.

"Well, look at what the cesspool of the universe coughed up... a jealous bitch. What took you so long, Mercy? I was starting to think you lost your nerve. With all that muscle behind you, I expected you to show your ugly mug about two months ago. Oh, but wait, you had to escape your cage first, poor little thug."

Her eyes changed from glittering triumph to pure hatred. She booted me in the ribs several times. I felt a familiar crack. Third times a charm. Her gang had done this before.

"Shut up, stupid girl, you are not in control here," Her eyes changed again, and this time wore an expression of malice. "You should have been dead months ago, but that selfish bitch Katya kept getting in my way with her inferior plans. Glad you finally caught on, dummy, and got her out of my way." I gulped and let down my guard, and she saw the questioning in my eyes, the vulnerability.

"That's right, silly girl. You thought I didn't know Katya was spoon feeding intel to my gang? I was well aware and used it to my advantage. Poor little brat, your childhood nemesis got the plan together to get rid of the famous Montana Stanford. Like, what a load of shit! I should have killed Adam a long time ago. Without him, you're nothing," she spat. I had underestimated her again. Or maybe not her but certainly the depths of her hate for me. I was afraid but kept my West End tough girl act up.

When her focus shifted to give orders, I glanced to the hallway behind Mercy and her goons. Declan and Eddy were tucked around the corner. My only chance of surviving would be to help the guys by distracting Mercy. Her gaze returned to me, which resembled a cat who'd eaten a bowl of cream, all happy and satisfied.

"I'm getting closer, Montana. When your family and friends are rounded up, you will watch me kill them all, except Alex. He will watch you die, and then when I'm done with him, I'll kill him too."

I laughed. It hurt like hell with the broken ribs, but I needed her off balance. What she said should have terrified me. But what she didn't know was there were no prisoners. They'd all gotten away.

"Good luck, crazy bitch! You have no one, and your goons are all dead or injured." I laughed again, a maniacal laugh. One of her guards came from the other direction and whispered in her ear. I could tell by the rage on her face that he had just confirmed what I'd said. I was out of time, her rage was too great to contain and would spill over into a death blow for me any moment. I prayed the guys had a plan of their own.

What came next was all in slow motion. As Mercy turned back toward me, as predicted, her rage evident, she pointed her gun at my head, and I heard the catch release, while simultaneously, a ruckus behind Mercy pulled all our attention.

I didn't waste my opportunity, I kicked Mercy's legs, and she fell to the ground. With my good arm I threw the gun that tumbled from her fingers. She wasn't going to let me go that easily. She pulled a knife out of her boot and crawled on top of me. She raised the knife and was about to plunge it into my heart when several shots rang out.

Mercy, a look of incredulity on her face, toppled to the ground at my side, dead. I heard Adam yell my name, and he suddenly appeared at my side. I smiled up at his beautiful but beaten face.

"Is it over?" I croaked. He nodded.

"Thank god, you're alive. I knew you had to be safe or they would have started killing the rest of us."

Alex, and Geoff were next at my side.

"Montana, do you know where Liza and the rest are?" Before I could slur out some words, Alex spoke for me.

"They are safe, Geoff. She saved them all. My sis kicked some serious ass today." Declan, done with tying up the last two assailants came over to check on me, wearing a proud papa look.

"Well done, lass." Alex kept his healing hands on me, and Adam had a compression on my shoulder to staunch the bleeding.

"I almost thought you were a goner for a moment. Eddy held me back from coming around the corner. He saw the advantage of having you distract Mercy." Adam admitted.

"Is she dead?" He nodded, "Thank god, it's over." The shock settled, and tears of relief, and gratitude seeped from my eyes and tracked down my cheeks.

Declan had gone to get the others out of hiding. It was a ragtag group of survivors that made their way out of hiding and into the light of the hallway. I was so grateful that we were all still here. Allyson, Dan and Ace would need medical attention. The others, maybe some post traumatic counselling.

It had been an all-out assassination attempt on multiple lives. It was harsh, and the reality of what could have been sank us into momentary silence. Sirens could be heard in the distance, the shrill sound getting slowly closer.

"I'm sick of getting shot, Adam. We may have to consider a career change for me." Despite the severity of the situation, he laughed.

"We have overcome the worst, Montana. I suspect things will calm down considerably, and life will become the fairy-tale it was meant to be. Besides, once the news gets out that you took down an entire gang of twelve, almost entirely on your own, no one will want to mess with you."

I was laying in my hospital bed, Allyson sat at the foot, and we took stock on the outcome of the day's activities. She had received nine stitches in her forehead. Her other injury was her ego. She was so pissed off at herself for getting caught off guard.

"Allyson, I never did find Mrs. Campbell, was she hurt?"

Allyson laughed. "Mrs. Campbell was hiding in a secret room behind the pantry. She was fine. Declan found her after everyone but her was accounted for."

"What about Danny? He was looking pretty bad when I saw him last."

She sighed, "He's in bad shape, and will be for a bit, I gather. Nothing is broken, but he has a lot of bruising and stitches in several places. He's already back at the castle, though, and Mrs. Campbell is clucking over him. I'm sure he'll be fine in no time with all those tinctures she has him drinking." We both laughed. Mine came out as a breathy hiss. My ribs were giving me more grief than the bullet.

In total, there had been twelve gang members that had infiltrated the castle, of which four were dead and the rest in jail. The papers had a field day with what had gone down. Quiet little town being infiltrated by a dozen assassins to take down one wee lassie. The stories and opinions were very biased and superstar status was mine. The tales, particularly in Scotland, were staggering in their exaggerations. As a good Scot's tale could be sometimes.

I was welcomed back to the castle the next day with a warm homecoming. The gang was all there, of course, and about fifty or so folks. They were, Mrs. Campbell explained, all that was left of the local inhabitants.

"In times past, the residents of this town were the families that sustained the lifestyle of those that lived in the castle. We were provided protection and support in exchange for our farming skills and the like." I nodded in understanding.

"Those living here now are the descendants of those who lived and served the castle. Most of Declan's friends couldn't wait to move on to the bigger cities. You'll see there is no one here his age. Mostly the folks are my age or older. The town is dying, lass. With no reason to be here and no means of income, the folks left now just exist. Your family and the attack are the most exciting event in their lifetime," she finished with a twinkle in her eye.

I rolled my eyes. Celebrity status with the locals, just what I didn't want. Mrs. Campbell led me to each person and made the introductions. She was amazing at controlling the length and content of my conversations with everyone. I found myself forgetting that I didn't know these people, and instead, earnestly engaged them in conversation.

So warm and friendly with the thickest accents. I listened to them as they talked about missing the young ones. And wishing they could see their children and grandchildren more often. They talked about the olden days and shared tales that had been passed down through the generations, father to son and mother to daughter. Stories you would never hear outside of the village.

I was reminded of Dad. He loved to tell stories and would regale us for hours with wonderful stories when he came home from the rigs. These people reminded me of what I was as well, and how I had started off in life, as a writer of songs. Before playing drums, before dance, even before cheerleading. I'd written songs and given them to my brother to turn into music. In that way, I was more like my father than I realized. I told stories, too. They may not be historical events or events at all, but they were real, and every emotion I wrote about I'd felt.

The locals had given me a gift. They reminded me that no matter what, I had family, a clan that loved me and that I loved in return. I had a gift for storytelling just like my father. I let the food and the laughter sink deep within me and felt so renewed. By the time we were due to sing a few songs, a usual part of any village gathering, I was filled with gratitude and wanted to sing, to honour their rich culture and traditions.

I'd been hesitating about my song choice. I was only singing one, and when I had agreed, it was more out of feeling obligated than because I wanted to. With a very sore shoulder and wrapped up ribs I was unable to play the drums, but I thought I could manage a song. I chose one that Declan had taught me. One he sang on a day of exploration not that long ago, when he showed me another outcropping of standing stones I had not yet seen. He had sung the song in Gaelic, and I had asked him to translate.

A lonely song that when sung on the moors sounded like the wind's lonely howl. Alex had played with the melody and turned the song into a rock ballad. That was the one I chose, about the laird and the lady, a story of their old chieftain and his wife, and hoped the locals didn't hate it.

I reminded myself to be very still as I sang. I needed all the breath I could get to sing the song. Alex, as if reading my mind, put a stool in front of the microphone. He grabbed a second stool for himself and set up with his acoustic guitar.

A hush descended over the group, as I took the mic from the stand.

When Adam and I were taking yoga classes as part of my recovery from being stabbed in the back and going through a few weeks of paralysis, we learned about breathing. Deep breaths that included all three parts of the diaphragm helped cleans the body, and release stored energy.

I took a deep breath and let it out slowly, visualizing letting go of everything that had been haunting me since I was fifteen years old. Letting go of Mercy, Katya, and all the pain both physical and emotional I'd had to endure. I was ready. I sang a tale, of longing, desire, and sorrow. I dug deep without straining. Any remaining doubts I had about singing the *right* song washed away. I was set free, and so was my voice. When the song ended, and I came back to myself, the audience was still. I was suddenly fearful that I had overstepped some Scottish custom that I was unaware of, until a boisterous applause broke out.

"When did you learn Gaelic?"

"Alex, I haven't learned Gaelic. What do you mean?"

"What I mean, Ms. Superstar, is that you sang half that song in Gaelic."

I was shocked, it just came out. "Probably hanging out with Declan too much." I laughed. Well, that got chuckles from those close enough to hear the conversation, except Declan and Alex, who clearly didn't believe a word I said. Truth was, I had no damn idea how I'd done that.

I stepped down, and the band continued for a few more songs. Adam was at the bottom of our makeshift stage.

Although it was only two steps, he held my hand, and once down handed me a glass of wine.

"That was beautiful, and I loved the Gaelic. It sounded sexy. So sexy in fact, I was hoping I could escort you back to our room." He waggled his eyebrows at me, and I giggled.

"Mr. Northrop, I do believe you are wanting to ravage me."

"Miss Stanford, that is exactly what I'm saying." He maneuvered us through the crowd like a pro and into our bedroom. Within seconds we were both naked.

"Adam, I'm sorry I need to be on top," I grinned. "You know I can't lay on my back with the ribs, and I can't hold you with the shoulder. So, I'm sitting and you're doing all the work." He grinned.

"Well then, I guess you're in for the ride of your life."

Chapter 20

The homecoming welcome marked the beginning of the best few weeks of our time in Scotland so far. We were high on the idea of freedom, even those who'd been less affected, found a new vigour and joy. Instead of hightailing it back to Canada, our group took the time to relax and enjoy the island, becoming tourists at last. Declan played tour guide for the group, except for Adam and me. We stayed pretty close to home allowing me the time I needed to heal. It was kinda nice having the entire monstrosity to ourselves most days.

  About a week in, I'd had enough coddling by my fiance and we decided to take our daily walks outside the castle perimeter. It was now summer, and the countryside teamed with life. Beautiful wildflowers were pops of color in the tall grasses of the moor, with insects happily buzzing through around them. The air itself seemed to shimmer with a fullness that I'd never witnessed back in Vancouver.

  Mrs. Campbell had mentioned checking out the standing stones on the property. I'd seen a few groupings already, but this one was purported to be magical like the fairy burn, which had done me a world of good. Adam led the way carrying a picnic basket Mrs. C had packed for us and I was tasked with the blanket.

Mrs. C had a twinkle in her eye when she'd packed the basket and gave us directions. I shook my head and wondered what she was up to now. We walked for about half an hour when Adam pointed. "I believe those are the stones we're looking for."

Unlike the remnants of the "henges" I'd seen, these rocks still stood tall and proud, like sentinels, in an unbroken circle. I felt an ancientness to the space. I'd noticed when Adam and I had traveled the more off beaten paths, when we'd traveled Europe, that many places felt really old. I always found it odd as isn't the entire planet the same age? Why did some spots feel so alien when compared with the rest?

I found a spot by what I assumed was the head stone and laid out the blanket. Adam set the basket down and pulled out our cameras, sketch pads and pencils.

"If the ground were a little louder, I swear I could hear its thoughts."

I stretched out in the warm sunshine. "I know what you mean. This is different from anything else, even the pool didn't feel like this. It's like the ground is alive and listening. Weird right?"

"That's a good way of describing it." Adam reached for his camera and snapped pictures of the stones. I rolled onto my tummy and watched him. A shimmering light from the sun had an odd effect on the surface making them appear to be dancing and the lines of minerals that ran through the rough surfaces shone like jewels.

Adam switched out his camera for his sketch pad, no doubt trying to capture something elusive. I didn't care about how anything looked, instead feeling compelled to touch the stones. I shifted my position and sat against the one closest to our blanket and leaned my head back.

With my eyes closed my other senses grew stronger and I heard whisperings on the gentle breeze. An entire tribe of souls spoke words I barely understood but the meaning was not lost on me. The stones had been here a long time and had seen thousands of generations of people. Like witnesses, they seemed to have absorbed and held these souls that had passed through.

I cracked an eye and watched my fiance sketch. He really was a different person when he created. Not Adam Northrop, only son of rich philanthropist Vancouver socialite parents, nor my fiance, or even Adam. He was an extension of his brush or pencil like my drum sticks were for me. It's when we disappeared and went elsewhere, becoming one with our art.

I closed my eyes and felt myself drifting. Within the circle, I was no longer part of the world, only the moment. Each moment that followed the last was conscious and not lost in thought or feelings. It was incredible and intense, each moment complete, and the fulfillment that followed was staggering in its simplicity.

When I opened my eyes next, the sun had traveled and was no longer directly above us. Glancing at Adam, I could see he had also fallen asleep and was pressed against me. I reached for my camera and snapped off a series of pictures of him. He looked ethereal in the setting, like the Greek god I always teased him about resembling. I felt safe inside the circle in a way that only Adam's arms had ever provided. I put the camera down and gently shook him awake.

"Let's have that lunch Mrs. C packed. I'm starving."

He grinned and sat up, and moving to the basket made quick work of setting everything out. "Adam, I had the strangest dream. There was a battle here. I saw soldiers in red and soldiers in tartan, and I felt like it was real, like I was watching a real-life battle. As they drew nearer to where I was standing, I saw a soldier who looked just like Declan. He saw me, and he recognized me. He called me Kate and told me to run to the castle. Isn't that strange?"

"Was it upsetting?"

"Not in the least," I yawned. "The only thing strange was how real it was."

"Maybe the landscape inspired a rendition of a battle that took place here a long time ago."

I nodded in agreement. Adam placed the contents of the basket on the blanket. The bannock and beef sandwiches with cold apple cider were delicious. We ate everything she'd packed, and when we were done, I cleaned up the wrappers and glass jars and placed them back in the basket.

With the basket items cleared, I lay down on the blanket and gazed up at Adam. He leaned over me, balancing on his fists so as to not press against my still healing ribs. He grazed his lips against mine. An all too familiar heat zinged through me, settling deep in my belly. I wrapped my legs around his hips. I took the lead, wanton abandon propelling my actions. This was not gentle love making, I needed to feel him deep within me. As we rode the wave to our mutual release, the stones seemed to groan, and a satisfied rustle moved through the grass surrounding us.

Panting, Adam rolled to his side and gently tucked me against him with my head held by his arm. I felt different, embraced by the land, the sun and air, imbued with a happiness I didn't usually have. The fact I was free and here with him... I could do this forever and be happy.

"I love it here, Adam."

"With the stones?"

"No, silly, Scotland. I like the stones too, but I mean this country, this land. It suits me. The air and the energy resonate inside like a deep thrumming. Maybe one day we can get that castle you talked about. Do you remember, Adam? Way back when we were lying in lounge chairs in my backyard, and you told me what my perfect life would be like?"

He nodded. "We had just started dating. I think it was my first sleepover."

"It was, and so far you've been right, about everything." In a softer tone I added. "I want you again."

Our pace was less frenzied this time, and when we were spent, we lowered ourselves onto the blanket. I watched a few fluffy clouds overhead until my eyes drooped and I slipped off into a doze. When Adam woke me the sky was deepening in color preparing food sunset. We returned to the castle all smiles and found Mrs. C.

"You two looked refreshed. Did you enjoy my stones?"

Her stones? Interesting. We told her we had and handed her back the empty picnic basket with thank yous. We then headed to our suite for a long romantic bath and a nap before dinner.

Adam was gone when I woke up, but I found his notebook open and read a few of his thoughts about our time today.

Montana, still sleeping, curled into my side, safe, with a smile of innocence enhancing her beautiful face. A sight I was beginning to wonder if I'd ever see again. A worry free, stress free Montana made me a very happy guy.

When I met her, I thought she was the most alive person I had ever met. She had a light that shone bright, and I was the moth that couldn't resist her flame.

What would my life be like without her? Who would she have met if not me? Would he have put up with her shenanigans, or tried to break her? I hold back my laughter so as not to wake her, but I can't imagine anyone breaking her. Sometimes, I thought that she would have ended up with Eddy. He was the only man outside of her brothers that she truly trusted with her life and, for Montana, that meant everything.

She'd been such a handful, but her brave unyielding path had always inspired me, even long before we started dating. As I say, her flame singed my pathetic wings long ago and I fell at her feet. I would and will give her anything because she is life, my muse, the part of me that is more alive with than without her... she stirs, and hopefully wakes as happy as was when she fell asleep.

I heard Adam in the bathroom and quickly put his book back the exact way I'd found it. I knew he knew I snooped but getting caught snooping was a whole other thing.

"Hey, Brat. Sleep well?"

"Uh huh, and I had the most amazing dream."

"Oh?"

"Mhmmmm. We were in this bed having a nap, and when I woke you made love to me."

Adam laughed. "Guess what?"

"What?"

"I had the same dream."

He joined me on the bed and pulled me up on top of him. They say the third time's a charm. I had to agree. Our session was different from earlier, not rushed, not slow, but quick with our senses so enhanced from our lazy day of lovemaking. I couldn't remember the last time we'd done this and I wanted to prolong the intimacy as long as possible.

"My god, woman, you're killing me. Do we have to move?"

I chuckled. "Yes, Mr. Northrop, I think you have a big scary brother to talk to."

"Huh?"

"Adam, with all of our friends and family here with us, what do you think about getting married in Scotland?"

I don't know what provoked me to say this and could tell he was completely taken by surprise.

"Mo, last week you wanted the big wedding, what's changed?"

"You."

"Me?" Again, I'd surprised him.

"Yeah, well me, actually, I want to be your wife now. I don't want to wait anymore, Adam. I felt it today, at the stones. I want you every possible way I can have you, even the paper that states it. It is time I became Mrs. Adam Northrop.

"Besides, your mom is like the ultimate event planner. She could make it happen. I'm sure Mrs. Campbell knows someone who could cater. Declan must know a silversmith that could make the bands. Your best man is here, as is my maid of honour. Your dad can emcee, and Ace can give me away just as we had planned.

"I never wanted a society wedding, Adam. I guess I felt pressured because your family has status, and you're rich. And rich people usually have society weddings. Here, I don't feel controlled by the obligation of said society. I'm not making a head choice. I am making a heart choice."

"Montana, if that's what you want, then that is totally fine with me. What do you need me to do?"

"I want you to ask Ace for my hand in marriage."

"Are you kidding? We already had a date. Besides, he's going to be so happy to have you hitched sooner, he's going to be thanking me," he joked. I punched him playfully in the shoulder.

"I should have asked before. Now that we are on the other side of all the crap that's been chasing us these past few years, I feel I've awakened from a nightmare that started with being stabbed all those years ago in the alley. For the first time in forever, my mind feels uncluttered. I'm feeling a strong sense of honour and respect for myself, for others, and life in general. It feels right."

"Sound reasons. I can picture Ace's expression when I ask. He'll probably laugh and offer me a scotch. Then, he'll tell me again that I'm in for the ride of my life, and I'll laughingly agree."

I laughed, envisioning the same thing. I got cleaned up in the bathroom and rummaged around in the wardrobe for an outfit, holding up two for Adam to choose from.

"It's getting cool, jeans and the white sweater."

"Okay. Adam, one other thing, can you help me announce it? And I want you to get the rings made. Design whatever you want."

"You've given me easy tasks. I already had the bands designed so drawing it for Declan will be easy."

After dinner, Adam approached Ace and they disappeared into the hallway. I made as if to grab a new game from the shelf by the door and shuffled close enough to overhear the conversation.

"What's up, bro?" Ace asked. He'd been calling Adam bro for a long time. That's why asking him probably felt ridiculous, but that is what I wanted.

"Your sister has made a request of me." I almost felt bad for Ace whenever anyone brought up *his sister,* his posture would change, his energy would shift, and he immediately would think the worst. "It's okay, big guy. I promise it isn't whatever you're thinking."

I held a hand to my lips to keep from giggling out loud.

"Well, spit it out, Adam. What is her request?"

"I am here to formally ask permission to marry your sister, whom I love and adore with every fibre of my being. She wants to get married here in Scotland with her friends and family, or as she likes to refer to us as, her tribe."

I pictured an ear-splitting grin filling his chiselled face, and softening it immensely.

"I'll have to give you the family paddle." My mouth dropped in shock.

"You don't have a family paddle." Adam replied.

"I know, but you'll need one, as you're in for the ride of your life. Montana is a force of nature and will keep you on your toes." They broke out laughing, and I would have been offended if it wasn't the truth. I grabbed a game and went back to my spot. Alex caught my eye. "I never took you for a Snakes and Ladders girl?"

I gazed down at the game in my hands and blushed. Alex smirked knowing exactly what I'd been doing. Luckily, Ace and Adam entered the room, before Alex could question me further.

"May I have your attention, please." Everyone stopped what they were doing and turned their attention to Adam. I took a moment to appreciate his beauty. The man had an unearthly handsomeness, and my breath caught. He stood by the fireplace, the dancing flames casting a glow that only added to his otherworldly image. Sexy as fuck in his low slung jeans that hung on his hips and clung to his muscular thighs. I licked my lips. Maybe four times was a charm. I imagined his hands running down my back and squeezing my ass.

"You all know Montana has agreed to marry me. What you don't know is we've decided to get married here in Scotland while the people we care about most are in residence with us."

"About time," Geoff called out.

Adam grinned. Announcement over, everyone was buzzing with questions and suggestions.

"All right ladies, we have some planning to do!" I cried out happily.

Chapter 21

Liza and Mrs. Campbell grabbed pens and paper. Allyson, Sonya—Otter's mom, Stella, Kris, and Chrissie joined us. Mrs. Campbell volunteered to gather the local talent. She felt, and we agreed, that using our money within the town first would certainly help their tiny community a great deal. She knew just who to talk to about food, flowers, decorating, the minister and, she said, there would be no shortage of volunteers.

Free of the big city wedding plans meant I could choose things that truly resonated with me. "Mrs. C, what about a seamstress? I think I want a tartan gown and Adam will need a matching kilt."

"Och, nae worry lass, I know exactly who to talk to. Did ya nae have something already in the works?"

"No. I was told I should pick a wedding gown because of the alterations required. I should have done it before we left on tour the last time. I just didn't want to as I hadn't a clear idea of what I wanted. I was never that little girl who dreamed of the perfect wedding. I mean, I had a few ideas when Adam gave me the promise ring, but they were very juvenile. Now that I'm not obligated to stand in a reception line wearing five hundred dollar pumps with a jewel encrusted veil, I can honestly say I don't want anything stuffy, a few chairs, and a lot of beer sounds pretty good to me." The ladies laughed.

"Only five hundred? Adam was getting off easy," Kristine joked.

"Right? I'd be in vintage-style Louis Vuittons," Allyson added.

"I want to be barefoot," Chrissie said dreamily.

"That's funny, so does Alex," I said and immediately regretted it. That created an uncomfortable silence. Liza quickly deflected the conversation. "You should have told me you were struggling with the wedding. I could have helped more."

"More? You were already doing all of it. I was just a *yes* girl." That garnered more laughter.

Liza lowered her eyes, gathering her thoughts, "I guess I assumed with being shot, the trip to the Caymans, and starting the charity, your focus was busy elsewhere. I'm sorry, Montana."

"Now I feel like a shit. Please, don't be sorry for anything. Like I said, I never really thought much about my wedding. I mean really, did any of you really believe I'd live to have one?" Whoops, another joke gone south, "Or Adam still wanting to marry me after all I've put him through?" Another oops, no-one was laughing.

"Sorry. I keep putting my foot in my mouth, I guess I'm a little nervous." That broke the ice and the ladies got back to discussing the plans while I leaned back, beer in hand, enjoying all their clucking like a gaggle of hens.

An hour later, I faked a few yawns and Adam, reading me like a book, said good night for both of us. We retired to our room and proved that the fourth time was the charm. We were talking about the showdown that had taken place.

"If I haven't told you yet, Brat, I'm super proud of you."

"You are? For what?" I wasn't digging for a complement but I was curious as to what part of that day made him proud.

"Who would have thought that this tiny, fierce, drumming machine would take down almost an entire enemy gang on her own." I rubbed my face into his chest.

"I think Declan is the true hero. Without him I could have never done what I did. Without him I wouldn't have been out of the castle witnessing the takeover. Really, Declan is the hero of the hour."

"I suspect he has a crush on you."

I broke out in laughter. "Adam, you can't be serious."

"Oh aye, lass, verra." Adam's impersonation of Declan had me cracking up.

"Okay, suppose for a second you're right. How does that make you feel?"

"First off, it's true, I watch him watching you and it's not the same way Eddy looks at you, like a sibling. That man has eyes only for you, Mo. It doesn't bother me at all. I'm sure half the world feels the same as he does."

I frowned. I'd never considered anyone's feelings for me to be anything other than mutual friendship.

"The papers have done a fine job of painting him as the new William Wallace."

"Seriously?" I laughed until tears spilled from the corners of my eyes. "Oh, I can't wait to tease him about that."

The next day, Declan took the men to town. With them out of our way, Mrs. C brought in her seamstress friend. After several bottles of champagne, I chose an opaque whimsical material that reminded me of the Scottish mist. It wasn't white, but appeared so in the sunlight. The material had grey undertones that made one think of mist. The gown would hug my body but give me leg room for walking. The bodice would be off the shoulder, and a little low cut, accompanied by a wrap of McGregor tartan.

All the girls chose styles and fabrics for their bridesmaid dresses. The dresses would all be different and reflect their personal taste. Allyson chose a calf length, figure-hugging design in a soft forest green with a white chiffon wrap. The green would match the leaves in the bouquet. She added a very delicate silver filigree to the edging of her wrap and the bottom of her dress, which would give a hint of glitter to her overall look.

Kris chose a light pink, her signature colour, with classic lines that I knew Ace would love. Jaimie decided on a calf length mermaid style purple dress. Chrissie chose blue, ironically, the same blue that was my brother, Alex's favourite colour. As she was more on the slender side, with a small bust, her dress would have a plunging neckline almost to the waist with a strap of material across the back to hold it all in place. Stella went with a knee length ruby red silk number that showcased her pale nordic skin tone. Ann was last and by that time I was completely hammered and only vaguely aware she'd chosen.

Our seamstress left, with Liza and Mrs. C to help her transport all her items back to the car. Good thing, too, as I was way too drunk to do anything responsible. Chrissie turned on some music and the wedding was forgotten. I wasn't the only one drunk as we weaved around, under the guise of dancing, until we collapsed in fits of giggles on the couches. Someone turned up the music in the games room where we'd been doing measurements.

Wedding preparations kept our lives busy and exhilarating. As the days passed, and we moved closer to our wedding date, things became more intense. Last minute everything, as the entire wedding was last minute. Two days before the big day, Geoff and Liza arranged for a catered dinner with a group of locals who unofficially had a catering service.

They were the towns' organizers, a group of women who provided food for events using the only local pub kitchen to accomplish the task. This was a courtesy to Mrs. C, who wanted to do it all herself at the castle, but knew she'd hate having her kitchen overrun. That and we all considered Mrs. C and Declan as part of the family and wanted them to enjoy the wedding festivities.

The rehearsal dinner was fun, but didn't alleviate my nerves in the least. I was going to get married. It sounded so strange when I said it out loud. Whatever heat I'd felt that day at the stones had burned out pretty fast. Not that I didn't want to be Adam's wife, but the finality of it set my nerves on edge a bit. I needed time alone and went seeking solace the next day in the great outdoors.

Being outside was the best way to ground myself and alleviate my stress. As I traipsed over the landscape, deep in thought of vows and dresses, I almost tripped into a bush when I rounded a hillside.

When I righted myself and looked around, my jaw fell. Before me was the most beautiful glen I'd ever seen. The faint tinkling of a stream, and the moisture in the air was a dead giveaway that a stream lay ahead.

I followed my ears and found a crystal-clear burn. I decided to take a naked swim, feeling safe from prying eyes, as the land belonged to the castle and therefore was private property.

The place was peaceful and ageless. The surface was clear enough to be glass. I scooped some water into my mouth and tasted it before I entered. Once in, I luxuriated in its soothing embrace, swearing a better spot couldn't be had.

It felt like only minutes had passed when I exited the water and went looking for a warm rock to dry myself on, but I knew better. The sun had traveled, and I bet I'd been here two hours already. Finding a large flat stone, I lay on my front and sighed contentedly.

I was jolted out of my warm lethargy by a noise that didn't belong to the burn.

Cocking my head, I heard it again, shuffling in the brush to my right. I dove into the pool and to the other side, looking for something I could use as a weapon.

"Lass, it's all fine now."

Declan. He emerged from the bushes, while I remained rooted, naked and thoroughly embarrassed. He stood there staring, while I walked with as much dignity as I could muster to my pile of clothes, which were laying inches from where he stood. I bent over to retrieve my shirt when I noticed him laughing.

"You bloody Scottish bastard, you think this is so funny, don't you?"

"Well, lass, I wasn't the one noodling about in the water, eh."

"I wasn't noodling, you crazy Scot. I was enjoying my time alone before I'm a married woman, aye?" I added that last part sarcastically. Dressed, I started back for the castle, and passed two men who were knocked out, obviously by Declan. I was suddenly unsure as to my safety.

"Who are they? Please say they weren't trying to kill me."

"Yer okay, lass. They are bloody bastards who thought to take pictures of yer naked body, and slap them all over the tabloids, aye."

That stopped me in my tracks. I was an idiot and despite my feeling free to do as I pleased on the property, clearly my lifestyle choices said otherwise. I was still famous, and there were two escaped convicts back in Vancouver that had yet to be caught. Cameras lay on the ground at their feet.

"What happened to the film?"

"No worries, lass, I've taken care of it."

"Thank you," I replied simply and continued out of the bush and back toward the castle.

"Declan, I would appreciate it if you didn't share this with anyone. I'm stupid for assuming that I wouldn't be noticed."

"I'm here for you, lass, not as a job or a spy, just for you. We are friends, aye?"

"Yes, Declan, we are very good friends. You're kinda like Eddy, but different. Deep down I know that you are my friend before everyone else's in the group. I know it is me you are loyal to, and I'm thankful for it. I don't have many close friends. In fact, all my friends are here." I laughed.

"I know it. Can I ask you something, Montana?"

I stopped walking and sat down on a rock to give him my full attention.

"Yes, you can ask me anything."

"Lass, you have a lot of scars, more than just the last attack on the castle, or even the explosion that brought you here. I saw your scar by your spine that Adam said came from being stabbed. You also have been shot in your other shoulder. Why, may I ask, are you so marked?" I sat back down on a nearby rock.

"I guess you could say that I don't back down from challenges or fights. I've paid for my choices. Some weren't my fault, more bad timing. The girl," I corrected myself, "the woman, that Eddy shot, Mercy, she has hated me since we met in grade nine. She liked Alex, and she dated a guy who beat me up. She dated another guy, and he jumped me and sent me to the hospital with cracked ribs. She stabbed me in the back after getting me removed from the band and crippled me. I couldn't walk, I was paralyzed."

I stopped talking. It felt strange sharing with someone who didn't know all my stories. And because they did, sharing it with him now was surreal. It was cleansing, and I decided to continue. I got up and walked, Declan following patiently beside me. I think he'd been a good listener for others before me as he didn't hurry me to continue.

"It was Adam who got me walking, and in record time. He and Dan had been traveling around Europe and came home early to help me get the best doctors in the country. Within two weeks I was walking. A full recovery took much longer, of course. Adam never left me, wouldn't leave me. He pushed me and still does. He keeps me healthy and regulated."

I paused again as my feelings and words sorted themselves out.

"I'm impulsive, Declan and I always have been. I guess today was another example of that. I don't think about repercussions. I just act, you know what I mean? That's why Adam calls me *the brat*."

He didn't say anything for a bit. As we continued our walk back to the castle.

"How many times has he saved yer life, lass? Has he always been there for ye?"

"Since I was fifteen, he has been there for me. Before that it was Eddy, and Alex and I always had each other's back. Adam became a much needed buffer for me and Dan and Ace. It's no secret Ace and I, we've always butted heads. I've been told we're a lot alike. I always got into trouble, but mostly because I got caught doing things that, at the time, made sense to me, but not to my brothers."

Declan chuckled. "I can imagine you as a little urchin, running around and terrorizing your neighborhood."

I smiled. "I always knew what I was doing—that's not entirely true. I didn't care about what I was doing or how it turned out. Do you know that song, *Only the Good Die Young*, by Billy Joel?" He shook his head no. "Anyway," I continued, "That was my motto. I didn't care about the repercussions of my choices. I figured I live, I die, what's the big deal?"

His eyebrows rose, but he remained silent, "Listen, Declan, I have never said this to anyone before, so please don't... well, it's a secret. But back in those days I didn't care much about what happened to me. Life was a gamble, and I had no problem gambling mine. Especially if it meant keeping someone safe. Usually Alex." I could see him digesting this new information about me.

"That's why Ace used to get so upset with me. I was fearless, but not because I was brave, because I didn't care if I lived or died. That has changed now, with everything that's just happened. I've been beaten many times, shot, stabbed, and I've broken my ribs at least three times. Aging is overrated. Imagine the kind of pain I'll have when I'm old, if I live that long." He laughed.

"Being attacked on the street by five guys was the worst. I was terrified after, when I thought about how easily it could have gone the other way. I could have been raped, tortured, and killed like all the other victims."

"Yer speakin' of those men that escaped?"

"Yes, there were five, three escaped, and two were caught. The two I testified against were broken out of their transport. Eddy and Adam thought for the longest time that the notes were from them. They would, *finish what they started*." I shuddered. I didn't think I would ever be able to hear those words and not think about Katya. "Now that Scotland, and you, have woken the warrior in me, I will fight for life."

"I understand, ye, lass, I feel similar."

"Do you ever feel like a bad person, Declan?"

We stopped walking, the clouds that had been gathering overhead getting dark, and ready to pour down on us. But then the sun emerged, and a ray shone down directly on me. I lifted my face to it, welcoming its warm embrace.

"I see it now," he finally spoke. That was an odd thing to say. I opened my eyes and looked at him quizzically.

"What do you see, Declan?"

"I see why he loves ye so. You are quite a woman, Miss Montana. There is a force inside ye that is bigger than ye. I see why you're his muse. He's a verra lucky man."

I blushed in embarrassment, "That's high praise from a proud highlander."

He gave me a gentle shove, "Don't let it get to yer heid, lass."

We continued our walk. playfully shoving or attempting to trip each other like a couple of kids. This little outing with

Declan confirmed what I'd been thinking when discussions of going home began. He would be invaluable to me in Vancouver. Until the escaped criminals were caught, I would still need protection. Eddy would be going back into his detective job with the force, so there was a space for Declan to step in if he wanted it.

"Declan, I have an offer for you. Please give it some consideration before you give me an answer. Alex and I will be signing many bands and will require a large-scale security team when touring begins. We need someone with brains and skill to head up this team."

I paused to see if he had anything to say or ask, and as he said nothing, I continued, "I also need someone to keep me safe until those men are found, someone that Adam can depend on.

"The threat to me isn't over, as I said. Those men are free, and Eddy feels that they will want to remove me, so I can't testify against them ever again. At the very least, I'm sure they will want revenge. Seems to be my lot in life." I paused, waiting for his answer.

"Ye still have not asked me a question, lass."

"Declan, I am asking if you would come back to Canada with us? You can name your price. We all know your value, and I know Alex would love it if you came and helped out with our new company."

We continued walking. He was silent for a while, weighing out my proposal. He asked me if Alex was aware of my offer to him. I knew what he was doing. He wanted to know if I was being impulsive again. Well, I wasn't going to let him know that was exactly what I was doing. Having him with us felt right, and I always went with my gut.

Instead of answering, I focused on Alex sending him a vibration, a connection with a vision of what I intended. I know he got it, I always felt peace when Alex and I connected.

"Yes, he knows."

"Well then, lass, ye got yerself a deal."

He extended his hand, and we shook on it. I felt that rightness when our hands connected. It was more than a deal. At that moment, Declan and I had made a solemn pact. I only felt the first stirrings of that connection then. Later, I would look back and realize that a handshake was the beginning of a friendship that would last a lifetime.

"Don't you want to negotiate terms first?"

He laughed. "Lass, I have been around your family long enough to know you are honorable people. I am sure whatever I am offered will be more than fair. I like to go where I am needed and keeping you safe is a big job."

I punched him in the arm but laughed, as he was making light and not insulting me.

"Ye know, lass, ye may come to regret your decision on me as your choice."

"Oh, and why is that?"

"Because, this last year, you've had Eddy in charge, aye? He has his way, and I have my way. I see what I see. I'll be keeping ya on yer toes, aye?"

I sighed, then laughed. I had finally gotten rid of Ace as my guardian and Eddy as head of my security, trading both of them in for a giant Scottish guy, who was much deadlier than either. Bitter irony. But with most of the heavy trouble past us, I felt optimistic.

Chapter 22

The little chapel had been transformed into a fairy garden by Mrs. C and her band of merry women. The space was full of wildflower wreaths and garlands. Rose-scented candles were added to wall sconces, and everywhere you looked twinkling lights brightened every nook and cranny.

Dan and Adam had painted a scene of the West End on the stone behind the altar. That way we could have a little bit of home to oversee our vows. I took pictures before heading to my room for hair and make up.

The girls chattered excitedly while one of the villagers did my hair. I had a glass of champagne that remained full. My stomach was doing somersaults and I didn't trust myself to drink or eat anything.

My hair had grown long over the last several months in hiding. We decided to keep it down and Caitlin, a very talented young woman, wove wildflowers into my glossy locks. The last step was the dress. Kris kept me steady as Caitlin helped me step into it. I straightened and looked in the mirror. The result was stunning. I'd never looked so together. The grey undertones provided me with that stormy look I was after.

A knock at the door, "Can I come in?" It was Ace, that meant, it must be time.

"Sure, bro, come on in."

"Wow," Ace's jaw dropped. "You look like a princess, but not the fairytale kind."

A frown creased my brow, "What do you mean?"

"You look powerful, a perfect storm, a whirling dervish, ageless, beautiful."

Suddenly unsure of myself, I asked. "Will Adam like it?"

"Are you kidding me? He'd have to be blind not to see how beautiful you look. You picked the perfect dress, rock goddess."

I smiled in satisfaction.

"Are you ready m'lady?"

"I am," I took his outstretched arm and wrapped my much smaller one around his. He felt solid and secure and I was glad he was here for me. On our walk to the chapel, Ace told little jokes about how nervous Adam was and kept things light. But as we got closer, he stopped and held my gaze.

"This is it, Peanut. Are you sure you're ready? Is this what you want? Because I'll put a stop to this if you're unsure."

I wasn't sure of anything and wondered if he could hear my knees knocking together. Beyond the door, Stella and Ann's beautiful voices sang one of our songs. One I'd written for Adam. The music infused me, a reminder of who Adam was to me. I put a big grin on my face.

"I am totally ready. Let's do this!"

Ace chuckled. The doors parted and there was Adam, standing at the altar with Dan and Alex at his side. Eddy and Chrissie, my two besties, waited for me on my side. Their grins changed to admiration when they took in me and Ace.

Stella and Ann changed the song to *Going to the Chapel*, acapella style. Ace walked me down the aisle of the tiny chapel. Liza and Mrs. C had tears in their eyes. Chrissie was practically balling her eyes out at the altar, and Ace's grip tightened.

"I love you, little sister," His eyes were moist as he handed me off to Adam, who tugged me to him and claimed my mouth.

"My god, Montana, I'm overwhelmed. You look incredible. Thank you."

Dan and Alex chuckled. I gazed up at Adam.

"For what?"

"For this dress, for this day, for picking me. You are the most extraordinary woman." A ray of sunshine broke through the stained glass and shone directly on me.

"See, even the gods agree."

Everyone in the chapel laughed, including me and Adam. Our vows felt magical, each word spoken felt like an invisible thread weaving its way around us, joining us, connecting us in a way we hadn't been until this moment.

"Adam, you know you are the sun, moon, and stars for me. I fell in love with you the moment I got in your car that first time, and you drove me home. You are the most generous human being I have ever met. I don't know what I did to get you to notice me, but I'm glad of it. Without you, I'm pretty sure I wouldn't be half of what I am. You always believe in me. I'm sure all the eligible Vancouver socialites are in tears right now, as the most gorgeous eligible bachelor is officially off the market." Everyone laughed.

"I want to thank you for saving my life. For as long as I live, it won't be long enough, to express my love and gratitude that you picked me. You had everything, The Golden Boy, and I was a little nothing. Somehow, you saw me. Without you, I don't know where I would be. Without you I don't know who I would be. Without you, life would be empty. You, Adam Northrop, are the best man I know, the most honorable, and I am so happy and grateful to be yours, and I promise you, it will never be boring."

Again, our small group of guests laughed as Adam placed the ring he designed on my finger.

"You may kiss the bride."

"Finally," Adam muttered, to more chuckles. He took my lips and savoured them for our first kiss as man and wife.

"Whoa cowboy," Ace said loud enough for the whole room to hear. I tried and failed to stifle a giggle. My eyes glittered with merriment but Adam's were full of arousal. I was pretty sure his mind was on consummating our contract. He wasn't the only one.

When Adam kissed me. I felt a stirring in my belly. A picture of mine and Adam's carnal session at the stones played in my mind. If I didn't know better, I'd say I was pregnant, despite the dire warning from the doctors. This was the best news and I knew exactly how I wanted to tell Adam.

Two hours and hundreds of photos later, we headed to the game room for the reception. As the party got underway with Champagne and appetizers, I pulled Mrs. Campbell aside.

"Mrs. C, do you have any pregnancy tests in your medical station?"

Her eyes twinkled, "You won't be needing one of those to tell you what you already know, lass."

"I know, but I want to give it to Adam as a surprise."

She nodded her head in understanding. I followed her to the first aid station, and with the test in hand, headed to the bathroom. When the two lines showed up, I was ecstatic. I came back to the reception in time for the speeches to begin. The champagne was abundant. So far, I'd only had a sip of mine. I looked to Mrs. C, she held up one finger. Okay, one drink, I'd be nursing this for a while then.

After the speeches from Geoff, Liza, Adam, Alex, Eddy and Chrissie, accompanied by spoons tapping crystal for the groom to kiss the bride, it was finally time to eat. My appetite was back and I felt like Henry VIII, inhaling everything set before me.

We'd asked for no gifts, but still there were plenty to open after the wedding cake and coffee. Geoff stood and gave a second speech, not in the plan. The man was up to something and I could feel Adam's anxiousness. I squeezed his hand and whispered, "It's going to be fine, you'll see."

"Adam, I have often been unfair toward you. I provided you with stuff and opportunity, but never invested in who you were as a person. Thank goodness, your mother had more foresight and encouraged you. My son, you make me so very proud. You have incredible talent and are self made. There is no better gift a son can give to his parents than that. If that wasn't enough, you have brought us an exceptional daughter, as your wife. Your mother and I are so very proud of you, son. Congratulations."

Adam let out the breath he'd been holding. He was so unused to praise from his father, although Geoff had gotten much better this past year.

"To Adam and Montana," Geoff said, raising his glass.

"To Adam and Montana," everyone followed. Geoff handed us an envelope. In it was a deed. A deed to what? I scrolled down. To the castle.

"This castle?" I blurted out, not able to hold back my shock.

He nodded.

"Oh my god, oh my god, I can't believe it!" I squealed.

"What is it, lass? Tell us all what ye got."

I could tell that somehow Declan knew already, because his eyes were all twinkly with mischief, just like his mother's. Those two, they seemed to always be in the know.

"Geoff and Liza have bought us a castle. This castle," I broke out in tears. "Oh my god, how? I hope you're not broke." Geoff and Liza both laughed.

"Rest assured, Montana, we are not broke. Mrs. Campbell has agreed to stay and oversee the castle, its running and maintenance."

We gave them each a hug. "Well, I guess this is a good time to share my news. You may recall me and Adam had some fireworks a few years back. He immortalized our loss with a beautiful statue, the statue that now sits on our piano back home. We were told that I may never have children."

I was being bold, as what I was about to say could go totally wrong, if I had a miscarriage. There were no guarantees, but I knew he, and his parents, would be happy with the news. I handed him the stick. His eyes grew big when he realized what he was holding.

"Apparently, they were wrong. Congratulations, Adam. You are going to be a daddy."

His eyes shone with excitement. The stones, he mouthed to me. I nodded. His eyes closed, and a look of peace came over his beautiful face. Geoff and Liza were out of their seats congratulating us with hugs.

I glanced at Mrs. Campbell who was beaming. She had known all along, of course. Then it dawned on me, did she know this would happen? Has it happened for others? I made a note to talk to her later, as the more I thought about it, the more questions I had.

Later that night, Adam and I snuck out to our standing stones and made love, in thanks for our blessing. The moon was high, and it shone down on us. Adam leaned over me, his gaze holding mine.

"You are my greatest gift, Montana, but a child is the greatest gift a woman can share with a man. Thank you for being my wife and sharing your life with me. I love you."

"I love you, too."

Chapter 23

We were back in Canada and life was back to business as usual. Being away for five months had changed my perspective on many things. It was being away that allowed me to see that I was viewing my incredible career as a burden. My perception was ruling my life, not my schedule.

Being in Scotland all that time made me see it. In the back of my mind, I had always entertained the idea that life would calm down. I figured after we signed our first record deal, life would be peaches and cream.

When that didn't happen, my thoughts shifted again, and figured once we resolved the issue with the Mercy connection and dealt with it, things would calm down. Now I knew every new road brought with it a set of challenges and that was life. *Calming down* was not part of my reality. If that's what I wanted then I needed to create it, because circumstances weren't just going to provide it for me.

I admired Alex. He didn't see or treat things the way I did. To him, life was a journey, one long adventure. Where every piece was part of the bigger picture. I was not graced with that mindset. My brain was wired like a pinball machine, always bouncing and rolling where the paddles pushed me.

In this case, Alex and Adam did most of the pushing. One dragging me along for the ride in our career, and the other directing and shaping my daily life. The tide may have turned without a direct death threat hanging over my life, our lives, but when I fell victim to swirling thoughts and others noticed and questioned me, I simply blamed the pregnancy hormones.

To keep Declan close, Adam rented him an apartment in our building. As my new bodyguard, Declan drove me and Alex to work every day, and he took over as the head of security for our new label, Twin Spin Records.

The three-way dynamic of Alex, Declan, and I was easy for us all. Very natural, which made our demanding lifestyle run smoothly. Eddy had trained Declan how to translate what he knew of being a bodyguard into how to run security in British Columbia.

Our security team was primarily for local concerts and tours, which he would be spearheading for the five bands that we'd signed so far. Declan seemed inexhaustible. He trained everyone we hired and spent time with Eddy and the bomb squad, learning to recognize what was in current use and how to disarm them.

When Declan was busy learning the ins and outs of bombs, which was way more than your average bodyguard training, Otter and I would assist Alex in nailing down tour dates. Allyson was instrumental in assisting Alex with ironing out details. Personally, I hated the logistics of what we did.

It gave me a headache and I often passed the duty off to Chrissie, who found it easy.

Alex was reminding me more of Ace everyday, at least in his business acumen. In the temperament department, while Alex had Ace's business sense, I had his temperament. We got stressed out, and reticent, in Ace's case angry. Whereas Alex was more like Adam. Cool as a cucumber. Nothing fazed either of them. Dan was the most laid back of us all. I used to imitate him by acting like I didn't give a shit about anything.

I laughed thinking about how upset Ace used to get with me. I acted like I didn't care, but I really did. That is why, in so many ways, my life appeared destructive. I channeled my inner brat all the time in the old days. I liked *that* Montana, she didn't take shit from anyone.

Deciding she needed to strut her stuff. I decided to take a stroll. I hadn't been out for a walk on my own since Scotland, but by the end of the first block, a gigantic highlander was at my side.

"Declan," I acknowledged.

"Montana," he acknowledged. "Whit you up to, lass?"

"Just going for a walk, you know, like normal people do."

He was quiet for a few blocks, "But yer not normal, lass."

I stopped walking and looked him straight in the eyes, "I know that, Declan, I am pretending. Surely there is a Scottish word for that, aye?"

I was being a pregnant bitch, and he knew I knew it. But I wasn't apologizing for it, instead choosing to stew in self righteousness. "We have a tour in six weeks, and Adam is driving me nuts. He doesn't want me to go. The only silver lining in all of this is, he is more worried about the baby than me for a change." Declan didn't talk but quietly laughed. I punched him in the arm and continued walking, picking up the pace.

"I feel good, strong, in shape, a little tired, but that is to be expected. He has become the most taxing part of my day. I need advice. I wonder if Liza is free this afternoon?"

"Are ye hungry, lass? Let's get some food, it will help ye ask the right questions," That sounded good to me. We continued our walk down to Denman Street to the Vina Vietnamese restaurant. I was dying for noodles and spring rolls.

"So, question fer ye lass. If you dinnae mind me askin'?"

"Shoot," I mumbled through my enormous bite of spring roll.

"What do you think is the best way to get Adam off yer back?"

"Oh, hell if I know, that's why I need advice."

"May I speak freely?"

"Like I could stop you. What is it you're doing the rest of the time, if you aren't speaking freely then?"

"Aye," He laughed, "I guess I am. But I dinnae wish to offend ye, so I'm asking." I sighed and took another huge bite, considering whether I would get a second order. I was starving all the time. At this rate, I'd be a Hungry Hungry Hippo. It was a positive the drum kit did a fairly good job of hiding my body.

"Please tell me."

"Lass, Adam, he is worrit about yer energy and regulating. All you have to do to get him off yer tail is to utilize your most powerful tool," I put my fork down, he had my attention.

"And that is?"

"Me."

"You, how so?"

He rolled his eyes, frustrated at me missing the obvious.

"We, me and ye, come up with a plan that will work for you, that Adam will accept. Then, we let him know that I'm in charge of the plan and instead of bothering you, he'll come to me."

I was seeing the light. It was so simple, no wonder he'd been rolling his eyes. I laughed until all my stress melted away.

"Declan, you're a wily bastard, you know that?"

His expression changed to mock innocence, "I dinnae ken whit ye mean, lass."

"As if! You ken just fine. All I had to do was tell Adam to give his list of what he needed to you, and you would take care of it, thereby getting him off my back. Instead of telling me right off, you made me sweat," I accused.

But, with nothing behind my meaning, the entire situation was humorous, and laughing at myself was the best remedy.

It was his turn to laugh, "Aye. It's all true lass, I cannae tell a lie. But ye had it coming, aye?"

I grinned, "Yes, I did, and now we are going to come up with a plan that will get him to tell you everything and me nothing, right?"

"Right," he agreed.

Declan came through, and even had multiple suggestions that Adam had not thought of, Adam was thrilled to have someone he could rely on to *keep me in check* as he called it. I was thrilled to not have to listen to him nag.

The morning of my twelfth week into the pregnancy, I woke up with the worst morning sickness. I decided to stay in bed and go into the studio late, maybe even pop by and see Adam with a surprise lunch on my way.

Declan had gone to the studio with Alex in the morning and was coming back to pick me up at one pm to take me to work. I snuck out of the apartment at eleven-thirty with lunch in hand. I took a cab to the gallery and was feeling proud of my sneakiness.

The cab pulled up out front and I could see Adam leaning against his desk, with Katya in his arms. What! How the hell? She was in prison last I heard, and now here she was, and in my husband's arms, kissing him.

My stomach plummeted and all thoughts of lunch evaporated. I dragged my eyes away in time to see Dan look at me from his office window and could tell by the guilty expression on his face that this was no accident. That son of a bitch! As he rose to come and talk to me, I had the cabbie take me home.

I told the cabbie to wait while I went upstairs to get my identification. When I came back down, we headed to the airport. I expected to see Declan when I returned to the cab and was a little surprised when I didn't, but that just made my plan easier.

On the short ride there, my mind replayed the scene in a vicious loop. Katya's smug expression taunting me. Hadn't we been hiding in part due to her involvement with the Yakuza and Mercy? How could he betray me like this?

I was off on the next plane to Glasgow, feeling elated to be taking control and doing what felt right to me. From the airport, I took another cab to the castle. When I found Mrs. C in the kitchen, she looked concerned but didn't ask questions, just clucked her tongue.

"It's late, lass. Why don't you go relax and I'll bring you a spot of tea." When she brought me tea, she sat down on my bed and I told her everything.

"I was so angry and hurt that I headed straight for the airport after grabbing my passport. I mean, Katya of all people! She slept with my husband on my living room rug. Granted we weren't together then, but she knew how I felt about him. She tried to have me *assassinated* so she could have her Adam. Well, looks like she got what she wanted. I caught my husband holding that bitch in his arms and I'll never be able to erase that image."

I knew that my family would be freaking out. Mrs. Campbell calmed me down and encouraged me to call someone back home and let them know I was okay. I sighed in resignation, "You're right, I'll call Alex, at least I know he'll be on my side and not try and tell me I'm overreacting." If Mrs. C thought my action was of that nature, she never said a word. just patted me on the arm and told me everything would work out.

"Montana, I know where you are," Of course, Alex knew where I was, he could have found out at any time, I guess. I hadn't thought to try and block him.

"I know you do, Alex, but please don't tell anyone. I'm not ready to talk to Adam. I mean, how could he do that with her of all people? I feel betrayed by him and sorry that he's too dense to realize she's such a fake and a phony, and a damn criminal, for Christ's sake." He was silent, but I felt his calming vibe. I breathed, trying to relax.

"Mo, I don't know what is going on, but I'm sure it was not what it looked like. Adam is completely in love with you. Everyone knows that."

"Oh yeah, *we* all know that, but I guess a bit of action on the side is okay. I mean, his arms were around her, and her tongue was down his throat. Listen, I just need some time alone to think. You know where I am if you need me."

"Montana, listen, just please stop stressing, it's not good for the babies."

"Babies?"

"Are you so disconnected from your own pregnancy that you didn't realize that you're pregnant with twins?"

That took me back, I guess I was disconnected. "I promise you, brother, I'll be fine, Mrs. Campbell is here taking care of me. It's quiet, and I can think without Adam, Declan, or whoever bombarding me."

He told me he loved me and hung up the phone. Exhausted, I decided to have a nap and ended up sleeping for fifteen hours. Which did me a world of good, feeling better than I had in weeks. Out to the castle garden, with tea in hand, I sat among the plants, and sunk my fingers into the dirt, and sighed contentedly.

Large breaths of the fragrant country air, increased my feeling of overall well-being. After lunch, I took a walk to the stones, where Adam and I had made the two little bundles that were growing inside of me.

I sat against the same stone as before. I must have dozed off, because I woke to the sounds of a war being fought. Opening my eyes, I saw men in funny hats and red coats, and men in kilts, just like the first time. The clang of weapons clashing rang out. The images disappeared as fast as they appeared, but the faint echoes of battle followed me on my walk back to the castle where I found Declan there waiting for me.

I marched up to him and grabbed his hair pulling down his head. And then I kissed him, and not a peck either, a full-on, tongue delving kiss. It was hot, passionate and demanding. Guilt swept through me and I pulled away.

"I am sorry, Declan, I don't know what I was thinking." I sat down opposite him and placed my head in my hands.

"Lass, are ye alright?"

What I wanted to say was *yes, I'm just teaching my errant husband a lesson.* But the truth was I was very upset, and I began to cry. The one sure thing in my life I could count on other than my family's love, was Adam. Now that I'd seen what I couldn't unsee, that stability felt like a lie and that was what was killing me. How could I ever trust him?

"There, there, lass. It will be alright. Ye just need to let it all out, aye, just let it all out." And then he began to talk in Gaelic, and I didn't understand a lick of what he said, but it was so soothing I drifted off to sleep, my head against his shoulder.

Hours later, I woke up in my bed. He must have carried me. I showered and went in search of food. I found a note in the larder and a stack of very nutritious foods waiting for me. Declan and his mother were nowhere in sight.

I ate like a starving woman, and then headed to my turret to stare at the night sky. I could just make out the tallest of the stones in the moonlight. It was captivating. I sighed, content for that moment to just be here. When I grew cold, I moved to the great room. The balcony there would have the moonlight streaming through the windows, and I could enjoy the moon and stars without the cold.

With my Walkman on, I danced and sang along to the music. The light infused me with energy and I felt alive. When the candles I'd lit were burned down to nubs, I blew them out and went back to bed, where I slipped into a deep sleep.

Chapter 24

My sleeping schedule was way off since I'd arrived and I wasn't surprised when I woke a few hours later. Hungry, I headed down to the kitchen but stopped when I heard voices.

"Declan, how is she?" Adam on the speakerphone.

"Och aye, Adam, the lass is fine. No need to worry, pal."

"What has she been doing? Is she eating?"

"Like a horse and sleeping a great deal. She just left the great room a few hours ago and headed to bed. She's not aware that I've been watching her, ensuring she's safe, Adam, dinnae worry."

"Was she wearing her Walkman?"

"Aye."

"Please tell me she was wearing clothes." I felt a blush stain my cheeks and remembered the kiss Declan and I had shared. Adam had been right to ask if I'd been clothed and thank goodness I had been, not that the giant Scotsman hadn't seen me naked, but the idea of him seeing me covered in nothing but the pale moonlight was too embarrassing to fathom.

"Aye, she was, and seemed better, you know, pal. She glows in the moonlight, eh. What a fine thing to see."

"Yes, the moonlight infuses her somehow. A story for another time. When do you think you can get her back?" Get me back? Like I was a missing piece of luggage that he needed back in his possession. The last few months of being home hit me like a sledgehammer. I was done with being told where and when and being followed every step of the way.

"I cannae say, Adam. She was pretty upset, still is. I dinnae think that will change until someone tells her what all the Katya business was aboot. I dinnae know this Katya lass, with the exception of her role in hurtin' your wife, but Montana can't get past the idea that you cheated on her, betrayed her with what she calls her worst enemy after Mercy."

There was silence from Adam's end.

"Ah dinnae ken what ye done, Adam. Ye dinnae seem like the philandering type, but your lass, she's carrying your barins. Me mum says her hormones are all out of whack, and well, you may want to send someone other than yourself to smooth things over. What about Danny? He knows this Katya and yer feelings, aye? And as ye have said many a time afore, he is her hero. Surely, she will listen to him."

"You're right, Declan, thank you. I will send Danny, expect him sometime tomorrow."

I hid while Declan took the hallway to his suite. On silent feet, I went back to my room, dressed, grabbed my purse, and made sure I had my passport. Adam had a safe installed in our bedroom closet, so I opened it and took out a stack of cash. He could track my whereabouts by my credit card transactions, and where I was going next, I wanted to ensure no one would be coming to visit.

Back in the kitchen, I called for transportation from town and made my way out the back of the castle and followed the deer path around to the front. I slipped out and walked fifteen minutes to town arriving at the same time as my cab. I had him drive to Edinburgh airport. Declan would assume I'd flown from Glasgow which was closer and get stuck checking for me at the wrong airport. At the gift shop, I bought a baseball cap and a tacky jacket I'd never be caught dead in and headed to the ticket counter, purchasing a ticket to Grand Cayman.

An hour later, my flight took off and I sat back in my seat with a sigh of relief. They'd infiltrated my favorite place, the castle, hopefully it would take more time to find me this time round.

I didn't use the Northrop house and opted instead for what we jokingly referred to as Alex's shack. When we'd been here last, he'd found a little beach house in a private cove about a mile down the beach from where we'd been staying. As far as I knew, he hadn't done anything with it yet, and expected it to be rough, but I knew where he hid the key.

When they finally figured out where I'd gone, they'd assume I'd go to Geoff and Liza's, but I'd make it a little harder. Declan and Eddy didn't know about Alex's shack and I blocked myself from Alex's radar.

When I got inside I was happy to see it was still the same down bachelor pad it had been when Alex bought it. There was something comforting in the ratty conditions that reminded me of home before I'd met Adam.

"Finally, peace." I found clean bedding, albeit a bit stuffy, and hung it outside to air out. Under a tarp on the back deck, I found a moped in working condition. "Why, you sneaky..." I laughed. Finally I'd get to ride a Vespa I'd been wanting since I was sixteen.

I started it up and rode to town, wearing a big ass grin on my face. Finally, freedom! I went to the poorer sections to purchase a few things to wear and buy some essential groceries. What I couldn't stuff in the basket of the moped head fit inside the seat which had a bit of storage. I quickly headed back to my new sanctuary.

Wearing a new bathing suit, I grabbed a towel, and a snack and headed onto the sand. The breeze and salt air cleansed my soul and I drifted off to the sounds of gentle waves lapping onto the shore.

My skin prickled with unease. Someone was watching me. I cracked one eye open, and gazed as far around me as I could without moving my head and alerting whoever was here that I was aware of their presence.

"Did you really think that would work?"

I screamed and sat up. Dan peered down at me looking annoyed. "I've been on planes for almost twenty-four hours, thanks to you." He plopped down on the sand beside me looking exhausted. I felt bad for all of a split second.

"I don't recall inviting you to join me, so you can give your guilt trip to the person responsible." He scrubbed his face, looking decidedly less annoyed when he dropped his hands.

"Adam should have spanked you more, instead of spoiling you rotten."

He didn't just say that. "What the hell, Dan? Go fuck yourself."

"I'm sorry, okay? I've had too much time to think and my anger has me contemplating murder right now."

No. I wasn't taking this, "You know what your problem is, bro, you're a fucking pushover. Adam asked and of course you couldn't say no to your bestie. It's him you're pissed at, not me."

He sighed, "Not even him, it's the entire situation, Katya, you running off, but I have to give you credit, purchasing in cash was smart."

"Apparently, I wasn't that smart because you found me pretty damn fast. How did you know?"

Dan chuckled. "I said you were smart, but unfortunately that wily Scotsman is smarter. He checked in on you to make sure you were okay. He followed you to town and watched you get in the cab. He followed you to the airport and saw where you were going. When you weren't at your in-laws place, I phoned Alex. He said before you blocked him, he picked up on this being where you were headed. So, I walked a mile down the beach and here you were."

"I see." I wasn't feeling so clever anymore. We sat in silence for a bit and I thought Dan had fallen asleep.

"Are you ready to hear the truth about what happened, Mo?"

I rolled onto my side so I could see his face, "If I was, bro, I wouldn't have tried so hard to be alone."

He rolled onto his side and faced me, "I'm sorry about what happened. I know this is going to sound like a cliché, but it wasn't what it looked like."

My stomach growled. The little aliens inside me, demanding their next meal. Dan heard it too and smiled.

"How are you feeling?

"Better than I have in a while. I was having a lot of morning sickness back home and that's why I wasn't at the studio when that bitch showed up and ruined my life, again."

"I get it, I really do and if that ever happened to Jaimie, I would expect her to react the same way." Good, at least he understood that much about my feelings.

"The thing is, Dan, that would never happen to Jaimie. It's one of the reasons I needed time to think without someone trying to persuade me to go home. Katya should have never been there and no excuse explains how she managed to get so close to Adam if it was really *not what it appeared to be*, as you say."

He rolled onto his forearm and leaned his head on his fist. "Neither Adam nor I knew Katya made bail. Had we known, we would have been vigilant to her possibly showing up. Neither of us have spoken to her since Italy, the day after you were stabbed.

"She shouldn't have been there, Montana, and I think she may have broken her parole agreement. She waltzed into the gallery. As you know, Jaimie wasn't there, and I happened to be at the front desk. When she headed into Adam's office, I went to mine, to call Eddy and let him know that she was in the gallery. She's dangerous, Mo, she shouldn't be on the loose. Anyway, she leaned into him while he was on the phone with a client and kissed him."

"Eww! I just can't ever remove the image of them, even if I scrubbed my soul, that will haunt me for the rest of my days. I'm not stupid, I know what I saw."

Of course Dan rushed to Adam's defence, "She was trying to push him back onto his desk. When he regained his footing, with the phone still propped between his ear and shoulder, he held her in place, so she couldn't get any closer. She must have seen you in the cab and ripped the phone from Adam and kissed him. She was laughing about a child when she exited his office a moment later. I knew she meant to hurt you, and when she left, I told him what you saw."

He collapsed back on the sand. "I've never seen him so worked up, Mo. I'm afraid he is going to have a heart attack. You know Adam, cool all the time. He is really upset and worried about you and the baby. Please, just talk to him."

"Babies."

"Excuse me?"

"Babies, Dan, there are two."

"Congratulations, Mo, that is brilliant news."

"Thanks, but I won't speak to him."

"Seriously?" Dan rolled up to a seated position. "Why?"

"Because half the shit that has happened to me has been because of Adam. I said all along, women obsess over that man and I've been paying for that obsession."

His eyes narrowed, "I'm sorry, I spent six months of my life in hiding because of a situation you created on your own with Mercy, because the tough brat act got you into shit that not even Eddy could get you out of. Everyone's lives changed because of what, the world according to Montana? Tell me why you should get a pass, and not Adam?"

He had a very good point and I'd asked myself that very same question a thousand times on the flight from Scotland to the Caymans.

"Been as we're coming clean on shit. If you'd listened to me that night of the Hallowwen dance five years ago, all of this may never have happened. Instead you punished me when I was telling the truth and put a friggin alarm system on my window. So maybe, Dan, this is all your damn fault!"

I was livid, and bringing up the past was driving me to a place I didn't want to go. Rising to my feet I stared down at my brother whose jaw hung open in shock, "We both need some time to cool off. I'm going for a swim."

The water was a balm for my battered heart. I floated on my back, eyes closed and soaked up the energy from the sun and sea. Thoughts swirled about Adam and Katya and this entire messed up situation.

When I exited the ocean hours later, no wiser to what I should do, I saw my brother hadn't moved from his spot. Upon closer inspection, I saw that he'd fallen asleep.

After another snack and a shower, I called Ace.

Chapter 25

"Ace Stanford here, how can I help you?"

I giggled. "Hello, Mr. Important."

"Hello, Brat, how are you?"

"Hanging in, I just wanted to check in and say hello," I felt tears well up in my eyes, just hearing his voice.

"Are you still in Scotland?"

"No. The Caymans, I guess no one has brought you up to speed."

He remained silent for a moment.

"Montana, do you believe for one second that I wouldn't know where you were?" My eyes crinkled in a smile, a tear escaping and sliding down my cheek. "I wasn't going to step in unless someone asked me for help. As no one asked, there was nothing for me to do."

"Dan is here, passed out on the beach like a cat in the sun."

Ace laughed, "Are you coming home?"

"You know when I first thought about where to hide from the world I thought of Kristine's house, but as it's also your house, it wouldn't have worked out this time for me."

He laughed again.

"It worked pretty good the first time though, when you were fifteen, didn't it? Has it been that long since Katya infiltrated herself into our lives? Anyway, kiddo, I have to run, let me know when you're home."

He hung up. Weird, Ace was being too cool about the situation. With Adam being the one freaking out, it made for a total role reversal. What else was going on that no one was saying? There had to be something. I woke up Dan.

"Hey, bro, wanna go for a walk?"

"Absolutely," he jumped to his feet. "Just let me call Jaimie first and let her know I found you."

"How is Jaimie?

He grinned, a nice big shit eating grin. "We're having a baby."

"Eeek! Congratulations, brother. I am so excited. You and Adam, best friends and partners, and now your babies can be pals. How adorable."

"It will be cool, just don't tell anyone. I promised Jaimie I would wait until she passed the dreaded twelve-week mark."

"How far along is she now?"

"Eight weeks. I keep wondering if it was the stones."

Holy crapsicles, they went to the stones too. "What do you mean?" I asked casually.

"Mrs. C told me and Jaimie where the stones were the night before we flew home. Not to sound crude, but it was the best sex of my life. I'm just going to give her a quick call, I'll be right back."

When he rejoined me to say things were good, we started our walk down the beach.

"What's on your mind, sis, you seem lost in thought."

"A few things. Dan, I got pregnant at the stones as well. Adam and I swear, we had sex like four times that day, and it was crazy good. When I announced the news at the wedding, Adam said it was the time at the stones. What do you make of that?"

"Hell, I don't know. Coincidence? Maybe it's the timing. I heard that the stones were to signify things like the seasons, but also the equinox. There are different times in the month when women are potent, ready to conceive. Maybe, being a nurse, Mrs. C knew that it was a good time, and maybe, the added romance of the stones made conception easier because of the sheer rugged romance of the place."

That made perfect, logical sense to me, "That makes total sense. I swear hormones are making me bat shit crazy."

He laughed, "Things to look forward to." We continued for a few minutes in silence.

"What else is bothering you?"

I sighed. "I had a strange conversation with Ace earlier when you were asleep."

"What was strange about it?"

"He answered in his usual way but was way too relaxed. He asked if I was still in Scotland and then admitted that he knew exactly where I was."

"And that's strange how?"

"I expected him to do what he always does and treat me like a child and tell me I'm selfish and blah blah blah. Instead, he said he wasn't going to step in unless asked. Then he said, 'See you later, kiddo,' all chipper like and hung up."

"I repeat, what was strange?"

"Really, Dan? Has Jaimie's pregnancy made you loopy? That's not Ace, which means he is covering something up, and I want to know what. Adam freaking out and Ace as cool as a cucumber is a total role reversal. Tell me what is going on because I know that you know."

"Damn, sis, you are so very perceptive. Stanford vs. Stanley."

I froze. This was about the guys I had helped put away that had since escaped, broken out at transport time by their fellow rapists/murder pals.

"As you know, they have been in hiding since they escaped on the way to the trial. There is a warrant out for their arrest, but there has been for two years now. As they never got sentenced, the case was dismissed the day you left, before Adam could tell you.

"There is a lot at stake because the evidence Eddy and his team has is circumstantial. With you they can be brought to justice, but the case would begin again. Without you there is no case.

"Now that they have this new chance, they will, no doubt, come looking for you. They won't want this to ever go to trial. When you saw Adam with Katya, he was on the phone with Eddy receiving the news. I lied earlier when I told you he was on the phone with a client because he wanted to break the news to you himself.

"At the time, Katya was the lesser of the two situations. In Adam's mind, he can handle what's in front of him. The missing criminals are a much larger stressor for him because he doesn't have control of that. When you disappeared so quickly, we were all worried that they may have gotten ahold of you. That is why Adam was freaking out. Even now, he doesn't want you under any extra pressure. We were told that, if you got a hold of us, not to tell you. Anyway, now you know why Ace was acting out of character."

My breath came out in a low strangled gasp. I felt heavy and lifeless with the news.

"Adam wanted to tell you himself, funny that it was Ace's behaviour that gave it away."

"That's why Adam was so different, he wasn't altogether sure that you weren't kidnapped. Even after Declan found where you went, you were out in the wind for a while, where anything could have happened, and no one would have known, Mo. We couldn't have saved you."

The enormity of his words sunk in. Unwittingly, I had played the fool again. The danger was back, and unlike with Mercy, there was no emotion involved, no personal vendetta. Just cold-blooded murderers that wanted to ensure they could continue being just that. I thought the manhunt to bring them in would have turned up something, but I guess not.

Images of the cops arriving at my car where I'd been fighting for my life. My attackers scattered and only two were caught. I identified them the next day in a line up. Eddy had been working on a murder investigation, and the two in custody had been primary suspects in his other case.

Those two had been sentenced to maximum security holding cells until the trial, but they escaped during transport. I had wondered many times since that night if they were under orders to go after me specifically, or if it had just been a random attack.

Back then, my misfortune had seemed like a stupid mistake. I had picked Adam up at the airport a few days after in his Porsche, as my car was in getting a new soft top. I had worn a baseball cap, so he couldn't see the stitches in my forehead, and long sleeves, so he couldn't see the stitches in my arm. He was so angry at me that I couldn't stay out of trouble that he hired my first bodyguard. A huge guy, Charlie, who escorted me everywhere, even to the bathroom.

I smiled remembering Charlie. He had stayed with me up until the Sechelt weekend. He had been out of town for his mother's funeral and hadn't been with us. So he had not come to Scotland. I'm sure he had moved on to other jobs by now, as I hadn't seen him since our return to Canada.

"What are you smiling about, Montana?"

"I was remembering when the incident happened. Remember Adam got so angry, he hired Charlie, and Ace thought it was so funny."

Dan smiled, "Yeah, I remember, it seems like so long ago now, and so innocent compared to what has happened since."

"Yes, that is exactly what I was thinking. What am I supposed to do? I can't hide, you know that. Life goes on, and I have a job. There is no proof to say they will come after me. But as you say, knowing my luck, they will. If we anticipate the likelihood, then we won't have any surprises... aye?"

He grinned. "You spend too much time with Declan."

I laughed, "You're telling me. The Scottish inflections are so easy to pick up. Sometimes I speak and feel like such a phony because I sound Scottish, but I'm not. Well, not born anyhow. What right do I have to speak like a local? Then I think, screw it. You just pick that stuff up easily, not your fault, just go with it."

He laughed, "It's nice to see you have lightened up on yourself a bit. I swear, sometimes I think you are by far your own worst enemy." His smile was wistful, not his usual movie star smile. "Life is marching onward, sis. Let's be brats together and stuff our faces, what do you say?"

We ordered pizzas and cake and stayed up late eating, telling stories from the past. It was loads of fun and easily my favourite evening with Dan, ever. The next day, we flew home.

Chapter 26

"Montana, promise me you will be careful."

I sighed. "Yes, Adam, for the hundredth time, I will be careful."

We were on our way to the airport and alone in his Porsche. The rest of the crew was meeting us there, and Declan was in the car behind us keeping close. I wasn't showing yet, but by the end of the tour I should be getting my baby bump on. I felt okay, better now that I was in the second trimester. It was a short tour, then home for Christmas. Our first album would come out during the tour to help hype sales.

The recording of our next album would be in the New Year, but not released for several months. We wanted to get as much done as possible before these babies came along. I would be close to thirty weeks when we arrived home. The twins would come early, either from being induced or C-section as is standard with a double birth when one or both are breech. I figured with our mini tour and album one done,

I would have about five weeks to relax before they came, and I was looking forward to the down time.

"No, I said."

"No, what?" Adam looked confused.

"No, I won't overwork myself, I will nap. Stop worrying. I'm twenty now, and I feel forty, so don't worry, I'm a grown up."

He laughed, which was my intention. "Okay, okay, I'll stop worrying. Besides, if you screw up, I'll kidnap you and tie you to the bed until you give birth, and it won't be all sex and games either." His eyes twinkled with mischief, but he wasn't joking in the least.

"If there are no sex games then count me out, it sounds very boring." I smiled. Everything had been good between us since coming home from The Caymans. Adam and I were good, life was good, the band was good, and the family was good.

No criminal element had reared its ugly head yet. We had an uneasy truce with the world. Alert, but taking things one step at a time. We had been through so much as a family and as a band. We seemed to know our place and how to be, and the usual stress that would normally be with us seemed to abate. I was taking a passive role with our situation. I was not resisting or trying to control anything, just along for the ride, and ever watchful.

I waved to Adam one last time as I took my seat on the plane, "Earth to Mo, hello." Startled, I looked across at Alex. "Sorry, I was zoning out, what did you say?"

"I said we had a pregnancy scare, but it was a false positive."

"It will happen when it's meant to. Did you hear about Jaimie?"

"No, what about her?"

"She's pregnant, too."

"I didn't know they were expecting."

"They're keeping it a secret until twelve weeks, just in case anything happens. Remember, Dan was the one helping me with my miscarriage. Poor guy, with all the blood, he's scarred for life. He's not taking any chances with Jaimie."

"I guess not. Allyson and I are over." I was beginning to nod off but his statement woke me right up.

"What? Why?"

"She was offended by my reaction to her false positive. Frankly, I felt relieved. As much as I want children one day, I'm not entirely sure I would want them with her."

This was news to me. Chrissie walked by and Alex's gaze followed her down the aisle.

"Is this about Chrissie?" I whispered, "If so, you know she's with Eddy."

He frowned, "I guess you two haven't talked. They haven't been together since we left Scotland. Eddy moved out the day after we got home and has been buried in a new case."

I shook my head. Chrissie walked past us once again taking her seat closer to the front. I noticed she seemed less chipper than usual. How had I not noticed before?

"You're pregnant and busy, that's how."

"Alex, stop reading my mind, geez."

He chuckled, "Sorry, sometimes your thoughts are loud and I can't help myself."

"Whatever, now tell me what's going on."

"I know she's your bestie, Mo, but Chrissie learned to trust me a long time ago and she confided in me what was happening with her and Eddy's relationship."

"And? Spill it, bro."

"Eddy wants her to step down as your PA and be a stay-at-home mother."

"What? I didn't even know she was pregnant."

"That's the thing, Mo, she isn't."

"Ohhh, and that happened in Scotland?"

He nodded. "Eddy loves you but he's tired of Chrissie's life being in danger because of you always being in danger. He didn't want her on this tour either. She told me last week."

"Okay so what, you're staging a coup? I thought you loved Allyson?"

"I did, I do, but after the false positive, and my reaction, she told me she wanted a family, now. She's a strong woman and has always had her own mind. That is one of the things I admired about her the most, but she is stubborn as hell and wouldn't budge on her position. I'm not bringing life into this world until I'm damn ready."

That was fair, "So Allyson isn't here because she is recovering at home?"

"No. She flew home to Japan. Her parents found her a man who wants as many children as she wants to spit out and will keep her in a life of luxury."

"Holy crap! She works fast, who is it?"

"Sun Akito, the second son of the current emperor of Japan."

My stomach sank. "Wow! That is reaching really, really high. So it's over, like over, over?"

"Yeah. Chrissie and I are both free. If she can be your PA at home and on tour, why not be with me? Unlike before, we're living the same lifestyle now and she is my first love, Mo. I've always loved her."

My heart softened, "I know bro, and I'm sure she feels the same. I hope it works out for you." I took his hand and held it in mine. We stopped talking and I must have nodded off. Alex woke me when it was time to seatbelt up for our descent.

We landed in London at Heathrow airport and were immediately shuttled to our hotel, which was close to Wembley Stadium, where we would be playing the next evening. We made sure everything had arrived and left the roadies to set everything up for the next day.

The band, plus security, and Chrissie all headed to the hotel to check in. Then we went down to the dining room for dinner. I was famished and was eating like a horse, but thankfully everything I was eating was so healthy. I wasn't gaining extra weight, just what I was supposed to gain, but my breasts were getting bigger. Adam liked that part.

Up to the room after dinner for an early night before things got crazy, I called Adam to check in, and then Declan came in to make sure I had everything I needed. An early rising followed by a quick sound check had left us with spare time. We decided to go tour the Tower of London.

I had gone years earlier with Adam and was super excited to take Alex, Otter, the girls, and Declan. We also visited Madame Curie's Wax Museum, on the bottom floor of the tower.

We were hoping to see ghosts or something, but all that happened is Declan became grumpier as the tour continued. He started cursing in Gaelic when we passed through to the cells where the Scottish rebels had been held before being beheaded during the Bonnie Prince Charlie rebellion.

Poor Declan, he was in a rage by the time we left, going on about Sassenach and their bloody twisted history. We decided to stop in a pub and get the man a drink before heading back to the hotel to get ready for the concert.

The concert went off without a hitch, and we were optimistic for the rest of the tour. The rest of the United Kingdom was one great concert after another. The weeks flew by and everything was good. I stayed regulated, there was no drama. We played Ireland, Hamburg, Munich, Stockholm, Budapest and, three cities in, we finally reached the last stop on our tour in France. We arrived in Nice and checked into our hotel. Declan scanned my room and found a bug on the hotel phone and a gift waiting for me.

A rag doll that had seen better days. It was devoid of clothing, its eyes ripped off, and hair burned. Declan went on instant alert and wouldn't leave my room. I'd had a bad feeling about France and was anxious to be done here and go home.

Katya was from Paris, and her connections were bountiful there, but her family had a summer home in Nice and Jean-Pierre's family resided here all year. He was a total predator, we found out, after he'd commissioned Adam to decorate a family castle with my face. He'd become obsessed with me, and Adam had cut him off. He potentially could be helping Katya, being her eyes and ears while she was in jail. Or... this was the predators from back home trying to get to me before the tour ended.

Declan had the security footage from the previous evening and that morning sent up. While he was waiting for the footage, he put Eddy on speaker phone so we could both ask questions and listen.

"How's the tour going?"

"Seamless so far, until today."

"What happened?"

Declan told him what was waiting for me and asked if dolls had ever been part of the Stanley gang's MO.

"No, but be careful, Declan, it could be a crazy fan, there have been plenty of those. Just remember you're in Katya's part of the world. She has proven to be crazier than any fan, and using her local connections should be expected."

The conversation switched to tactical arrangements, which was too boring for me. My thoughts strayed to Jean-Pierre. I had forgotten all about him. Would he do something so distasteful? I didn't think so, it was not his style. I didn't know him well. But my gut said if he struck, it would be more sophisticated than this.

Eddy continued, "Listen, if you're really worried, Declan, make it known that you are moving to the hotel across the street, pack up and make it obvious. Make sure that the rooms around the ones you supposedly rent are empty. We wouldn't want innocent people possibly getting harmed.

"Then find a way to secretly get back to your hotel, but this time stay in different rooms. You will know if someone in the hotel is behind this if they go to deliver another gift to your new rooms. Be careful, no one knows she is pregnant. Any major stress could have her losing those babies."

Declan hung up the phone, and we got busy making the ruse look real. Alex had made it clear that we were not impressed with the lack of security, while the hotel manager played along. We checked into the hotel across the street from our current hotel with empty suitcases, while our actual belongings were being moved into a new set of rooms in our current hotel.

I was exhausted from our little escapade and laid down for a quick nap. I woke to Declan muttering in Gaelic. I opened my eyes and saw he was reading a magazine. Something had woken me. I looked around the room, nothing seemed out of sorts, but something was wrong.

"Declan, how long have I been sleeping?"

"About an hour, why?"

"Something feels wrong," As I spoke a shattering explosion was heard outside. Declan ran to the window and peered out. The small hotel across the street was burning, only the top floor south west corner, where we pretended to be staying. Within the hour, we were on a private jet, courtesy of my father-in-law. The plane was taking off down the runway when Alex gripped my arm.

"Everything is okay, isn't it? Montana?"

A sense of impending doom set me on edge, an image of our apartments back home blowing up had me reach for a barf bag. We were airborne and Alex was out of his seat grabbing Declan.

"Montana needs you."

Declan was kneeling in front of me, looking concerned.

"What is it, lass?"

"Call Eddy, tell him to evacuate our two buildings, they're going to blow up."

Declan's eyes widened in surprise but he hustled to grab an airfone. Goosebumps broke out and covered my entire body. It was happening. Please let Adam be okay. I silently prayed. I began to rock in my seat, trying to block out the awful vision of the buildings on fire, people screaming.

"Well?" I asked when Declan hung up.

"It's done, lass, I called Geoff as well. Adam is already leaving and Eddy is on his way with a team of people. How do you know it will blow up?"

"I can see it, that's how."

Hours later, everyone moved to a window seat when Vancouver came into view. Our vantage point showed a part of downtown in flames. Shit! I'd been right! I prayed that no one had died, and gripped Alex's hand in mine. We landed and made our way out of the hangar into the waiting vehicles. Our driver pulled out and we were instantly swarmed by reporters.

"Montana, Montana!" They yelled, each vying for my attention. "Is it true that you had knowledge of the bombing, how did you know to get everyone out?" I opened the window and made our driver stop.

"Is everyone safe? Any casualties?"

The reporter for Georgia Straight appeared surprised, "Didn't they tell you? Everyone got out safely, from both buildings. You're a hero."

Alex, who had been holding my hand in a death grip since the plane, eased up and we held each other in relief. The group took a collective sigh of relief, while the cameras went off all around us. We took stock of what could have been the biggest nightmare of our lives.

"Declan Campbell, is the real hero, and all those on the ground who were instrumental in getting everyone out of the buildings."

Geoff's limousine rounded the corner, Adam was out the door and running toward me. The reporter from the Georgia Straight opened the door and helped me out. Adam and I were both in tears when we collided.

"Thank god you're safe Adam, I've been so worried."

"You've been worried, silly girl, I've been terrified that something else would blow up, like the plane, and I'd never see you again." Cameras clicked like crazy but I didn't care. Let them see how much this man meant to me.

Ace and Kris were out of the limo next and Adam stepped back giving Ace room to me up in a bear hug, "We're okay, Mo, stay calm." I buried my face in his chest, relishing his solid frame and warmth before he set me back on my feet.

"Where are we going now?"

"To the mansion," Geoff replied, stepping in to hug me. "Adam's apartment has been renovated and is ready for you two. Alex and Declan can stay in the guest rooms until we figure out our next move." The four of us had lost our home, and until the fire department had combed through everything to see what was salvageable, we had nothing, other than what was with us.

I was getting into the limo when the idea of so many recent homeless were not as lucky as me and Adam.

"Adam, what about everyone else?"

"Who, sweetheart?"

"The other tenants, surely some of them are completely without means?" I turned to Adam's mother, "Liza, the other tenants, they will need help."

She smiled at me, "I knew you would feel that way, dear. Friends of the Ocean has put everyone up in hotels around the city for a week to help. That is partly why I think all these people are here, darling, to thank you." I waved and blew kisses to the crowd from the safety of the interior as we pulled out of the tarmac and headed for the West Side.

When we arrived at his old apartment, Adam carried me up the stairs, stripped me naked, and put me in bed. He climbed in behind me and snuggled in tight, his arm draping over me protectively. I sighed happily.

"How are the babies?"

"They're fine."

"Let me have a look at you, wife."

He pulled the blanket back and took in every inch of me.

"Finally."

"Finally, what?"

"You look pregnant."

I looked down, he was right. Somewhere between Germany and Sweden my baby bump had developed, and it stuck out far enough that certain parts of my anatomy were obscured from my vision. I smiled.

"That's right, look at me, proud and pregnant with the best man in the world's babies. Did you hear about Allyson?"

"Yeah, through Dan, that really sucks. How is Alex holding up?"

"Holding out is more like it."

"I wondered why Chrissie came home with us when her apartment wasn't affected at all."

I laughed, "My brother works fast when he wants something. Who knows—this may be just a relationship of convenience... only time will tell, I guess."

"Yeah, interesting timing for them."

"Adam, what will happen with our building, with our home?"

"Well, I was going to surprise you, but since you asked, I bought us a little house."

"You did? When?"

"I'd been looking for a while and bought it when you were on tour. I guess the timing was good as I'm pretty sure the apartment building will be condemned."

"When can I see it? Can we go now, pretty please?"

He laughed, "In the morning. Right now, it is time for you and my babies to rest."

I closed my eyes, remembering how the apartment looked when I left it last. So many personal items destroyed but losing the art was by far the hardest hit.

"Adam, my photos, your art, they are gone, forever." A tear slid down my cheek at the loss.

"No, not your photos, Mo. I have the negatives at the gallery and every piece of artwork was well insured. I have my muse, that's all I need." He held me, and I inhaled him, and instantly, relaxed. He was right, of course. We had each other, and that was most important.

The next morning, we showered, dressed, and headed into the main house for breakfast. Chrissie, Alex, Declan, even Ace and Kris, and Dan and Jaimie were there.

"A family breakfast?" I sat down on the chair Adam pulled out for me.

"Montana Northrop, you're in trouble," Ace said in his unique 'you're in trouble' sort of way.

Out of habit I sat up straighter, "I am? What did I do now?" I reached for Adam's hand under the table.

Ace's stern visage gave way to a teasing smile, "We need help."

"Sorry, what do you mean?"

"I mean, Mo, that Vancouver's most beloved daughter has created the biggest charitable mess in history. Money is pouring in for the displaced residents of the two buildings, and not just money, but stuff. Word has gotten around that Friends of the Ocean is helping those that lost their homes and they want to help."

I didn't know what to say, I was in shock. The human condition, which had always seemed so frail when I was young, as there was always so much lacking in humanity, suddenly seemed fruitful and alive.

"We have sold out the art gallery, as well, Mo. Everyone wants anything connected with the saviour," Dan spoke.

"Come on Dan, surely you jest. All I did was get a vision, and I wasn't too late. I'm no saviour, I'm just me."

"I've hired extra staff and found more volunteers for our foundation," Liza added.

"I have a logistical nightmare," Chrissie added, and Kristine nodded in agreement.

I didn't know what to say, but being pregnant and in hormone overload, I began to cry. Not because what they said was upsetting, but what they shared was so real. I had heaped a big plate of stress on every one of them. Proving to myself again, that I always messed up, even when unaware of it.

Alarmed, Liza tried to comfort me, "Montana, darling, we're only teasing. All those things are true, but in the best way. Don't be upset."

Adam squeezed my hand, then lifted it and kissed it, "It's okay, Mo, we're on it, and we're all making it happen. There is only one of you; safety for you and the babies is a priority."

I smiled through my tears, "I'm hormonal, what else can I say? Speaking of," I looked at Jaimie. "Are you ready?"

She and Dan smiled.

"What's going on?" Ace said, swinging his gaze between me and Jaimie.

"What's going on brother, is that Jaimie and I are expecting to have our first addition to our little family about six weeks after Adam and Mo."

A huge grin split Ace's face, "Congratulations!" He held up his orange juice, "To Dan, Jaimie, and the little heathen."

"Hey!" Dan said but he was laughing.

"To Dan, Jaimie, and the little heathen," we enthusiastically repeated.

With the news out of the way, I dug into my breakfast and ate enough for three people.

Chapter 27

It had been three weeks since moving to our new home. I was in my office at Twin Spin Records, privately celebrating the completion of our album. I checked in with Liza to see how the temporary residences were going. The project to rebuild the towers would be two years running. The good news, the folks that had lived there would get first crack at moving back in. The other good news, many of them had moved on, with the help of our charity.

Letters came in every day from those that received support, thanking us for our intervention. The situation was now controlled, and the overtime of the hard-working staff had come to an end. I hung up the phone from the update with Liza as Declan walked in.

"Ye be looking like a cat who's had her cream. Good news, lass?"

"Yes, but I'm starving, let's go for perogies."

"We're going fer whit, now, lass?"

I smiled at his accent of which I never grew tired of hearing. "Come on, Declan, are you going to tell me that you have never heard of perogies?"

"Weil, I ken, but I'm no' familiar with payoogie ."

I broke out laughing at his way of saying perogies. I had to stop walking and hold my stomach, which was huge now that I was so close to my due date.

"Do it again," I cried.

"Do whit? Say payoogies?"

Oh my god, I was laughing so hard. Then I started to panic because I couldn't breathe. I was grasping at his arm, wheezing. He turned me around, so we were spooning while standing. He placed his hand on my sternum and gently pressed.

My breath came back. I sighed in relief, "I'm excited about sharing my childhood with you."

"Aye, but I think it's better if I drive, the way you're wheezin' an' all."

We got in the car he used for shuttling me around and drove to the West End. The last time I desired to be home this badly, I went to Ceperly Park at Second Beach and got attacked by the Stanley gang. The next time I'd felt nostalgic, I had a party in the penthouse and was shot. What could possibly go wrong?

Declan parked on Denman Street, and we made our way to Hunky Bills. Everyone noticed me, but no one accosted me or asked for autographs. I smiled, but spoke to no one. *That's it, move along, and don't get in between a hungry mamma and her perogies.* We got our food and sat down at the only table they had inside.

"Lass, how are ye able to be here unmolested? You get bombarded at every turn. Why not here?"

"Because, Dec, this is my home, this is where I'm from. These people knew me when I was nothing, before I became famous, and to them, I'm still that girl. That's why the West End is special. Because I'm just me, the bratty, brave, youngest Stanford."

He nodded but said nothing else. His demeanor relaxed somewhat. But his body language spoke another story, he was alert and ready in case of danger. I really felt we would be fine.

"Tell me about you, Declan, tell me about what you were doing in life before I saw you on the field outside the castle walls that day."

"Well, I was thinking about what I wanted to be when I grew up, of course. What else does one do in Scotland, in a field, in a tartan, with a sword?" We both laughed at the image, and I encouraged him to continue with his story. "I had sold my business and was at a loss as to what I wanted to do. Then you showed up, lass, and gave me purpose. Now, I'm here in Canada."

"What was your business?"

"Newspaper business, I sold ma' wee paper."

Our food had arrived, and I was so looking forward to it that my mouth was watering. I took my first bite, and then asked through a mouthful, "Which paper?"

"The Scotsman, lass."

The Scotsman, why did I know that name? I had read about the young man who had taken a flailing paper and built it to a net worth of ten million dollars. I chewed distractedly, completely immersed in my thoughts. I was scanning the article in my mind that I had read in Scotland, in my early days of recovery. There was a picture. It was Declan. I almost choked when I looked at him. He had been watching my face closely and laughed when he saw the truth dawn on me.

"Aye, lass, I am that Declan."

Food forgotten. I took a good look at him for the first time. Who is this guy, really? And why was he here with me?

"Why didn't you tell anyone, Declan?"

"Really, lass, you think no one here knows? More like no one chose to tell ye. Geoff and Adam know who I am, as of course, being the safety conscious gentlemen they are, they ran checks on me. As to why they dinnae tell you, I dinnae know."

I chewed on that for a moment. That wasn't my question. I guess what I really wanted to know was why he had agreed to work for me, for us.

"Declan, you're a rich man, why did you accept my offer and come to Canada?"

"That's an easy answer, lass. Ye needed me."

I thought I had heard wrong, "Pardon?"

"Me ma had told me about ye, aye? She adores ye, lass, she loves ye, I think right from the first moment they brought ye to the castle. She said to me, 'Declan, lad, she is a special lass, and I think she needs ye.'"

The enormity of what he had just shared was not lost on me, and I had been right, Mrs. Campbell had been orchestrating something, but it was not something secretive or deceiving, it was my safety. What a dear woman she was. He had come for me, not the money, not the band or even Alex or a career, but for me. I was overwhelmed and tears threatened. Damn hormones.

"Declan, do you have siblings?" I deflected to a safer topic.

"Nay, lass, I dinnae."

"So, you are telling me that your mother wanted you to risk your life and protect a stranger?"

"Aye. But you're no stranger, lass. You met Kate, we are family, albeit verra distant, but you have almost as much Scottish blood flowing through your veins as I do. And surely you saw all those old family portraits. Who did they look like?

"I did," Yes, I do share a strong resemblance with those crusty old dames in the paintings. I was about to ask a question, but I got a bad feeling, and a shadow passed, leaving me with a chill.

"Declan, I think we are in trouble."

He stood and grabbed my hand and headed to the front door. Outside five men stood on the street acting like they hadn't a care in the world, but we knew different. I recognized them. It was Paul Stanley and the rest of his crew, and they were here to finish me off.

We stepped back inside. "Bill, call Eddy, tell him the Stanley gang are here. Hurry, Bill," I managed to get out as Declan hustled me to the back door. He nodded as Declan pulled me out the door. How the hell was I going to fight with my tummy so big? We headed down the alley, away from Denman Street, toward the park. Declan was on the walkie talkie with someone.

I grabbed his arm, as two of them rounded the corner in front of us. We turned to go back toward Denman Street, but only got a few feet. When the remaining three came around the other corner. We were right back behind Hunky Bills. I looked around the dumpster for a weapon and found a piece of pipe. Declan had a knife and a gun. All we could do was hold them off until help arrived.

As they approached us, I could already hear the sirens approaching, and knew the gang would act fast, in hopes of ending this and getting away. I wish they hadn't used the sirens which alerted their approach.

"Well, lookie what we have here, that rotten little bitch that tried putting us away, Paul. She thinks she's so smart. Thinking her rich boyfriend could save her, thinking this giant can save her. Thinking her cop buddy could save her. Well bitch, don't think anyone is going to be saving you."

Declan moved me behind him and forced us back, so the dumpster was shielding me from the ones behind us. He faced off with the two closest. I kept my eyes on the three, as they moved closer.

Then everything went to hell. The three from the other end came running down the alley as the two in front of Declan pulled their guns. Declan fired before one got his gun fully out of his pants, and he went down, the other however, got off a shot and hit Declan in the arm.

As I was bending down to grab the gun that had fallen from his hand. Someone grabbed my arm and spun me around. That gave me momentum, and I had the advantage as they had no idea that I was now a trained fighter. I swung with my pipe as I squatted, and my leg swept the one who grabbed my arm.

I caught the other one with the pipe, and he, too, went down. That left us with two assailants. Declan recovered enough to grab his gun and aim it at the third assailant that was now holding a knife to my throat. The last assailant from the two that had approached Declan was holding a gun, and it was pointed at me.

"Don't move, highlander, or she dies."

Declan carefully put down his gun, "She's pregnant, ya daft wee bastard, leave her alone."

It was Paul, he was the last one standing. It was then I saw Eddy, he motioned me to duck in three. I leaned back into the guy holding the knife to my throat, and then dealt him a blow to the nose. I heard it break as I quickly ducked, and Declan threw himself over me for protection from the bullets.

Moments later, I was being pulled to my feet, "Lass, are ye alright?"

"Yes, I think so. I—ohh! Declan, somethings not right, my stomach." He carried me down the alley to where the ambulance stopped. He placed me down on the stretcher.

"I'm fine," I panted, "just contractions. I, AAAAAAAAAAA, that was a bad one. I've been having contractions for days, but the book said they were Braxton Hickssss... argh!"

"Hold on, lass, there's Adam. It's going to be alright, lass. Do not fret, aye?" Then things moved in slow motion. Declan started rambling in Gaelic as paramedics looked him over. I was placed in the ambulance and Adam hopped in after me.

"It's over, sweetheart, four are dead, and one is going to prison. It's over, we're free."

"Adam," I grunted, "I know that should make me happy, but right now I... aaarrgh... I'm having babies."

Within minutes of our arrival I was in the delivery room getting prepped for a C-section. One of the babies was going into distress during contractions. The decision had been to go in and get them out. This was not a shocker, there had been concerns that I may need a C-section anyway.

I was terrified of having an injection in my spine. After having a knife shoved in my back, I had a little anxiety about sharp things touching me there. I wanted the babies out, but I was scared to let them take them.

"Montana, this is a standard procedure, it is okay. You know I would only let the best doctors in the world touch you."

"I can't help it, Adam. When I try bending forward for them to get into the right part of the spine, the contractions hit and I move. I can't do it."

"Yes, you can, you just need something else... hmmm, what about the music you and Alex have that sounds like the sea, would that help?"

Would that help? Good question. Sound, though, I think was the ticket. Then I had it, "Adam, is Declan here? He was shot, is he going to be alright?"

"The bullet went clean through his arm, and they just finished stitching him up."

"I need to hear Gaelic. You're right, sound is the answer. I need to hear it, it relaxes me every time. Please, can you see if he is okay enough to come here?" I panted out the last word.

He nodded and left me writhing in pain. In a moment, Adam and Declan were in my room and ready to help. Adam held one of my hands and put his other arm behind my back in support. Declan held my hand with his good one and leaned in. First, he just started talking, then he began a quiet crooning in Gaelic. I wasn't sure what it meant, but the longer he spoke, the more feeling went into his words. They took me to a deep place of relaxation. I saw sword fighting and images of a long forgotten time.

My body let go, and when the contractions came, they felt more subdued, as if the babies were relaxing as well. A part of my addled brain realized that is exactly what was happening. Declan was relaxing all three of us.

I melted into a semi-conscious state of relaxation. Declan kept murmuring as I was folded forward. I felt a prick, but nothing painful. I was laid down, and they began. Adam released my hand to go and watch our twins be born. Declan stayed and was still holding one of my hands, murmuring in Gaelic. It was different now, more like conversation then meditation. Fifteen minutes later, I was holding two babies in my arms; Daniel Geoffrey Ace Northrop, and Alex Declan McGregor Northrop.

"Congratulations on yer lovely babes." Adam and I were grinning from ear to ear.

"Thanks, Declan, I couldn't have done it without you." He smiled and went off to call the troops. I was wheeled into a private room and the babies were brought in shortly after. They were so adorable. One looked like Alex and me, and one looked like Adam. I prayed they would have his temperament and not mine.

It wasn't long before the family started to arrive. Geoff and Liza, Ace and Kristine, Alex and Chrissie, and Dan and Jaimie. They all crowded into the room and took turns holding the babies. Adam was taking pictures with a permanent smile fixed on his handsome face.

Seeing Ace hold the twins together was the best. The big giant cooing and talking babytalk, had the rest of us in stitches. He reluctantly passed one on to Dan but held possessively onto the other. I grinned. I loved watching the expressions on everyone's faces as they held the babies.

"I want one," Ace said.

"Want what?" Kristine asked.

"A baby, I want a baby."

"You can't be serious," I answered. "You just got rid of Alex and me like what, two years ago, and you want to get saddled down already?"

"That's good news," Kristine cut in, "as I'm eight weeks along."

Ace's face went from shock, to wonderment, to pure happiness. "Really?" he asked with a little boy look I had never seen before. She nodded.

He passed off baby Alex to his namesake so he could give Kris a hug and a kiss. We congratulated them. So many babies, we'd have to get our retreat finished.

The conversation turned to the early arrival of the twins. They grabbed chairs from the hallway and sat down while I told the story of mine and Declan's adventure leading up to the twins being born, including the part about him being a millionaire.

That initiated lots of speculation on how long he would stay employed with Twin Spin Records or if he would go back to Scotland, now that the danger was finally over. Declan appeared at the door and looked desperate to get out of the hospital.

We welcomed him in. He sat and was promptly bombarded with questions about himself. Not used to being the center of attention, he looked a little embarrassed at first, then he warmed up and regaled us with stories of how he became the owner of the paper.

He was a very interesting man, Declan Campbell, and I was suddenly reminded of the first day we had met. He, Dan, and Adam had been standing in the hallway talking. I had turned and studied them for a moment on my way to find Eddy. The three of them had looked so different from each other, but something else about them seemed the same.

I hadn't been able to put my finger on it back then, but I could see it now. They were cut from the same cloth, they were purely what they were, nothing more and nothing less. They would be the same people twenty-five years from now that they were right now. For some reason, I found that very comforting.

I knew the same couldn't be said for me or Alex, or even Ace. Some people grew and changed with circumstances, and some were what they were meant to be right from birth. That was those three. I wanted an image to immortalize the moment.

"Adam, pass me the camera. I need you, Dan, and Declan to stand right there," They looked puzzled but did as I asked. I took the picture. They relaxed, and I took a few more. Then passed the camera back and relished the tight family moment. Looking at my sons, my brothers, and my new sisters, was truly my West End life at its best.

The End

Acknowledgements

Thank you to my West End tribe for a speedy childhood and one I wouldn't trade for the world.

Thank you to my friend and publisher, Deborah of Rottie Books for being invested in my vision.

Thank you to L.G. Knight of Alluring Blurbs for her work on the blurbs for this anthology. I love them!

Thank you to my Alpha Team, Angie Goodin, Lori Smith, L.G. Knight, Rose Chaplan, Denise Holder and Anice Walker, and my ARC & Street Team for taking the time to review and share my work.

Thank you to my readers for your ongoing support. Last but not least, a shout out to Western Sky for all her hard work and creative genius.

In love & light,
Rogue London xoxo

Join the Inner Circle

Join The Inner Circle Series Fandom Group on Facebook
Join The Inner Circle on Discord
Follow The Inner Circle on TikTok

facebook.com/groups/theinnercircleseries

tiktok.com/@circle_series

About Rogue London

Rogue London is an International bestselling author of sassy, steamy, suspenseful romance that features alpha men with a soft spot for the women they inevitably fall for.

Rogue's imagination is limitless for exploring the power exchange dynamic in her stories.

https://linktr.ee/RogueLondonmedia

About N.M. McGregor

N.M. McGregor is a Canadian author born in the east and bred in the west. Despite the huge shifts to her beloved Vancouver over the past few decades, she still loves the place that helped build who she is today.

The Inner Circle Series is a dedication with her connection to a time and place that will always hold a special place in her heart.

About the Publisher

Rottie Books was created to help developing and experienced authors take their books from draft to finished product. Our team of authors have the expertise to help you finish and launch your new creation from blurb writing to covers.

We at Rottie Books appreciate your taking the time to leave a review on the site where you purchased the book, and on Goodreads or Bookbub. Your feedback is important to our authors.

Contact us at deborah@rottiebooks.com
https://rottiebooks.com/

Made in the USA
Columbia, SC
13 May 2025

57648781R00200